# STARSHIP THESEUS

## THE HIVE INVASION – BOOK 3

JAKE ELWOOD

This is a work of fiction. A novel. Totally made up. Any similarity to actual persons, places, rebel colonies or alien invaders is purely coincidental.

ISBN: 1541001796
ISBN-13: 978-1541001794

# CHAPTER 1 – HAMMETT

Richard Hammett stood in the bathroom of his villa on Ariadne, rubbing No-Beard carefully into his cheeks and trying to figure out who the hell was looking back at him from the mirror. The weathered face was the same, but he no longer knew who that weary-looking man was.

Washing carefully, he dried his hands and returned to the villa's tiny bedroom where the single biggest source of his disorientation lay draped across the narrow bed. It was a uniform, which was nothing unusual. Hammett had worn a uniform almost every day of his adult life. It had always been a Spacecom uniform, though.

This uniform was not the sober dark blue of Spacecom. It was green, the green of lush forests and the countless trees that filled Harlequin, the city that had become Hammett's new home. They'd promised him a jacket and cap, but for now his uniform consisted of a shirt and a pair of trousers.

He dressed reluctantly, fidgeting at the touch of unfamiliar fabric. Spacecom uniforms were made from a sophisticated synthetic. They were nearly impossible to tear, and you could wear them for weeks if you had to, day and night, without odor or much in the way of wrinkles.

This uniform was made of cotton grown not fifteen kilometers from the villa. The tailoring was hurried, the shirt looser than he was used to. Which might not be entirely a bad thing, he reflected as he buttoned the shirt across a stomach that was larger than it once was.

Instead of rank bars across the chest, the shirt had three fat stripes running the length of each sleeve. It marked him as an admiral, and he shook his head as he tucked in his shirttails. Never in his most grandiose dreams had he expected to reach the rank of Admiral.

No more than he'd imagined serving anywhere but in the Spacecom navy.

He checked his appearance in a wall mirror, decided he looked respectable, then turned away before the strangeness could overwhelm him. He buckled on a gunbelt, checked the safety on his rail pistol, tucked a small bundle under his arm, and headed outside.

"Good morning, Richard." Sinda Leitch, his next-door neighbor, could never seem to look at him without sadness in her eyes. She'd been friends with the villa's former resident, a man who'd died fighting the Hive invaders in the long weeks before Hammett's tiny fleet had arrived. All the Navy personnel were taking the places of the dead.

He gave her a distracted nod and moved past her, heading for Garibaldi Plaza. Once a lovely park in the heart of the city, the plaza now held a massive gun emplacement and an outdoor market where the colonists swapped or shared everything from bolts of cloth to electronics. Hammett passed a table with heaps of plums and cherries and a sign that said, 'Free'. Cooperation came as naturally as breathing to the people of Ariadne. Even before the alien invasion life had been tough here. They pulled together and helped one another when they could, and Hammett felt a familiar mix of pride and frustration that he was now one of them.

It was ten days since the showdown with the EDF when he'd renounced his rank in Spacecom and accepted a new role in the brand-new Colonial Forces. Ten days, but he still felt shocked, dislocated, like he was dreaming and waiting impatiently to wake up. He wondered if he'd ever get used to this new reality.

Ahead of him a plume of smoke rose skyward, and instinct made his arm tighten protectively on the bundle he held. He caught his first whiff of synthetic fibers reluctantly burning. *I can't do this. This is wrong. I can't-*

A circle of solemn figures stood around the perimeter of a dry fountain. It made a great site for a bonfire, he realized. The low concrete wall and tiled bottom would keep the fire from spreading. He recognized shipmates and fellow displaced officers in the circle, familiar figures made strange by their new green uniforms. Hayat Sanjari turned and gave him a smile as he approached.

She had family back on Earth, he remembered. Dozens of them, apparently. She could go on at length about siblings, aunts, uncles, cousins … His own discomfort was suddenly trivial as he realized how much more difficult this must be for her. For most of them.

Hammett had no real ties left in his former home. A younger brother he traded messages with once a year at Christmas, and visited every five years or so if he found himself planetside during December. Some old friends he hadn't seen in more years than he cared to remember. His life was the Navy, had been for years. If he couldn't go back to Earth, he'd barely notice the difference. What must it be like for the others?

Sanjari edged sideways, making room for him in the circle. Dozens of people ringed the fire. Scores. Even in the bright morning sunlight, firelight made flickering patterns on a wall of green uniforms. A pyramid of wood burned ferociously, the bones of a ruined building by the look of it. All over the timbers and scraps of lumber, dark blotches smoked and smoldered, burning only reluctantly.

Uniforms.

Ken Hardy, the fighter pilot who'd come over

from the EDF fleet, stepped into a gap on the far side of the fountain. Hardy held a shirt in each hand. One shirt, impeccably tailored, featured a black band around one arm. That shirt had barely been worn, and Hardy chucked it on the flames without a pause.

He hesitated with the next shirt. Hammett had seen him wearing it, a baggy thing too short in the sleeves that Hardy had mooched from some other crewman. It lacked the damning stripe of the EDF. Hardy clearly saw it as a symbol of his inclusion in the rebellious fleet. He sighed, then tossed the second shirt after the first one. It landed on a burning timber, arms flung wide like a martyr, and the blue fabric slowly began to blacken.

A pair of dark blue uniform trousers lay draped over Hardy's shoulder. He balled up the trousers and tossed them after the shirts, then retreated.

A boy stepped into the gap. His name was Vicente Ramona, and he was all of sixteen years old. He wore a green uniform with self-conscious pride, and he squared his shoulders as he stepped up to the edge of the fountain.

Instead of a Naval uniform, Vicente held a set of coveralls in his hands, rust-colored fabric bright with reflective strips. By the look on his face, this ceremony was as significant to him as it was to anyone present. He hesitated, fingering the coarse fabric, then took a deep breath and consigned the coveralls to the flames.

Vicente was from Dryad, a much less

hospitable planet sharing the Naxos system with Ariadne, the only planet in the system with breathable air – at least within one deep crater. A week earlier, the Colonial fleet had evacuated several hundred people from Dryad, where they had survived the invasion of the system in perfect serenity, ignored by the Hive. Now the boy was in the Naxos military, and he wasn't even the youngest new recruit.

Hammett pushed that unsettling thought from his mind as Sanjari nudged him with her elbow. He took his old uniform from under his arm. He'd worn it with pride, used it to define himself, and he desperately wanted to pause a moment, maybe unroll the shirt and look at the Captain's stripes one last time. His people were watching him, however, and he needed to send a clear message.

Without so much as a flicker of hesitation, he lobbed the bundle of fabric onto the fire.

After that he stood for a few minutes, watching as more uniforms fed the flames. He was careful not to overstay his welcome, though. He knew what sort of damper an officer could be at a gathering of enlisted personnel, and his new rank could only make things worse. Before long he edged back from the fountain, Sanjari following.

They strolled away from the fire, and he heard a gradual rise in volume behind him as crew began to relax and talk. He headed toward the tower-like structure of the alien gun emplacement, now a hodgepodge of alien and human technology. Christine Goldfarb and her team of scientists had all but rebuilt the thing from the ground up.

A handful of figures waited near the base of the tower, each one with rank stripes along their sleeves. They were captains and commanders and lieutenants from Spacecom, with one exception. Ronald Faraday, lean and middle-aged, was one of the shortest people in the group, but he had an aura of quiet authority that made him seem larger than he was. His brand-new title was Military Commander of Colonial Forces, and his sleeves had the same three stripes as Hammett's, plus an additional pinstripe.

The tall, craggy man at Ron's elbow gave Hammett a nod, murmured, "Admiral," then smirked. James Carruthers, captain of the *Indefatigable*, had served with Hammett for far too long to be in awe of his new rank.

Hammett grinned back, grateful to his friend for taking some of the starch out of the air. He joined the circle of officers, looking around at the familiar faces in unfamiliar uniforms.

"The evacuation of Dryad is complete," Ron said. "We've pretty much scouted every piece of rock in the system, and we've got the *Theseus* ready to launch. All our ships are back. We need to decide how to deploy them." Ron had an excellent leadership style, in Hammett's opinion. The man owned up to his lack of military experience and listened carefully to his officers, but he had no trouble asserting his right to make final decisions. He'd been a colony administrator before the invasion, and it showed.

Lieutenant Nicholson cleared his throat. "We could blockade the Gate, but I'd advise against it." He tilted his head, pointing at the gun emplacement beside him. "This is our biggest advantage. This, and the other ground guns, and the new satellites, once we launch them. We'd be fools to fight anywhere else but above the planet."

Ron nodded. "What's the status of the new weapons?"

A young lieutenant named Krill spoke up. "All four guns on the north polar ring are online. The south polar ring needs at least another week." She made a face. "That's pretty optimistic, actually. A month might be more likely. We put everything into the north ring. I think they've barely started on the south."

The gun emplacement beside them was a powerful weapon, but it could only cover a limited area. The colony was installing similar guns near the north and south poles, where they could cover every side of the planet.

Ron nodded. "How about the satellites?"

Krill gave him a helpless shrug. "They thought the first satellite would be good to go three days ago. Then they were going to launch last night." She shook her head. "I really don't know when they'll be ready."

Ron flashed a gallows smile. "Well, let's hope the EDF and the bugs give us a little more time." He looked around. "Anyone else?"

No one spoke. Ron turned to Hammett. "Admiral? What are your thoughts?"

It was a subtle bit of political handling, Hammett thought. Let the other officers speak first, then the admiral, with Ron speaking last. That way, no one would be contradicted or corrected by a subordinate. He wondered if the man had done it consciously. Not that it mattered too much, not with this group. These were seasoned officers with a high level of professionalism. Still, every little bit helped.

"It's high time we scouted the enemy," Hammett said. He gestured upward. "We know they're out there. We even know roughly what direction. We don't know what they're up to, and we should." He folded his arms. "It would also be nice to take the fight to them for a change. I'm tired of scrambling around, reacting to whatever they throw at us. Let them react to us for once."

Ron nodded. "Makes sense to me." He swept his eyes over the gathered officers. "I hesitate to send too much of the fleet into deep space. The *Theseus*, though, is far more effective against Hive ships than EDF ships."

Several officers nodded. The *Theseus*, a converted freighter, was covered in heat-shedding hull plates that made her all but impervious to the Hive's favorite weapon. She wouldn't fare so well against the missiles and rail guns of Spacecom, though.

Ron's gaze landed on Jean Harrington. She commanded the *Gideon*, a Jumper designed to generate wormholes. "The *Gideon* is the obvious ship to send on a scouting mission. You can open wormholes for the *Theseus*." He glanced at Hammett. "One more ship, do you think? A corvette, perhaps?"

Hammett remembered Ron's words before the last battle. *The* Theseus *is immune to heat weapons. Your corvettes are not. If you launch with us, you'll die.* The problem was, the Hive had a nasty habit of adapting. The *Theseus*, alone, had prevailed once. The Hive would have a strategy by now for dealing with the refurbished freighter. A corvette, its fighting style so different from the *Theseus*, would mix things up. He nodded reluctantly. "One corvette."

"Right." Ron turned to a dark-haired, fierce-eyed woman with a silver bracelet on her wrist and a small knife at her waist. "Captain Kaur."

Meena Kaur nodded. She'd held the rank of Commander in Spacecom, but Ron had made her a captain.

"What's the status of the *Tomahawk*?"

"She's ready to fly," Kaur said promptly. "The heat plating isn't complete, but it covers the most vital areas." Crews were coating the ship with a fine mesh of Fourier metal to spread and dissipate heat.

"Good," said Ron. "Is there any reason not to launch immediately?"

Hammett said, "I'd like an hour or so to get the crew aboard and bring in some fresh produce." The ship was stocked with a week of food, but Hammett, after a lifetime of dried and processed rations, was now accustomed to having fresh fruit every day. He was getting spoiled, he realized. He didn't care, though.

"That works for me," Kaur said. Jean Harrington, captain of the *Gideon*, nodded as well.

"Good." Ron nodded. "You can launch at eleven hundred, then."

Sanjari headed for the bonfire to spread the word among the crew. Hammett moved away from the group, shoving his hands in his pockets to keep himself from fidgeting. The familiar knot of fear and anticipation stirred in his belly, and he was grateful that he had so little time before he launched. He'd be too busy to fret.

*Maybe we finally get to call some shots. If only they'll wait for us to get there.* He looked around at the city that had become his unexpected new home, the stone buildings and the lush profusion of plants, the colonists who just kept plugging away without complaint in the face of adversity and terrible danger. The colony seemed so homely, so quiet and safe, but one big rock from space could turn it all into a lifeless wasteland in the blink of an eye.

If the Hive came to Ariadne while Hammett was on his scouting mission, the battle would be over before he even knew it had begun. And the Hive wasn't the only danger.

*Maybe you shouldn't leave. Tell Ron you think the whole fleet should stay here to defend the colony.* He shoved the thought to the back of his mind. The scouting mission was his own idea, after all. *You have your orders, and it's the right thing to do.*

*I just hope there's still a colony here when I get back.*

## CHAPTER 2 – HAMMETT

W e're through. Looks like it worked." Eddie Walsh, helmsman of the *Theseus*, looked over his shoulder and gave Hammett a strained smile. Eddie had been a freighter pilot for more than a decade, but wormhole jumps were still pretty new to him. He seemed astonished and relieved every time a jump succeeded.

"Thank you, Eddie," said Hammett, suppressing a grin. He looked at Sanjari.

"All clear, Sir." She leaned back in her seat and sighed. "Nothing to do now but wait for the *Gideon* to recharge."

Hammett nodded. The *Gideon* would need fifteen minutes or so before she could generate another wormhole. The *Tomahawk* could also generate wormholes, but they were saving the charge in case they needed a quick retreat.

Hal, the co-pilot, swiveled his chair around.

His fingers drummed on the arm of the chair. "I don't know you stand the tension. Nothing's even happened yet, and I'm wired like I drank a pot and a half of coffee."

Hal wore a green uniform shirt, but he wore it unbuttoned to display a bright red singlet underneath. His sleeves were rolled up past his elbows, and he had yet to use the words "Sir" or "Ma'am" when addressing the officers. Eddie had his shirt buttoned up, but he showed no more concern for traditional military protocol than Hal did.

That was just fine with Hammett. Neither man had asked to join the Colonial Forces, but here they were, in uniform, flying into mortal danger without a word of complaint. They knew the *Theseus* backward and forward, and they knew their duty. Hammett was glad to have them, and he wasn't about to pester them for salutes or any of the other trappings of military life.

No rank stripes decorated their sleeves. They held the rank of Private, not a traditional Navy designation. The Colonial Forces were all of ten days old, though, and entirely free of the weight of tradition. Ron wanted a unified military, with ground forces no different from shipboard forces.

He wanted things simple, too. The only ranks were Private, Sergeant, Lieutenant, Captain, and Admiral. That he was mixing traditional Army and Navy ranks bothered Ron not the slightest, and Hammett, on reflection, decided he wasn't bothered either. Everyone knew their job, and everyone respected the chain of command. The rest was details.

Hammett looked at the fifth and final member of the bridge crew, and felt a tremor of disquiet. Vicente Ramona sat along the port bulkhead, fidgeting with the sleeve of his uniform shirt. The boy kept unbuttoning the sleeve, then buttoning it back up and smoothing the fabric. Every few minutes a determined expression would cross his face and he would fold his hands in his lap. Before long, though, he'd be fiddling with the sleeve again.

Vicente saw Hammett looking at him, flushed, took his fingers from his sleeve, and said, "Any messages, Admiral?"

"No," Hammett said patiently. "No messages." He moved his gaze to the stars outside. Maybe after another jump or two the kid would calm down. In the meantime, ignoring the boy seemed to be the best way of dealing with him.

Vicente and his family were Hammett's new Signals Corps. Like most of humanity they spoke New Standard English, but they also spoke Mayan. Hammett was pretty sure English was enough to keep the Hive in the dark, but the Ramona family gave him a way to send messages that would be incomprehensible to Spacecom.

Rosalina, Vicente's mother, had assured him that the K'iche' dialect was all but a dead language back on Earth, and that her children, who had never set foot on the home planet, spoke with an accent so thick it would be practically unrecognizable to her community anyway.

She'd also promised to murder Hammett if he didn't bring her children back safe, and he was pretty sure she meant it. She was aboard the corvette *Epée*. Her youngest child, a girl of twelve, was at Colonial Forces headquarters – formerly the spaceport terminal – back on Ariadne. Her husband and other children were distributed among the ships protecting Ariadne. Only Vicente was on the scouting mission.

Eddie said, "Uh-oh."

Hammett stiffened. "What is it?"

Eddie twisted around in his chair, eyes wide. "The *Gideon* is charged up. We have to jump again."

Letting a quiet sigh escape him, Hammett said, "It will be fine, Eddie."

"If you say so." Eddie turned back to his controls, making unnecessary course adjustments with tense, jerky movements.

Hammett sighed again, a bit louder this time. *Sometimes I really miss Spacecom.*

# CHAPTER 3 – BLOCH

Commodore! It's coming back!"

Commodore Wolfgang Bloch lifted his gaze from the tactical screen beside his seat on the bridge of the destroyer *Adamant* and fixed the lieutenant at Operations with a wintry gaze.

The young man flushed, said, "I guess you can see that, Sir," and turned back to his own console.

The tac screen showed a little robotic probe no bigger than a bathtub, looking none the worse for wear after its instantaneous journey through a wormhole to the Naxos system and back. He couldn't see the stream of data radiating from the little probe, but he knew it was there. He'd be getting a report right about ...

"No mines, Sir," said Remlinger, his tactical officer, without lifting her eyes from her own screens. "No ships in the immediate vicinity."

Bloch raised an eyebrow. 'Immediate vicinity' translated to a sphere of twelve thousand kilometers around the Gate. Apparently the door to Naxos was open and unguarded. That was sloppy of Hammett, very sloppy.

Well, a lack of professionalism was hardly surprising. Bloch glanced at his nav display and the blue orb of Earth floating not far away. Anyone with the criminally foolish gall to start a mutiny in the middle of an interstellar war could hardly be expected to show professionalism, common sense, or basic decency. His lip curled as the familiar disgust rose in his stomach. The mutineers were like people who went looting in the aftermath of earthquakes and hurricanes, counting on decent people being too busy saving lives to protect their property.

Scum.

*Maybe this will be easier than I expected*, he thought. The mutineers had an alarming number of ships and personnel, almost a match for the fleet Bloch was leading against them. If they were going to be sloppy and half-assed he'd be able to mop up this mess in a couple of days. Then he could get back to the real war, the one against the aliens.

Damn Hammett and his idiot followers for kicking off this ridiculous sideshow! What did they think would happen? Did they imagine Spacecom, strapped for resources in the face of invasion, would capitulate and negotiate with them?

Like hell.

He'd give them a brief opportunity to surrender. Then he'd crush them.

"They left a probe of their own," Remlinger said. "It's a safe bet they know we're coming."

"Let's not keep them waiting," Bloch said. "Take us through."

The displays on his screens changed, the Earth and the rest of the fleet vanishing. Ariadne appeared in the distance on the nav display, and the rest of the fleet began to appear, one ship at a time, as they followed the *Adamant* through the Gate. Six corvettes. Another destroyer. A supply ship. A carrier with a dozen fighters. And the *Cassandra*.

Bloch smiled coldly. The *Cassandra* was his pocket ace. He wouldn't even have to engage the mutineer fleet. He had the power to wipe the rebel colony from the face of Ariadne without going near the planet.

A quick laser burst destroyed the probe the mutineers had left. The *Adamant* and two corvettes quickly opened wormholes, and Bloch flexed his fingers as the destroyer jumped. They would be leaping ahead of any signal the probe could have sent, emerging from three points hundreds of kilometers apart. They would catch the mutineers entirely by surprise.

The stars didn't shift on the nav screen, except for Naxos itself. Whiter than Earth's sun, the star seemed to dart sideways in the sky, simultaneously doubling in size. The planet Ariadne loomed close, barely twenty thousand kilometers away.

"No ships," Remlinger reported. The words were barely out of her mouth when a warning chime sounded and Bloch saw a cluster of red circles on his tac display, just above the horizon of Ariadne. As he watched, more circles appeared. The mutineer fleet, nicely bunched together, wasn't quite visible to the *Adamant*. The tactical display was being updated with data from the other ships in Bloch's fleet. One group of ships had the enemy in sight.

"I'm getting some more signals," Remlinger said. Bloch saw nothing on his own screen, but the tactical station pulled in far more data. "Satellites," she said. "They weren't there when O'Hare and his people left."

"Maintain position," Bloch said. A few satellites were unlikely to pose a threat, but O'Hare had reported taking fire from a ground-based weapon left behind by the Hive. Clearly, anything was possible. *Let Hammett do the blundering. I think I can rely on him to do something stupid.*

"It looks like their fleet's in a geostationary orbit above the colony," Remlinger said. "They're not coming out to meet us."

That was unfortunate. He'd have preferred to fight them well away from that alien gun. Still, it hardly mattered. He checked his displays. Nine ships. He scanned the list of ship names drawn from transponder codes, checking against the ships that had fled their post to join Hammett in Naxos. The *Gideon* was gone, and the *Tomahawk*, the corvette Hammett had commanded when he left Earth. O'Hare had reported a converted freighter, too. It wasn't enough firepower to worry about. "Give 'em a shout," he said to Tomlin at Communications.

Lieutenant Tomlin nodded. He was a seasoned officer in his forties, just back from a crash course in obsolete radio and telephone communications. Tomlin's hands moved across his console. He nodded to Bloch, received a nod in return, and touched a final button.

"EDF fleet," said a dry masculine voice. "Welcome to Naxos."

"This is Commodore Bloch of the *Adamant*, commanding Spacecom forces in the Naxos system. Who am I speaking to?"

"Commodore. This is Captain Jamison, commanding the *Marlborough*. Tell me, who's holding your leash?"

Jamison was the senior captain among the nine recent deserters, with more years as a captain than any of the mutineers except Hammett. Bloch frowned. "I don't have a leash, Captain."

"Oh?" There was a sarcastic note to Jamison's voice. "Has Spacecom come to its senses, then? Are real military men commanding warships again? Or is there an EDF stooge standing beside you, telling you what to say?"

"In addition to my Spacecom rank," Bloch said, "I hold the rank of General in the Earth Defense Force."

There was a long moment of silence. Finally Jamison spoke, sounding shocked. "You put on a red shirt?"

Strictly speaking, he wore his Spacecom uniform under his vac suit, with a black sash signaling his EDF rank. "I did what every decent officer in Spacecom should have done," Bloch said impatiently. "I joined the EDF as soon as it was formed. If more Spacecom officers had followed my lead, there wouldn't be a need for inexperienced EDF personnel to command ships."

After another long pause Jamison said, "Unbelievable."

"Enough," said Bloch. "You've had your bit of fun, but vacation's over." He leaned forward, putting his mouth closer to the microphone on his console. "Now it's time to pay the piper. I'm not here to negotiate with you. I'm not here to talk. I'm here to accept your unconditional surrender, or to destroy you." The familiar fury rose within him, and he controlled it with an effort. "There's a war on, and you won't be allowed to disrupt the war effort any longer. If you want to still be alive this time tomorrow, you'll surrender now."

"You're on the wrong side of this conflict," Jamison said, sounding weary. "We're the ones actually fighting the aliens, remember?"

"That's enough!" Bloch snapped, slamming his hand down on the arm of his chair for emphasis. "You're traitors and cowards, and your little escapade is over! You've betrayed the entire human race, and you're going to pay the price."

For a long time there was no reply. Bloch sat

fuming, hearing his own angry breathing over the faint hiss of the ship's air conditioning machinery. At last Jamison said, "Well, you know where we are. Come and get us any time you like."

Bloch looked at Tomlin and made a curt gesture. Tomlin touched a button on his console, cutting the connection, and nodded. "Plot us a rendezvous course with Asteroid N581," Bloch said. "Transmit to the fleet. We'll stick together. Once they realize what we're doing, they'll come after us."

It would be an ugly fight, in the depths of space far from the protective fire of the captured alien gun. Bloch would win, though, and then he'd return to take control of whatever remained of the colony.

The *Cassandra* would make it almost easy. She was an experimental doomsday weapon, a ship designed to move cargo, given a hasty refit after the first Hive attack. The blueprints had kicked around Spacecom for decades, but there had never been the need – or the will – to implement them.

The original ship, almost a kilometer long, was in effect a giant flying rail gun, designed to lob cargo containers very long distances through deep space. Instead of using the current between the rails to directly propel a cargo pod, the newly-renamed *Cassandra* had an armature that would travel the length of the rails, stop, and be retracted.

Traditional railguns and their cousin

weapons, magnetic launchers commonly though incorrectly referred to as railguns as well, could fire a dozen rounds per second. The *Cassandra* was much slower. It typically fired a projectile every five seconds. The projectile, though, didn't have to be machined to precise tolerances. The projectile sat in the armature like a pebble in a slingshot, and the movement of the armature gave the projectile its velocity.

The projectile could be anything that would fit in the hollowed-out nose of the armature. The projectile could be a simple lump of rock.

Like the rock that composed Asteroid N581.

And, since the nose of the armature was five meters across, the projectile could be very, very large. The other part of the refit, the part that made the *Cassandra* a real threat as a weapon, was a group of articulated robots mounted with powerful lasers. They were programmed to swarm all over a piece of rock, cutting away rough cylinders of stone and loading them into the armature. Every asteroid, meteor, and dwarf planet was a source of ammunition, and the Naxos system was full of rubble.

One good hit inside the crater would be enough to devastate the colony. That kind of accuracy was nearly impossible without precisely-machined projectiles, but that was all right. A dozen or so hits to the planet should be enough to generate hurricane-force winds that would sweep away the fragile pocket of breathable air that filled the crater. The colonists, choking on a mix of methane and helium, would fall over each other in their haste to surrender and pledge allegiance to the EDF.

"Commodore."

Bloch looked at Tomlin.

"There's some communication between ships. They've encrypted it, but ..."

But it was Spacecom hardware and software. Spacecom encryption, which meant a good comms officer – and Tomlin was very good – would be able to decrypt it before long.

A hiss of static came from the bridge speakers. Then a man spoke, his voice garbled at first but becoming clearer with every word. "... least let me talk to him. It can't do any harm, can it?"

There was a long burst of static as someone replied.

"We can't fight them." It was the anonymous man, his voice firm. "They're Spacecom personnel. If there's any chance at all of avoiding a full-blown civil war, we have to take it."

"All right." The second voice belonged to Jamison. "I think it's hopeless, but I've seen how convincing you can be."

The speakers went silent, and Tomlin said, "We're getting a call from the *Indefatigable*."

Bloch gave him a curt nod and the same anonymous voice began to speak. "Commodore. This is Captain James Carruthers of the Colonial Forces Corvette *Indefatigable*."

"Your corvette belongs to Spacecom," Bloch said. "You don't get to keep it."

"Neither does the EDF," Carruthers replied. "In the meantime, I have a proposition for you."

Bloch remained silent, taking a moment to recall what he knew of the other man. Carruthers was a career lieutenant, one of hundreds of officers passed over for command, serving an unremarkable career at a modest rank. He'd struck Bloch as a sober, perfectly ordinary officer on the half-dozen occasions when they'd met over the years.

Carruthers had been on the *Alexander* during its historic final mission, and it had catapulted the man at last into a captain's uniform. Clearly the promotion and accompanying attention had gone to his head.

"I'm willing to listen," Bloch said at last. "But make no mistake. This will end with your surrender or your death."

"I don't think you really want to fire on your fellow human beings," Carruthers said. "I don't think you want to destroy the ships that have been fighting the Hive. They're your real enemy, after all."

"You won't hide behind the chaos of wartime," Bloch said. "You've crossed a pretty significant line. You WILL face the consequences."

"Well, we're not going anywhere," Carruthers said. "You can always kill us later. In the meantime, I have a suggestion."

Bloch frowned. He'd expected either bravado or groveling, or at worst the passionate rhetoric of fools who believe in a ridiculous cause. Jamison and Carruthers just sounded ... impatient, as if Bloch was a blundering fool they had to tolerate. It was insulting. Worse, in fact, than if they'd actually hurled insults.

Well, they'd take him seriously soon enough. In the meantime .... "What's your suggestion?"

"You must know that fighting the Hive would be a better use for your ships," Carruthers said. "But you have your orders, and the EDF is obsessed with controlling people. I understand. So here's what I suggest. Admiral Hammett has taken a small fleet on a reconnaissance mission. He's scouting Hive forces in the system. We're pretty sure they're out there, not far off. We even know what direction."

Bloch nodded, though Carruthers couldn't see him. He'd read the reports from O'Hare and Swanson.

"Why don't you go after Hammett?" Carruthers said. "If he's encountered the Hive, you might have a chance to do something useful. You can fight the real enemy for a change."

He spoke that last sentence with such disgust that Bloch felt his fists clench. *A traitor, criticizing me for doing my duty?* He pushed the fury down with an effort, and jerked his hand at Tomlin.

"Connection's closed, Sir."

Bloch took a deep breath, then another, fighting for calm. He wanted to shout at Carruthers. He wanted to bellow his rage and frustration. These self-important morons were making a huge mess, then judging him for cleaning it up! Only years of experience as an officer let him keep his emotions in check.

Slowly, deliberately, he walked around the

bridge. He paced out a precise square around his station, his hands clasped behind him, his anger largely hidden. Emotion had no place in command decisions, and he walked around his station, then around it once more, as the worst of his frustration faded.

Carruthers was a self-righteous fool, but it didn't mean he was entirely wrong. The Hive *was* the real enemy. It would be unfortunate if he had to lose ships and personnel combatting the mutineers. No ships could be spared. If the mutineers could be persuaded to surrender even one vessel, it would be a huge boon to the defense of Earth.

Right now, they were determined to stand their ground. Their morale was high, and they were ready to put up a good fight. He meant to take the starch out of them by destroying the colony.

However, firing on the colony, though it might yet prove necessary, was not without consequences. Every human being who died at the hands of Spacecom or the EDF added fuel to the fires of unrest. It made the ridiculous claims of the anti-EDF movement seem plausible. If he could persuade the colony to surrender without killing any non-combatants he'd make the EDF stronger, and weaken its enemies.

At the very least, he could gather some intel.

"All right," he said. "Where is Hammett?"

# CHAPTER 4 – HAMMETT

Hammett watched as a wormhole opened just ahead of the *Gideon*. A familiar dismay ran cool fingers up and down his spine as the Jumper went through. The *Gideon*, though poorly armed, was heavily armored, since it was constantly leading the way into unknown space. Its armor wouldn't handle heat weapons well, though.

The *Gideon* vanished, and the *Tomahawk* hurried through after it. The little corvette could open a wormhole for a quick escape, but Captain Kaur would wait for the *Theseus*. Hammett said, "Go, Eddie. Let's not hang around here."

Eddie, not looking much more comfortable on his seventh jump than he had for the first six, nodded and touched his console. The converted freighter surged forward and the *Gideon* and the *Tomahawk* abruptly reappeared.

"Admiral, we've got contacts." The voice

belonged to Jean Harrington on the *Gideon*, the only ship in the little fleet with military-grade scanning equipment that still worked. "I've got six unknown ships at a bearing of 47 degrees absolute, nine degrees up absolute."

"Absolute" meant a bearing in reference to the galaxy itself, with zero degrees lying along a line from the center of the galaxy to Sol. "Nine degrees up" meant nine degrees above a theoretical horizontal plane running through the middle of the Milky Way.

Hammett, with the ease of long practice, found the direction she indicated with his eyes. There was nothing to see. He looked instead at the screens on his console. "All I get is a single fuzzy blur," he told Harrington. "You'll have to be my eyes."

"Range is two to three thousand kilometers," she said promptly. "Actually, it looks like your display is about to become more accurate. They're glomming together. My best guess is it's six of the smallest Hive ships. They were spread across about two hundred kilometers of empty space, but they're grouping."

"Any other contacts?"

"None." She'd have told him if she'd seen anything else, of course, but every officer knew that assumptions bred mistakes at ten times the normal rate during crisis situations.

"We'll pursue," Hammett decided. "But we'll stick together." To Eddie he said, "Do you have the bearing?"

"Got it."

"Best speed, then." The *Theseus* was the slowest ship in the little fleet. She'd be setting the speed of the pursuit.

"They're all linked up with each other," Harrington said. "They're running."

"Try some laser shots," Hammett told her. "You might get lucky."

"Aye aye."

"Helmets on," said Hammett, and reached for the helmet rack on the side of his chair. They all wore the vac suits, but no one wanted to wear a helmet any longer than necessary. Hammett's vac suit was Spacecom issue, but they'd painted his helmet green to show his new affiliation. Beside him, Sanjari clipped her own green-painted helmet into place. Hammett kept the faceplate retracted and peered into the screen on his console.

He knew they were gaining when the blur on his screen sharpened into a white circle. It started to jerk left and right as the aliens evaded the *Gideon's* lasers, and he smiled. That would slow the aliens down.

"I'm scoring some hits," Harrington said. "It's hard to tell how much damage I'm doing, though."

"Interesting," Sanjari murmured.

"What?" Hammett turned. The converted freighter had a tiny bridge, crowded with five of them there. Sanjari was beside him, almost close enough to bump elbows, and he had no trouble seeing her screens. One display showed the *Theseus* as a green triangle and the Hive ship as a blue square. A white line bisected the square, extending off at an angle.

"They aren't running directly away from us," she said. "They're going kind of sideways." She put the edge of her hand on the screen, parallel to the white line. "They're a good thirty degrees port and down."

"They have a destination," Hammett said. "Reinforcements, or ..."

"We're getting close," Harrington said. "I'm trying some ballistic rounds."

Rail guns, in other words. The *Theseus* had vastly more ammunition than the Jumper, but the *Gideon* had computer-controlled weapons, and at long range that made all the difference. Hammett watched his inadequate tactical screen, wondering if he'd be able to see a hit.

Hal looked back over one thick shoulder. "Should we shoot too?"

Hammett shook his head. "We'll never hit anything from here." He gave Hal a grim smile. "Don't worry. We'll be doing plenty of shooting soon enough."

Hal nodded soberly and turned back to his console.

"They're losing speed," Sanjari said triumphantly. "I think they took a hit."

The ship broke apart on Hammett's screen, close enough now that he could make out the shapes of the little component craft. There were only four now, he was pleased to see. Three of them scattered, while the fourth wallowed in place. A moment later it disappeared, ripped apart by rail gun rounds or sliced up by lasers.

Eddie and Hal started talking excitedly, drowning each other out, until Harrington's cold voice cut through their chatter. "We've got more company inbound."

Hammett looked down. Fresh blips spread like a rash across his display, more than he could count, advancing from the direction the alien ship had been fleeing.

"Admiral, are you seeing this?"

He needed a long moment to figure out who had spoken. "Captain Harrington." She would have a much better view. "No. Explain."

"There's a big triangular structure," she said. "Hardly any mass, though. Sir, I think it's what the aliens use for a Gate."

His eyebrows rose. Gates were circular – but maybe they didn't have to be. He certainly didn't understand the physics involved. Maybe a Gate could be triangular. "Do you see ships coming through?"

"No, but there's a whole swarm of them gathering between the triangle and us. Like they're protecting it. And several dozen coming forward to meet us."

"We need to upgrade the scanners on this tub."

Hammett didn't realize he'd spoken aloud until Eddie said, "I hear that, Admiral."

"I can see the thirty or forty coming at us," Sanjari said. "The rest is just a blur, though."

"Thirty-four hostiles inbound," Harrington reported. The *Gideon's* computers would have counted the blips. "One hundred and nine hostiles guarding what I'll assume is their Gate. That's misleading, though. Quite a few of them are composite ships. They keep splitting and merging. The number keeps changing."

"Well, it's clearly a target-rich environment," Hammett said. "The exact number doesn't matter." He took a deep breath, channeling his stress, concentrating on the ways his body was reacting to alarm. A little awareness went a long way, keeping the adrenalin from controlling him. "Begin braking."

"My generator is charged up," Harrington said. "We could jump out of here."

"No." Hammett wiped his palms on his trousers, momentarily startled by the touch of cotton instead of artificial fabric. "Every moment we're in the neighborhood gives us valuable intel. We won't jump until we have to."

"Aye aye, Sir."

He wanted to flee. The swarm of ships ahead of him was terrifying. He also wanted to barge straight at them. Tear through the pack, rain destruction on all sides, and storm that Gate, if Gate it was. He'd never have another opportunity. Maybe he could dash through, jump to the enemy homeworld. Find out where it was, then run back before they could disable the Gate.

Pushing the thought from his mind, he stood, reached the port window in one stride, and peered through the hardened glass. A faint mesh of Fourier metal blurred the view. No ships were in sight. He knew they were out there, though. A hopeless number of enemy vessels. He'd never make it through the first wave that was coming to engage his fleet, never mind the larger group protecting that mysterious triangle.

He wanted to pace, but the tiny bridge was just too small. Stifling a sigh, he sat back down in time to hear Harrington say, "Contact aft."

Hammett looked at his screen, which showed nothing aft, then at Sanjari, who shrugged.

"It's faint," Harrington said. "Very long range. I can't actually tell what's back there. It's giving off energy, and it's at least several tonnes of mass. That's all I know for sure."

Well, it had to be tens of thousands of kilometers distant if that was all the *Gideon* could pick up. He could safely ignore it, whatever it was, for the moment.

The smaller group of Hive ships, the ones rushing forward to intercept them, began to merge on Hammett's screen. The level of detail grew sharper as the distance closed, until he could make out three composite ships and nine of the smallest craft.

"Use your own judgment, Captain Harrington," he said. "Fire when you've got targets. We'll be waiting until they're right on top of us. Captain Kaur?"

"Yes, Admiral?"

"Hold your fire until they're at point-blank range."

"Understood, Sir."

"Firing," Harrington said, and three of the smallest blips vanished from Hammett's screen.

The larger blips broke apart, and every ship in the swarm began to dive and dodge.

"They're retreating," Harrington reported. "The larger group is holding its position between us and that triangle. It looks like we've got ourselves a standoff."

Hammett spent a long moment just staring through the windows, his gut churning with a mix of relief and disappointment. He opened a channel to the other two captains. "We'll advance. Not too quickly. If they come at us, we'll retreat." To Eddie he said, "Take us forward. Not too fast."

"We've got a lot of forward momentum," Eddie said. "Do you want me to speed up?"

"No. In fact, slow us down a bit. I want to see how close we can get without starting a fight." It was a fight the humans would lose, he knew. But if he could get close enough to that triangle for the *Gideon* to scan it …

"They've stopped retreating," Harrington said.

Hammett looked at his screen. It looked to him as if the two groups had merged.

"They're advancing," said Harrington. "Slowly. But definitely advancing."

Hammett lifted his gaze from the screen. He could see the larger clusters with his naked eyes, glittering points of light, wobbling like fireflies. They would be zig-zagging to avoid incoming fire.

"Slow us down, Eddie." He looked at his screen. There was a new contact, displayed as a brown circle. It was the only thing on the screen that wasn't moving. "Let's get ourselves stationary in relation to that ... alien object."

"Right." Eddie touched his controls, and Hammett felt the tug of inertia as the ship braked. He could see the gleaming mass of the *Gideon* off to his left. Light flared from thrusters near the nose of the Jumper. To his right he could see the *Tomahawk*, also braking.

"The aliens are slowing down," Harrington said. "I guess we won't be – what the hell?"

Light flared in the void, ahead of the *Theseus* and high up. A ragged circle appeared in the darkness, glowing white, with rays of light shooting out in every direction. And ships appeared, tiny as toys. He saw a couple of destroyers, and corvettes so small they looked like snowflakes.

One ship after another poured through the wormhole, and the cloud of Hive ships changed direction, hurrying to meet this new threat.

"That contact behind us has disappeared," said Harrington dryly. "I guess we know what it was."

The newly-arrived fleet was spreading out, forming up, and advancing to meet the approaching Hive ships. The glowing wormhole shrank and vanished behind them.

"Let's get over there," said Hammett. "That's where all the fun is."

Eddie flashed him a grin, then turned to his controls. The deck tilted, and acceleration pushed Hammett against his chair.

"Stay with me," Hammett told his captains.

The *Gideon* and the *Tomahawk* were faster, but they'd be helpless without the *Theseus*.

He looked down at his screen. The EDF fleet – it was almost certainly EDF – had popped out on the far side of the alien Gate. Too far, unfortunately, to reach the Gate before the Hive ships could scramble back to defend it.

A couple of dozen Hive ships hung back to protect the Gate. The rest hurried to engage the EDF fleet. The *Theseus*, *Gideon*, and *Tomahawk* were left unmolested, and a traitorous thought flashed through Hammett's mind. *We could flee. We could go back to Ariadne. After all, what's the EDF done for anyone?*

But they were fellow human beings, and he'd be damned if he would abandon them when they were finally fighting the Hive. So he kept silent as the *Theseus* surged forward, wondering sourly if he was getting his people killed.

*It doesn't matter. If we sit idle while Spacecom battles the Hive, we're not worth saving.*

The EDF ships grew rapidly as the distance closed. Soon he could make out individual Hive ships, even the small ones. The fleet was having a rough time of it. He winced as he saw a corvette tumble away from the battle, spewing vapor from a breach in her hull.

Then the battle vanished from view and the stars whipped past in a blur. Eddie was spinning the ship around, flying her tail-first so he could decelerate hard. The back of Hammett's seat pressed against him. He stood and turned, leaning against the deceleration, watching through the aft windows as the battle raged.

Metallic clangs echoed through the bridge as multiple impacts slammed into the hull. The aft window starred not a meter from Hammett's face, and he flinched. *We really need steelglass up here.*

Vicente Ramona yelped, looking at Hammett with wide eyes. His hand went to the side of his helmet, poised to close the faceplate. "What was that?"

"Stray ballistic rounds," Hammett said calmly. "It won't be the last of it." Even as he spoke the words, a laser glittered against the window to his left. Scattered and diffused by the fine mesh of Fourier metal covering the glass, the laser left a wide scorch mark on the ceiling. The laser was gone in the blink of an eye.

"Jesus!" said Hal. "We're on their side."

"Well," said Hammett, "in a minute we're going to open up with the big guns – and I can just about guarantee we'll dish out some friendly fire of our own."

Hal gave a strained chuckle. "That's gonna be a shock."

Hammett nodded. The *Theseus* had as many rail guns as the entire EDF fleet put together, and some of those guns fired rounds fully a hundred times as massive as the puny round that had hit the window.

He tilted his head to peer between the cracks in the glass, and saw a cloud of small alien ships surging away from the main battle, coming to meet his little fleet. The *Theseus* tilted down, and then up. For a moment the approaching ships were dead aft, with nothing but empty sky behind them. In that instant, Hammett heard the thrum of the aft rail guns firing.

A ragged hole appeared in the center of that cloud of ships, jagged chunks of metal spinning away to vanish into the depths of space. Then the *Theseus* whipped around and charged head-first into the thick of battle.

For thirty long seconds the hive ships swarmed around them. The *Theseus* twisted and turned until Hammett was completely disoriented. Glittering streams of metal surrounded her, rail gun rounds from her own magazines and the other human ships. Hive ships broke apart, until the *Theseus* seemed to swim in an ocean of metallic scrap.

It ended suddenly. Hive ships pulled back, withdrawing in every direction. At first Hammett thought it was a rout, a panicked retreat, but the enemy ships stopped at a range of thirty kilometers or so. They formed a wide, loose sphere around the cluster of human ships, and they waited.

Something banged into the side of the *Theseus*. Hammett heard a metallic crunch, and he staggered as the ship lurched. He looked through the starboard window and saw a chunk of hull plate drifting away. It was from a Spacecom vessel, he couldn't tell which one. The impact had broken some Fourier metal loose, and he watched uneasily as bits of heat shielding floated off.

"All right," he said, suddenly weary, "let's see what's left."

# CHAPTER 5 – KAUR

For such a brief battle, the butcher's bill was horrendous. The *Gideon* had lost her engines and most of her air. The *Theseus* was a little banged up, but seemed mostly intact. The EDF fleet was a shambles.

Captain Meena Kaur sat in the captain's seat on the *Tomahawk*, listening as damage reports trickled in. There had been a bad few moments when Hive ships had surround the corvette on every side, like wolves trying to pull down a stag. Two different clusters had tried to burn through the hull. They'd been thwarted by the Fourier metal and had withdrawn.

She shivered. Much of the hull was unprotected. If the aliens had struck one of the many gaps in the Fourier metal ...

"Mr. Geibelhaus reports he can't charge up the wormhole generator," a sailor reported. "He's not sure why."

Kaur nodded, distracted. "That's all right. Someone in the EDF fleet will open a wormhole." *And not a moment too soon*, she thought. *I don't like being surrounded like this. I don't like waiting for their next move.*

A light flashed on the console in front of her, and she picked up the telephone handset. Hammett, his voice made scratchy and distant by the crystal radio, said, "What's your status?"

"We lost the top-side rail guns and the forward laser turret. Engines are good, and we're airtight."

"Good," he said. "I want you to dock with the *Gideon*. Offload everyone. We're going to have to retreat, and the *Gideon's* not going anywhere."

"Aye aye," she said, and put down the handset. "Touhami. Take us over to the *Gideon*."

As the *Tomahawk* moved through the wreckage-strewn battlefield, she watched the EDF fleet taking similar measures. Ships with minimal damage docked with ruined ships, or hovered close by while figures in vac suits sailed out from gaps in the ruined hulls. By the look of it, half the fleet was disabled. She doubted a single ship had come through undamaged.

The *Tomahawk* trembled ever so slightly as the docking ring in her nose met a matching ring on the side of the Jumper. She waited, wondering what she'd do if the aliens chose this moment to renew their attack. Silently she willed the crew of the *Gideon* to hurry. The *Tomahawk* was all but helpless while the two ships were docked.

"Oh, my God."

Kaur looked around. She couldn't tell who was standing at the starboard window – everyone looked the same from behind in a vac suit – but she knew immediately what the problem was.

The mysterious triangle, the artifact the aliens had taken such pains to protect, was just visible as a tiny gray line, shining faintly against the deeper black of space. She could make out a couple of dozen ships that had stayed back to protect the triangle. She could also see more ships forming a growing cloud in front of the triangle. No ships were visible behind the alien structure, but ship after ship kept appearing in front. There were dozens, then more and more, and a cold hand closed in her stomach and squeezed.

"Now we know," she said. "It's a Gate, all right."

"Here they come!" Touhami's voice came out shrill, and Kaur gave him a sharp look. He flushed and looked away, then busied himself with a handset. He was embarrassed. That was good. It gave him something to focus on besides his fear.

"Everyone's offloaded!"

Kaur glanced at the young sailor in the doorway of the bridge. It was a youngster, one of Hammett's cadets from the *Alexander*, a breathless, red-faced girl. Kaur lifted an eyebrow and the girl straightened up. "From the *Gideon*," she said. "They were uncoupling when I left."

"Back us up and bring us about," Kaur said. The corvette began to turn as the young sailor backed uncertainly out of the doorway.

A figure in a vac suit with rank stripes across the chest elbowed past the girl. It was Harrington, her face pale with a high spot of color in each cheek. "The *Gideon's* evacuated," she said. She sounded shaken. Well, it was her first taste of combat. Her first time losing a ship. Kaur, who had done both, felt almost calm.

Almost.

"Heading, Captain?" said Touhami.

"Queue up behind the *Theseus*," Kaur said. "Somebody's got to open a wormhole soon. We'll follow the *Theseus* through." The EDF might have the gall to arrest her after she'd helped save their collective ass, but she'd take a court martial over annihilation by the Hive.

A light flashed on her console, and she picked up a handset.

"Kaur." Hammett sounded harried, as close to flustered as she'd ever heard him. "Can you generate a wormhole?"

"No, Sir." She fought a sudden sinking feeling in her gut.

"Do you know why?" he snapped.

"No, Sir."

After a moment of charged silence he said, "See if you can fix it. But I think we're being jammed somehow."

Kaur stared blindly into space. *Jammed? You can't jam wormhole generators. It's impossible.* But the alien EMP weapon was impossible too. *Deal with it, Meena.*

"Aye aye," she said, and hung up. She rang the

engine room and reached a senior technician. "Tell Geibelhaus to fix the wormhole generator if he can. We need it badly."

By the despondent sound of the acknowledgement, the technician didn't hold out much hope. Kaur put the handset down, then looked around the bridge. "What's the enemy doing?"

"Spreading out to join the sphere," Specialist Jin said gloomily. "We're completely surrounded now." He gave her a bleak look. "And there's more ships still coming through that Gate. It doesn't look good, Ma'am."

Kaur surprised herself by chuckling. "We've never had so many targets to shoot at. We can hardly miss."

That earned her a thin smile. "You're right. What was I thinking? It'll be great."

Touhami snorted, then chuckled, and some of the tension on the bridge bled away. "We're about to have a hell of a scrap," Kaur said. "It won't be easy. But we're humanity's finest, and this is what we're trained for." She waved her hand to indicate the surrounding sphere of ships. "Those cockroaches have no idea what they've gotten themselves into."

The speech felt contrived, and it sounded absurd in her ears. But Touhami straightened up in his seat, and Captain Harrington, standing by the aft bulkhead, squared her shoulders and nodded to herself.

Kaur leaned back in her seat. *I've done what I can. There's nothing to do now but wait and see what happens next.*

# CHAPTER 6 – HAMMETT

Hammett stared through the forward windows of the *Theseus*, distantly aware that he was clenching and unclenching his fists. It was more nerves than he liked to show in front of crew, but for once he couldn't help himself. The entire mixed fleet, colony and EDF ships both, was about to be destroyed, and he couldn't see a damned thing he could do about it.

His eyes moved restlessly from one Hive ship to another. If he could just puzzle out which one was doing the jamming, maybe they could destroy the key ship and escape. But if there was any difference among the ships that hovered and circled, he couldn't see it. And for all he knew, the jamming came from the entire swarm.

Back and forth his gaze went. Ships were coming together, forming clumps of ten to twenty, big enough to pool their energy and melt holes in the hulls of every ship except the *Theseus*. When the converted freighter was the only ship left they'd find some way to deal with it as well.

It wouldn't be long now. He could sense it. Already ships were beginning to shift, move closer. By the look of it half the swarm was hanging back, keeping the fleet surrounded, while the rest, a mix of amalgamated ships and small individual craft, prepared to attack.

On the far side of that terrible sphere he could see the alien Gate, a dull metallic triangle still protected by a couple of dozen ships. No more ships came through, and his cheeks stretched in a mirthless grin. *Thank God for small mercies.*

"Admiral? Orders?"

"Hold steady, Sanjari," he said absently. It hardly mattered what they did. They would fight desperately, until they were overwhelmed and killed. The details weren't important. It wasn't as if there was some brilliant strategy he could pull out of the void that would give them an actual fighting chance. They could hand out a lot of damage before they died. And that was all.

*No more ships on the other side of that Gate.* The thought nagged him, distracting him. Any distraction from his rising terror was welcome, and he prodded the thought, trying to figure out why his subconscious figured it was important. "Every ship they've got came through," he muttered. "They all came through here to fight us."

Sanjari said, "Pardon me, Sir?"

Hammett turned. "N-" He paused, the word "nothing" sticking in his throat. *It's not nothing.* He turned back to the window. "They're all here."

Silence from Sanjari.

He whirled. "Call the fleet." He gestured. "The EDF fleet. And Kaur. Tell them to follow us."

Her eyebrows went up, but she reached for her console.

Eddie stared at Hammett over one thick shoulder. "Follow us? Where are we going?"

"Through that Gate," Hammett said, pointing. "It's the only way out of here. We'll run through and blow it behind us."

Eddie wasted a precious second staring at Hammett, open-mouthed. Then he grabbed the throttle control. Hal worked the nav thrusters, swinging the nose of the ship around as they surged into motion.

With no human ships in front of them the forward rail guns had a clear field of fire. The ship rushed the wall of Hive vessels, blasting one Hive ship to shreds in a single volley from the big guns. Smaller rail guns tore into other craft as the *Theseus* charged ahead. The sphere of Hive ships looked like a wall from this perspective, a wall that seemed to constrict as ships hurried to intercept the *Theseus*. Hal worked the nav thrusters, swinging the nose of the *Theseus* in a circle, and the rail guns thrummed. Alien ships blew apart, and then the *Theseus* sailed through the opening.

Hammett threw a quick glance over his

shoulder. The *Tomahawk* was right behind, close enough to pose a collision hazard, slightly above the *Theseus* to keep her out of line with the aft rail guns. The remains of the EDF fleet were rushing to follow, even as the sphere of Hive ships collapsed inward.

Hal let out a whoop, and Hammett turned back to the forward window. The cluster of alien ships guarding the Gate was hurrying forward to meet the *Theseus*, and the powerful forward rail guns were wreaking terrible carnage. The space in front of the *Theseus* turned to a glittering cloud of metal, spent rail gun rounds tumbling through a storm of shrapnel from destroyed Hive ships.

A chunk of debris thumped against the forward window, making Hammett flinch. Then they were through, and there was nothing between the *Theseus* and the alien Gate.

It looked nothing like the Gates humanity had built. Instead of a uniform circle of steel, he saw a giant rigid triangle, hundreds of meters on a side. At each point of the triangle a thick metal pyramid loomed, the size of a small house. Pale emerald light glowed from the seams where the faces of the pyramids met.

Would it work like a human-built Gate? Would it allow a ship to pass through from this side?

There was only one way to find out.

The nose of the *Theseus* swung around, and Eddie took a last frightened glance over his shoulder. Hammett gave him a curt nod, and Eddie pulled hard on the throttle lever.

The *Theseus* had quite a lot of lateral velocity, and for a terrible moment Hammett was sure they would smash into the side of the Gate, or miss it completely. Eddie knew exactly what he was doing, however. As the *Theseus* gained speed the Gate surged toward them, almost edge-on. It seemed to rotate as they neared and their lateral movement brought them closer to a perpendicular line. The *Theseus* was pointing straight at the center of the Gate as they finally shot through.

"Bring us about!"

Eddie and Hal reacted immediately as chaos swirled outside the windows. Hammett had a glimpse of tumbling rock, the gleam of metal, a blue-white glow as an engine flared. There was no time to take it all in. *You'll have plenty of time to see it all in a moment,* he told himself. *You're stuck here now.*

"I want us stationary relative to that Gate," he shouted, then made himself stop and take a breath. Eddie and Hal were barely out of arm's reach. There was no need to raise his voice. "Bring us in close," he said. "Not in line with the opening. But close."

A corvette came through the Gate, not the *Tomahawk*, an EDF ship trailing smoke from her port side. A bulky supply ship came through behind the corvette, a dozen holes gaping in her hull, none of them critical. Hammett looked around, eyes hunting the *Tomahawk*, and he felt a rush of relief as he spotted the little ship dropping into its familiar position just aft and above the *Theseus*.

Closer and closer the *Theseus* drifted to the Gate. Eddie braked, and the ship drifted to a stop no more than a hundred meters from the nearest side of the big triangle. More ships flashed into existence, another corvette followed by a strange-looking ship Hammett didn't recognize. It was painted Spacecom blue, but it was built like some strange cross between a cargo launcher and a warship.

"Point us at one of those pyramids," Hammett said, and the top pyramid seemed to slide down as the *Theseus* tilted.

A trio of Hive ships came through the Gate, one of them tumbling end over end. A destroyer came through next, and then Hive ships in a terrible wave.

"Fire!" Hammett bellowed, and Eddie echoed his command, speaking into his implants. The deck trembled as every forward-facing rail gun fired at once, and a storm of metal crashed against the Gate. The pyramid seemed impervious to the assault, one round after another striking it and bouncing away, spinning off to vanish into the darkness. A thick canister slammed into one of the bars extending down from the pyramid, though, and tore a great crack in the pale metal. An instant later a second round hit the same spot, and then a third, and there was an eruption of searing white light.

Hammett brought a hand up to shade his eyes, and when he lowered it, the pyramid, still glowing along the seams, was drifting away from the rest of the Gate. Two chunks of column jutted from the pyramid, the ends jagged and torn.

No more ships came through the triangle. The Gate was destroyed.

Small shapes darted among the battered ships of the human fleet. A dozen, two dozen …. The rest were gone, left stranded in the Naxos system, and Hammett felt a twinge of regret. *I've left you a nice surprise, Carruthers. You'll have to cope without me.*

He pushed the colony and its defenders from his mind. *Focus on the problems you can solve. Or at least address.* He turned away from the Gate. It was irrelevant now, so much scrap metal. "Who's left?" he said. "And where are we?"

"I count six EDF ships," Sanjari said, "plus the *Tomahawk*, and us." She glanced around at the windows. "It looks like the last of the Hive ships are pulling back."

The small cloud of alien vessels that had come through the Gate were having a rough time, suddenly surrounded by vengeful human warships. A last few survivors retreated out of easy rail gun range, twisting and dodging as they pulled well back from the little fleet.

"That was expensive," Sanjari said softly. "It looks like three corvettes, a destroyer, a supply ship, and that new ship made it through. And us and the *Tomahawk*. Nothing else."

*Made it through.* Hammett shook his head. *Made it through to where?* "Does anyone recognize any stars?"

"I see Orion," Hal said.

*Well, that's a relief. We aren't half way across the galaxy.* He turned, staring out through the starboard window.

Metal gleamed in the distance, thousands of kilometers away. Maybe tens of thousands. He saw a strange conglomeration of metallic shapes interspersed with massive chunks of stone. Without knowing the range he couldn't tell the size of the distant structure, but he sensed it was huge. Not planet-sized, but hundreds of kilometers across. By the look of it, the aliens had started by colonizing drifting chunks of stone. Eventually they'd linked the chunks together, probably to reduce collisions. They'd turned an asteroid field into a single massive settlement, a city of stone and metal drifting in space.

The whole mad structure was brightly lit on one side, and he turned his gaze in that direction. A blue-white star blazed in the sky, bigger than Sol looked from Mercury. If there were planets in this system, he couldn't see them. Had the aliens evolved here? Among the rocks, without a world of their own?

"Could this be it?" he said. "Could this be the Hive?"

"They're moving," Hal said, his voice high with alarm, and Hammett's head whipped around, searching for the little cluster of ships that had come through the Gate with them. They were, indeed, moving, retreating slowly from the human fleet. That couldn't be what had Hal so concerned. He scanned the sky, searching for enemy activity.

"Where are they going?" Sanjari said. "Admiral? Should we follow?"

"What?" Hammett looked at her. "Follow who?"

She pointed. The EDF fleet, all six ships, was in motion. He looked past the little fleet, trying to discern where they were headed. A cluster of asteroids floated in the distance, and the stars glittered bright and cold behind them. He could see nothing to attract the EDF ships.

He shrugged. *If that's where everyone is going, I guess we'd better go too.* "Signal the *Tomahawk*," he said. "Tell them to keep up." Not that Kaur needed to be told, but it was courteous to tell your allies what you were doing. A courtesy prominently missing from the EDF fleet. To Eddie he said, "Follow those ships, if you please. Let's not get left behind."

# CHAPTER 7 – CARRUTHERS

The satellite's deployed, Sir."

Carruthers nodded without turning his head. He stood facing the port window on the bridge of the *Indefatigable*. A shape floated beside the corvette, a lumpy sphere more than two meters across. It contained a miniature hydrogen fusion plant, a variety of electronics enclosed in nested Faraday cages, maneuvering thrusters for aiming, and a thermal cannon.

Most people called the alien weapon left behind in Garibaldi Plaza the "death ray", but Carruthers was trying hard to make "thermal cannon" catch on. He figured the planet needed a hundred or so of the cannons to be properly protected, some on the ground and some in orbit. The satellite floating on the other side of the window, the third weapon in orbit, brought the total to eight. He shrugged inwardly. It would have to do.

Every last cannon was vulnerable to missile fire from EDF ships. They were probably vulnerable to the alien EMP weapon, too, despite the Faraday cages. No one really understood how the aliens were frying electronics. Even systems with strong EMP shielding had failed. This hastily constructed and completely untested satellite might never get off a shot.

Of course, the aliens seemed to have abandoned the EMP attacks during recent encounters. That was good, but it was maddening not to know why. Was the attack expensive to launch? Did it use up a valuable resource? Were they blowing up chunks of plutonium every time, and now they were out? Or were they simply discouraged, because the *Alexander* and the relief fleet had taken an EMP pounding and kept on fighting?

It was one more exasperating puzzle in a long list, and he pushed it from his mind. Dealing with things he actually knew about was enough to keep him plenty busy. He had no time for pondering the unknown.

"I found them."

The speaker was Chavda, his tactical officer. She was doing her best to track Hammett's progress. With every jump, though, the fleet became more distant, the ships more impossibly tiny. It was harder to spot them each time.

"That's odd," said Chavda. She glanced at Carruthers, then touched her screen. "Let me show you."

A screen by the captain's chair lit up, and

Carruthers walked over. He dropped into his seat, then blinked, not sure what he was seeing.

Ships swarmed in the display, tiny vessels no bigger than specks. Little text labels appeared as the scanners picked up transponder data. *'Gideon'* flashed briefly beside one speck, then *'Tomahawk'*. Carruthers didn't know he was holding his breath until *'Theseus'* appeared, and he suddenly exhaled.

The other specks showed no transponder signals. They had to be the Hive, then, and he grimaced. There were so many of them!

Another text label appeared, then another. *'Adamant'. 'Kontos'*.

"It's the EDF fleet," he said. "But ..."

"There's too many of them," said Chavda.

Carruthers felt the blood surge fiercely in his veins. His gamble was paying off, better than he could have hoped. He had worried that he was selling out his old friend, sending the EDF after the little fleet. By the look of it, though, things had worked out perfectly. The two fleets had joined up, just in time to battle the alien swarm.

And it was working, too. One alien ship after another vanished from the display. He started to smile, until a sudden fear froze the expression on his face. He tapped at his display. "Come on, show me the *Theseus*."

No text label appeared. The freighter was gone. He searched for the *Tomahawk* next. It was gone as well.

"Oh, no." More tapping. He found the *Gideon*, her transponder still functioning, but she wouldn't last much longer. The *Adamant* was gone as well. It was a disaster.

"Maybe it's the EMP weapon."

Chavda looked up. "Captain?"

"Frying their transponders," he said. "Maybe they're not destroyed." But he could still see the signal from the *Gideon*, so that wasn't it.

"There goes the *Mercer*," Chavda said. "The *Gideon's* gone too." She looked up at Carruthers, her face bleak.

*We can't actually see what's happening. The screen shows nothing but a bunch of little dots. We don't know that they're all dead.* He knew, though. The Hive had adapted too well. The combined fleet had never stood a chance, not against so many ships.

"We should do something. We should go after them."

Carruthers wasn't sure which of his bridge crew had spoken. It's didn't matter. There was nothing to be done. That distant battle was over, and all those brave sailors were dead.

A different voice intruded. "I think I should tell him."

"You're crazy, man. It's the bridge! You can't just talk to the captain."

Carruthers looked up, glad for the distraction from the dark spiral of his thoughts. Two young men stood in the bridge entrance. They were young, barely out of their teens, and although they wore the same uniform as the rest of the crew, they were clearly not experienced sailors. They were gangly and awkward-looking, one with red hair and freckles, the other dark-haired and swarthy.

The redhead saw Carruthers looking at them and blushed incandescently. He hissed something to his companion and edged back.

The dark-haired man, however, held his ground. His fingers twitched and plucked at the seams on his uniform trousers, but he straightened up and said, "Captain. I've had a message."

Carruthers stared at him for a moment, trying to place him. The man shrank under his scrutiny. There were only a handful of colonists among the crew, and he wasn't one of the ex-crewmen from the science ship, so ... "Rigoberto, isn't it?" It took another moment for the last name to rise up out of his memory. "Sorry. Sailor Ramona."

Rigoberto nodded, apparently struck dumb by all this attention.

"Well, don't just stand there blocking the door. What's the message?"

Rigoberto took a hasty step into the bridge, clearing the doorway, then froze for a moment, clearly wondering if he'd taken an inappropriate liberty. Finally he blurted, "Vicente called me."

Carruthers waited, trying to keep amusement from his face. It was a long, long time since he'd been brand new to Naval life, but he still remembered those exciting, terrifying days.

"I was in the comms room," Rigoberto said. The ship had a tiny communications room on the lower deck so messages could be sent and received without disturbing the bridge crew.

"Vicente called." For a moment he squeezed his eyes shut. "He said there were EDF ships, and there were Hive ships, hundreds of them. He said there was lots of shooting. And then he said they were going through a Gate."

Carruthers felt his head jerk back. "What?"

"He said it was an alien Gate. He said they were going through. And then he just went silent."

Carruthers stared at him, processing the ramifications.

Rigoberto turned, took a step toward the corridor, then froze. "Oh. He said one more thing." His face scrunched up. "I'm sorry, Sir. I almost forgot. It's the most important part."

He stared at Carruthers in such misery that Carruthers didn't know whether to shake him or comfort him. Finally he just said, "Well? What is it?"

"He said they're going to blow the Gate from the other side. They're leaving all those alien ships on this side. He said we should get ready."

For a moment the two men stared at each other. "Is that all?"

Rigoberto nodded.

"All right. Thanks. You're dismissed."

Rigoberto nodded again and fled. Carruthers sighed, raked a hand through his hair, then looked at Chavda. "What are the Hive ships doing, Lieutenant?"

"Several ships have disappeared," she said, peering at her screen. "There go several more." She looked up. "More than half of them have vanished."

They might have followed the *Theseus* through whatever alien Gate she'd fled through, if she had indeed escaped. Or they might be opening wormholes and making smaller jumps.

And there weren't many places to go in the Naxos system.

"Contact Mr. Faraday," Carruthers said. "Tell him he should round up his gun crews. We might have company coming."

# CHAPTER 8 – BLOCH

P osition is confirmed, Sir."

Bloch, who had been leaning over the yac officer's shoulder, straightened up and looked at the navigation station.

"We're about forty light years from Earth," his nav officer said. She had to be rattled by that fact, but her voice was even, and he nodded his approval. "Thirty-five light years from Naxos," she added. "We went almost straight down. A few degrees toward the core."

That would be priceless information if he could bring it back to Earth – a possibility that looked painfully unlikely. "Signal Spacecom," he said, and she nodded. Forty years was a long time, but you never knew. Someone might actually still need the information by the time it arrived.

He turned his attention back to the tactical station. Scanner data was pouring in from every ship remaining in the fleet, and the map of the system was becoming clearer every moment. "Horowitz," he said. "Give us a summary."

Lieutenant Claude Horowitz nodded. He was a bulky man in his fifties, a career lieutenant who had accepted EDF oversight without a murmur. If anything could fluster Lieutenant Horowitz, Bloch had yet to see it. The man had let himself go over the years – he was hardly the picture of a fit military man, prepared for any crisis – but he was solid and utterly reliable.

"We've scanned pretty much the whole system," Horowitz said, pitching his voice so the entire bridge could hear. "There are no planets, although we've seen some distant objects large enough to qualify as dwarf planets. They're quite far out."

He leaned back, making his chair creak, and gathered his thoughts for a moment. "The volume of debris in the system suggests some kind of planet-forming activity in the distant past. The rubble is not a proper asteroid belt, like we've got back home. It's more like the Jupiter field. Close to a sextillion tonnes, not counting really small stuff. Most of it's in a field with a radius of about ten million kilometers." He gestured at the forward bulkhead. "We're heading for the thickest part, but the field is all around us."

Bloch nodded, waiting for him to get to the meat of the report. The rest of the crew just listened.

"We've catalogued more than a thousand

separate alien artifacts," Horowitz continued. "Most of it is concentrated in the settlement we saw, about fifty thousand kilometers from here." He shrugged. "We assume it's a settlement."

Bloch made an impatient gesture.

"There are ships," Horowitz said, unperturbed. "Over two hundred vessels. Some are grouped into composite ships. The computer is analyzing the composite craft and counting the component vessels." He glanced at his screens. "There are also objects with designs we haven't seen before. Some are ships. We can tell from their movement. Others are stationary; they could be habitats, or cargo pods, or ships that just don't happen to be moving right now."

With luck, Bloch thought, they'd be able to disregard the unfamiliar ships. Surely the aliens had passenger transports, cargo vessels, other craft that weren't equipped for war. Lord knew, he had plenty to deal with already.

"We've also detected nine more Gates," Horowitz said. "There's no way to tell where they lead, of course. Some of them we can absolutely confirm are Gates, because we've seen ship traffic move through. The rest?" He made a gesture with one thick arm, like a half-shrug. "They're built exactly like the Gate we came through. I suppose they could be decoys, or they serve some purpose we can't imagine. It's a safe bet they're Gates, though."

"Monitor those Gates," Bloch said. "Tell me instantly if traffic increases." He imagined reinforcements pouring through, making things even more difficult than they already were. "What are the rest of the enemy ships doing?" As Horowitz started to speak, Bloch added, "Start with the warships."

"They're gathering near the settlement," Horowitz said. "I'm calling that big structure with the rocks the settlement." At Bloch's curt nod he said, "I think they're protecting their home from us. I think they're scared to attack."

*Or they're waiting for reinforcements.* He looked at the forward bulkhead, imagining the thickest part of the asteroid field, still a good fifteen minutes distant. *Reinforcements would be a disaster. And if this is truly the Hive itself, the home of the aliens, then every ship we can strand far from home is a victory.*

He touched a button on the arm of his chair. "Missile bay."

"Wong here."

"Mr. Wong. I'm going to need nine missiles." He thought for a moment. "Better make that eighteen. Two per target."

"Right, Sir. What am I aiming at?"

Bloch looked over Horowitz's shoulder. "Check your tac display. Your targets are marked with white triangles."

"Got it," Wong said.

"Immediate launch, if you please."

"Aye aye, Sir."

Data flashed in the corner of Horowitz's screen. "Missiles are away," said Wong.

"Good. Stand by."

"Four minutes until the first strike," Horowitz

said. "Nineteen minutes, thirty seconds until the last one."

Bloch nodded, wondering how sturdy the enemy Gates were. Would conventional explosives destroy them? He had no nuclear warheads in the missile bay. Spacecom had offered him one. They told him it had an eighty-five percent chance of exploding on impact, and just under a one percent chance of exploding on its own. It was very old. He'd been tempted, but ultimately he'd decided to keep the stupid thing off his ship.

Well, the *Theseus* had taken the last Gate down with rail gun rounds, so conventional missiles would probably do the job. He still wasn't sure if he was pleased by Hammett's stratagem. He didn't care for being stranded, but if he could unleash all the destructive fury of the *Cassandra* without a swarm of Hive ships destroying her, it would be worth it.

"First impact," Horowitz said, hunching over his console. When he looked up, he was beaming. "The Gate's completely destroyed, Sir!"

"Good," said Bloch. He made himself return to his seat. Peering over someone's shoulder was undignified. "What are the aliens doing?" His own screen showed an eruption of activity, like an anthill poked with a stick. He wanted Horowitz's analysis.

"Well, we sure got their attention," Horowitz said. He tapped at icons, looked from screen to screen, then said, "A dozen or so ships are heading for the destroyed Gate. They're flocculating." He glanced at Bloch, who scowled. "That is, they're coming together. Forming one ship. To move faster, I suppose." He peered into his display. "Scratch that. They're turning back." He looked up. "I guess they figured out it's too late to do anything about that Gate."

Bloch drummed his fingers on the arm of his chair, then made himself stop. The enemy swarm still looked like nothing but boiling chaos to him.

"Second impact," Horowitz announced. He couldn't keep the glee from his voice. "The second missile's still going. The first bird smashed the Gate completely. The second bird didn't have anything to hit." His fingers flew across the surface of his console. "I'm telling it to swing back and target the biggest piece of wreckage it can find. Make it harder for them to do repairs."

Some of the tension left Bloch's shoulders. It was working. Even if the Hive destroyed all the remaining missiles, he and Hammett had smashed three out of ten Gates. At the very least it should throw the enemy into disarray.

"Uh-oh," Horowitz said. He pointed at the surging dots on his display. "They're thinking about what they're doing, now." He paused, checking two different screens, then said, "I think we'll get three more Gates. They can't intercept in time. There are ships on their way to intercept the other missiles, though. They'll save the Gates closest to the settlement, and the ones on the far side. They can get to those in time."

*We've done what we can. Staring at the missile*

*paths on the screen won't help.* "Listen up," he said, looking around the bridge. "Our little vacation is almost over. We're about to strike the biggest blow ever struck in this war." He swept an arm in the general direction of the alien settlement. "The *Cassandra* is about to get its first-ever field test. We're going to unleash Hell on the Hive."

A less disciplined crew might have cheered. A few people gave him fierce smiles.

"Right now they're keeping an eye on us, but they're staying back," he continued. "That's about to change. As soon as they see rocks starting to fly – and they realize they can't stop the barrage – they're going to come after us. So be ready."

All around the bridge people nodded and turned back to their consoles. Bloch nodded as well, satisfied that his people were as ready as they could be. *They can't stop the barrage.* He shook his head. *They better not be able to. If they can survive the* Cassandra, *we've dropped ourselves in the fire for nothing.*

It was an unproductive line of thought, and he abandoned it. He would do as much damage as he could in the time that remained to him, and then he would die.

Of course, if the opportunity to survive presented itself he would take it, if his duty allowed. It would be good if someone made it back to Earth. Spacecom needed to know where the Hive was, and what happened during the battle that was about to begin. If he could make it home ...

He thought of his family, of his wife who waited so patiently each time he was deployed away from Earth. It would be good to see her again, to see the relief in her eyes when she saw he'd returned to her once more. It would be good to see his children. They didn't live at home anymore, but they would come to see him if he made it back from such a dangerous tour.

After the damage he was about dish out to the Hive, they might even be proud of him. He grimaced at the thought. Both of them had joined the anti-EDF movement. They wore white and marched in protests, and risked death from a vengeful EDF. It was the foolish rebellion of youth, nothing more. When they were older they would look back on these days and be ashamed. For now, though, they were adamantly opposed to their father and everything he stood for.

But they were still his kids. Whatever hostility they nurtured, they would come to see him if he made it back to Earth. The four of them were still a family. They could put aside politics for an evening and be together once more.

"Another Gate is gone," Horowitz announced. "We might even get one more than I expected." He pointed at his screen, as if anyone else could make out the details. "I don't think they're going to be in time to save Gate Charlie." The computer would have assigned names to each target when the missiles launched. "The birds are too fast. They're going to be about twenty seconds too late."

Bloch nodded. "Good." Three Gates would survive the missile barrage, then. If the Hive ships were slow to respond, he might even have the *Cassandra* take a few shots at the Gates that remained. The system was target-rich, but he decided the Gates would be his second priority, after the destruction of the settlement.

"Missiles Eleven and Twelve have been destroyed," Horowitz said, and shook his head. "They crashed a ship into each one. Crazy buggers." He consulted a corner of his screen. "Missiles Nine and Ten made it past their interceptors, though. Looks like they'll go all the way."

Bloch checked his own screen. The fleet was decelerating as it neared the asteroid field. The *Theseus* and the *Tomahawk* were still with him, he saw. Well, under the circumstances he'd accept their help. If he and Hammett were both alive at the end of it all, that would be soon enough to deal with the man. Most likely, the Hive swarm would make their conflict irrelevant. *He's a good fighting man. I'm glad he's here. He's got a tough ship. I'd be happier if it was in the hands of a more reliable crew, but Hammett will do.*

# CHAPTER 9 – HARDY

Ken Hardy sat in the *Tomahawk's* tiny mess hall, bodies pressing in close on every side. The little room was completely jammed, mostly with crew from the *Gideon*. It occurred to him that he would have a hard time getting to his fighter if he was called, but he kept his eyes shut, riveted by the feed coming to his implants from the computers on the nearby EDF ships. That was quite a security breach, he reflected. Spacecom was woefully unprepared to deal with civil war.

The fleet was at rest, floating in the thick of an asteroid field. At first he'd thought the asteroids were for cover, but he could make out movement among the rocks. The *Cassandra*, the mysterious new ship, was drawing in chunks of rock and carving them up with lasers. He had no idea why.

He couldn't wait to find out.

Someone's hip jostled his right shoulder,

knocking him against the woman on his left. She turned to see what was happening, and caught Hardy in the eye with an elbow. He stood, clapping a hand to his eye. *To hell with this. There's just as much room in the cockpit, and I get to be alone.* A couple of blinks told him his eye was still functioning. He lowered his hand and pushed himself into the crowd, squirming and wriggling.

Reaching the door wasn't easy, but he managed it eventually. Sailors lined one side of the corridor outside, standing patiently with nothing to do but wait. Hardy hurried past them, suddenly grateful to have a destination, a role to play. Even if all he did was sit in the cockpit waiting for orders that never came, it had to be better than abandoning ship and standing in a corridor, wondering when the new ship would come apart around you.

It took him almost five minutes to reach the hatch leading to his fighter, a trip he could have made in forty-five seconds flat most days. He climbed a short ladder, squirmed his way into the pilot's seat, sealed the hatch in the floor, and heaved a sigh of relief. *Alone at last.*

He'd sat out the last battle, before the mad retreat through the alien Gate. It frustrated him that he'd missed the action, but the truth was, he was pretty sure he'd be dead if the order had come to launch. The little fighter was terribly vulnerable. He'd flown it in combat once, and survived by the narrowest of margins. The odds now were much worse, and there would be no ground-based death ray to save him this time.

The fighter perched on top of the corvette like a nestling on the back of a swan, giving him a panoramic view of the asteroid field through the cockpit windows. He couldn't see the alien settlement, or any other alien technology, which disappointed him. It was also a bit comforting, he had to admit.

The *Theseus* was dead ahead, reassuring him with its massive bulk. The former freighter bristled with rail gun turrets of every size and configuration. It looked lethal, and he was glad of its presence. *I'll have to give it some space, though. Maybe stay on the far side of the* Tomahawk. *It's going to be throwing out a lot of flying metal.*

Almost directly above him he could see the *Cassandra.* From his perspective the big ship looked like a gleaming steel tower, painted dark blue. At the near end rocks came drifting in, captured and controlled expertly by the ship's tractor beams and force fields. He caught the dazzle of a laser as hovering robots carved pieces from a rock almost the size of the *Tomahawk.* Along the side of the tower a wireframe sleeve held half a dozen rocks that had already been cut. Each of the rocks, though smaller than the behemoth currently being sliced up, was still enormous. The *Bumblebee*, Hardy's fighter, could have sat inside that sleeve with clearance on every side.

The *Cassandra* was clearly going to do something with those rocks. They were queued up in that sleeve almost like ...

*Like ammunition in a magazine.*

He almost missed the firing of the weapon, even though he was looking right at it. The motion came so quickly that it was over before he registered it. He wasn't sure he'd actually seen anything until he made out the shape of a metal block travelling rapidly from the tip of the tower back to the base.

Rapidly, but much, much slower than it had gone up. He stared, perplexed. The metal block, almost as wide as the tower itself, reached the bottom, and the rocks in the sleeve shifted. He couldn't quite make out what happened, but now there were five rocks in the sleeve, not six.

The metal block vanished. He spotted it a moment later, dropping rapidly toward the base of the tower, and understanding washed over him. It was a giant slingshot, lobbing boulders the size of cottages. His jaw dropped, and his mouth remained open as the *Cassandra* fired again.

*They could smash the alien settlement with that gun. They could obliterate it completely. Good God. It's a doomsday weapon.*

*And it's in the hands of the EDF. What will we do when they run out of aliens to shoot at?*

He pushed the thought from his mind. *They would never do that. It would be unthinkable. They wouldn't fire that thing at our fleet. Or at Ariadne.*

*Would they?*

*Well, they won't have the chance. It's not as if*

*we have a way to get back.* He craned his neck as the *Cassandra* fired again, trying to see where the rocks were going. The target was somewhere aft, though. He couldn't make it out. He closed his eyes instead and brought up a tactical display.

The alien settlement still glittered among the rocks, untouched. Hardy frowned. *Did they miss? Do the aliens have some kind of shield?*

*What kind of shield could stop a rock that size?*

The *Cassandra* was still firing, one rock after another hurtling out into the darkness of space. He instructed the tactical net to show him the path of the rocks that had been fired.

He had underestimated the scale of the system, he realized. The first rock was still on the way to its target. He tried to calculate how many rocks would be in motion by the time the first rock hit, then abandoned the effort and decided just to watch.

The first impact was disappointing. The rock slammed into a much larger lump of stone between two sections of glittering steel. By the look of it the rock from the *Cassandra* vaporized on impact. It jarred the entire settlement structure, though, and Hardy saw bits of metal and plastic break loose and float away in a cloud.

The second rock was a miss. It whipped past the narrowest part of the settlement, missing stone and steel by scant meters. Hardy gaped, his mouth open, wanting to shout a protest. *We finally have a weapon that can hurt them, and it missed? It's not fair!*

Rock Number Three collided directly with one

of the structures that connected two chunks of asteroid, and the effect was everything Hardy could have hoped for. The stone blasted a jagged hole in the front of the settlement, and shock waves washed outward. Debris and vapor poured from the entry hole, and the entire settlement shuddered.

Rock after rock slammed into the settlement. Each one moved on a slightly different trajectory, its path altered by irregularities in the shape and density of the stone missiles. This was magnified by the huge distance, so that rocks struck as much as half a kilometer apart. There were several more misses, but most of the barrage found its target.

A nav thruster glowed on the top of the tower. The *Cassandra* was swinging her nose over so she could rake the settlement from end to end. The destruction was glorious and horrible, and Hardy drank it in. Some of the asteroids that anchored the settlement were breaking apart under the barrage. He could see large manufactured sections that, so far, were undamaged, but other parts were all but wiped out.

The blaring of an alarm jerked his attention back to the *Bumblebee*. He opened his eyes. Every screen in the fighter was live, and he soon saw why.

The aliens were on the move.

A cloud of ships surged out from the settlement. After a minute or so of indecision the aliens had figured out they only had one way to stop this lethal barrage.

They had to destroy the ships that were causing it.

Hardy spent an intense moment with his hands hovering over his controls, adrenalin sizzling in his blood as the alarm blared in his ears. He sat like that, poised and ready, as the seconds ticked past. Then he shook his head and lowered his arms. The aliens were coming, all right, but they were a long way off. Sure, he was doomed, but there was nothing he could actually *do* for several minutes at least. He closed his eyes again, this time not viewing anything on his implants, and concentrated on breathing in and out. Massive adrenalin dumps when you couldn't act on them were worse than useless.

The fleet began to move, ships turning and arranging themselves in a kind of staggered grid. The *Adamant* moved in close to the *Cassandra*, edging forward so she was ahead of the gleaming tower but well out of the path of the rocks, which were still sailing out at five-second intervals. The EDF corvettes took up positions around the two larger ships. The point, from what Hardy could see, was to protect the *Cassandra* and keep her firing for as long as possible.

At first there seemed to be no place for the *Theseus* and the *Tomahawk*. After a long pause the *Theseus* began to move below the *Cassandra* and *Adamant*, the *Tomahawk* keeping station just behind and above the freighter. Hardy stared up at the gleaming length of the *Cassandra*, watching as the stone launcher flashed past, then returned.

He could see the alien settlement with his naked eyes now. It was too distant for him to make out the details of the damage – until he saw one end of the long, meandering structure begin to turn, while the other end remained stationary. "We broke it in half," he murmured, hardly daring to believe it. "We busted it in two."

At first he couldn't see the approaching Hive ships. When he spotted them, all he really saw was a red and white haze that blurred parts of the distant settlement. Only when individual ships emerged from the haze, appearing as black dots, did he realize what he was seeing. The Hive ships were plunging toward him, decelerating hard. He saw the glow of their engines as they braked.

There were fewer ships than he'd expected – no more than a couple of dozen at the most – and he experienced a brief moment of optimism. Then he glanced at his display screens and groaned. Each ship was an amalgam, roughly a dozen ships joined together to boost their acceleration.

*I'm doomed. I'm a dead man.* The thought had been in the back of his mind for a while, solidifying when the *Tomahawk* went through the enemy Gate. When the *Theseus* destroyed the Gate behind them, the thought had become a cold certainty. He'd pushed it from his mind, though.

Now it was back. He tried to push the thought away, found it wouldn't leave, and examined it instead.

*I'm going to die. I'm dozens of light years from home. Hundreds, maybe. I'm in the Hive's home system. In fact, I'm looking at the Hive itself. I'm guarding a weapon that's demolishing their home. There's nowhere to run, and no way I could let myself run even if there was somewhere to go. This is the day I die.*

*But I get a rare privilege. I get to die giving the* Cassandra *a few more shots at those filthy skittering little bugs. We're giving them a good pounding. We might be making all of humanity safe right now. At the very least we're setting them back. Giving every human being alive a chance to recover, regroup, prepare.*

*I get to be a part of that. History may never know what we do here today, but I'll know. I'm going to keep the* Cassandra *firing for just a few moments longer.*

*This will be a good death.*

"Hardy," said a voice in his ear, and he felt a cold prickle go dancing across his skin.

"Hardy here."

"Launch," said the voice. "And good luck."

He reached down, grabbed the handle that controlled the grapple holding him to the hull of the corvette, and pulled.

And the *Bumblebee* launched.

# CHAPTER 10 – CARRUTHERS

H ere they come," said Chavda. "If they keep braking, they'll be here in five minutes, nineteen seconds."

*And if they stop braking,* Carruthers thought, *they'll whip past at high velocity and slam into the planet. So I think they'll keep braking.* He didn't voice the thought. He'd served as a lieutenant under a captain, now mercifully retired, who'd mocked his officers for stating the obvious. The result had been silent, strained hostility, the last thing he wanted on his own bridge. The galaxy didn't need another horse's ass in a command position.

"It looks like eighty-three individual ships," Chavda added. They were formed into nine composite ships at the moment. *Sharing their thrust while minimizing their vulnerability to missile strikes,* Carruthers thought.

"Thank you, Lieutenant. It should be an

interesting scrap."

She glanced back at him, her lips quirking in a strained smile. "Yes, Sir."

"This isn't a planned attack," Carruthers said, addressing the entire bridge. "They didn't decide they were ready to tackle us. The admiral caught them by surprise. He shot up their fleet and blew up their Gate. He stranded them here, and they've panicked." He gestured at the forward bulkhead, in the general direction of the approaching ships. "They don't have anywhere else to go. They don't know what to do. So they're making a last, desperate, ill-advised attack."

He watched the bridge crew exchange glances. They wanted to believe him, but he sensed they figured he was just trying to buck them up.

Which he was, of course.

"If they were thinking," he went on, "they'd throw another rock at the colony. Then we'd have to fly out there, and fight them in deep space. But they're not doing that." He gestured again, this time toward the planet below. "Instead, they're fighting us here. In range of all those thermal cannons." That entirely inadequate, tiny number of thermal cannons. Eight of them, only six of which actually covered this stretch of sky. And that included the satellites. If any of the satellites actually hit an enemy ship, Carruthers would eat his new uniform.

"They're desperate," he repeated, "and we're ready for them." *Please, God, let us be ready for them. Eighty-three ships, and us without a single square centimeter of Fourier metal in the entire fleet.* "This is what we've been waiting for. They're making a mistake, and we're going to capitalize on it. We're going to destroy the enemy threat, once and for all."

It sounded thin to him – what wouldn't sound thin, with eighty-three ships bearing down? – but there were no more shared glances among the crew.

"Enjoy this moment," he said. "You'll tell your grandchildren about the final battle for Ariadne, when the Hive was finally wiped out in the Naxos system."

That, he thought, had to be too much, but Chavda turned and flashed her teeth in a nasty grin. Then she said, "One of the composite ships has stopped braking."

That was odd. What in space could that mean? "We'll ignore that one for now," he said. "There's more than enough to keep us busy until they get back into the battle."

She nodded, started to fidget, then stilled her hands with an obvious effort. Carruthers smiled. He knew exactly how she felt.

"They're closing," said Chavda a moment later. "The ships are breaking up."

On Carruthers' screen the alien ships seemed to disintegrate, breaking into a cloud of smaller ships. They were forming groups of three, by the looks of it. Just enough to provide a bit of shielding. Well, if they weren't going to fire their EMP weapon, he wasn't going to pass up the opportunity to make use of advanced combat computers.

"Signal the fleet," he said. "I want two ships firing on each target. I want to overwhelm their shields."

In the corner of his eye he saw a flash of movement, gone almost before he could register it. It was the one amalgamated ship, he realized. The one that hadn't braked. "Signal the colony, too," he added. "Tell them they might be under attack."

The starfield tilted as the *Indefatigable* turned, controlled by the ship's computer. On his display he saw colored lines as the corvette's lasers and rail guns fired. Similar lines shot out from every ship in the little fleet. The *Indefatigable* and the corvette *Stiletto* concentrated their fire on a cluster of ships almost a hundred kilometers distant. A white circle around the three-ship cluster showed the shields holding for a moment as laser fire burned in. Then twin streams of rail gun fire slammed into the cluster and it vanished from the display.

The battle became frustratingly automated, ships' computers reacting faster than any helm or tactical officer could, pouring coordinated fire into one cluster after another. The *Indefatigable* helped destroy three composite ships before the enemy was suddenly among the fleet.

Now the enemy clusters clumped together, three clusters joining to form an attack ship nine strong. These raced in close and used their heat weapons on the hulls of the colony ships. Chavda stopped watching, working now in close cooperation with the computer. She targeted a ship as it rushed the hull of the *Stiletto*, and the *Indefatigable* opened fire.

It took longer to break through the shields of the larger cluster, but the time was still measured in seconds. The cluster broke apart, and the *Indefatigable's* lasers, choosing targets with inhuman speed, burned into solitary ships before they could flee.

"We've got one on us!" cried Jarvis, the lieutenant at the helm. He jerked sideways on the main control stick, the ship swung down and to port, and Carruthers saw the gleam of metal as a dark shape covered the front edge of the starboard window. Alarms blared as the alien heat weapon burned into the hull.

Jarvis lifted his hands from the controls, looking as if the effort was all he could endure, and the *Indefatigable* swung around under computer control. The *Marlborough* loomed through the starboard window, and Carruthers saw sunlight glitter on a stream of rail gun rounds. The troopship wasn't terribly well armed, but she wasn't entirely toothless either.

Laser light sparkled on the hull of the alien ship. For an instant the laser shone through the steelglass window, leaving a deep scorch mark on the forward bulkhead of the bridge. Then the alien dropped away, smaller ships scattering to flee in every direction.

"Let's return the favor," Carruthers said. "There's a couple of bogeys on the *Marlborough*."

The aliens hovered amidships, far from any critical systems. Empty passenger compartments would be depressurizing, but the ship could survive a few hull breaches. It gave the rest of the fleet a good opportunity to focus their fire on attackers who kept reasonably still.

The *Indefatigable* swept in low over the hull of the troopship. The angle made it easier to fire on the nearest alien cluster without hitting the *Marlborough*, and Carruthers watched on his tac screen as the *Indefatigable* opened up with lasers and rail guns. When the cluster finally broke apart the nose of the corvette tilted up, and several of the individual ships blew apart or went spiraling off into the dark, disabled. Others rose until they were in range of the troopship's guns, and came to a nasty end at the hands of vengeful fire from the *Marlborough*.

The *Indefatigable* tilted, and Carruthers glanced through the starboard window. The *Marlborough* looked terrible, great dark trenches burned into her hull. She'd need a major overhaul after this. The *Epee* and the *Stiletto* were ganging up on a cluster on the *Marlborough's* port side, and Carruthers watched the cluster break apart. By the look of it, not a single component ship escaped.

"Starboard!" cried Chavda. Carruthers' head whipped around. A composite ship dropped toward the starboard window, the heat weapon on the underside already glowing. It was a scant few meters from the corvette when a flash of white blinded him for an instant. A moment later, scraps of wreckage clattered against the window.

"I guess the death rays are working," Chavda said. She glanced to port. "There's another one."

Carruthers turned, too late to see the white flash lancing up from the surface of the planet. Instead he saw a litter of ship parts as a cluster broke apart. The *Marlborough*, not the most maneuverable ship in the fleet, managed to swing her nose around in time to pour a volley into the survivors.

"The *Balisong* is disabled," announced the sailor at the communications station. "They're in a decaying orbit. Captain Jeung says their situation's not urgent."

Rail gun rounds slammed into the starboard window, a quick clatter loud enough to echo through the bridge. Carruthers flinched – the whole bridge crew did – and stepped closer to the window, inspecting the damage. The steelglass was dented, distorting the stars in a line of five evenly spaced depressions the size of his palm. The ship was still airtight, though, despite everything. The faceplate on his helmet was still retracted.

Looking out through the window was an invitation to nausea. The corvette kept swiveling and twisting, bucking and rolling, as it evaded attacking clusters or, more often, targeted enemy ships. The computer was doing nearly everything, coordinating with other ships, unleashing barrages as part of a volley from multiple ships. One alien cluster after another broke apart, and the surviving ships seldom got far.

*We're winning this.* He resisted the thought, but it was getting harder to deny. His speech about the aliens being desperate and making a mistake had been largely bravado, but it seemed to be true. The aliens were fighting in a panicked frenzy, as if they knew they were doomed but had nowhere to flee.

A chunk of wreckage, an alien ship sliced in half by a laser, banged against the window and floated away, disappearing when the *Indefatigable* rolled to meet a new threat. Scraps of alien ships filled the sky. There would be beautiful meteors in the skies over the colony for weeks. Carruthers looked at the wreckage of dozens of ships and felt something almost like sadness. It seemed odd to pity such merciless, savage foes, but this battle reeked of desperation. He was seeing a last stand by warriors with nowhere to go. He had to destroy them, but he could mourn them as he did it.

The corvette turned, and a new shape filled his view, a metallic bulk almost as big as the troopship. Carruthers saw one alien ship after another race in to join the behemoth, and watched a stream of rail gun rounds slow and turn as it neared the alien hull. The rounds bounced harmlessly away, repelled by magnetic shielding.

If the aliens had formed a single massive ship at the start of the battle they might have prevailed. Now, however, not enough ships remained. The *Indefatigable* turned, and the alien ship disappeared from view. It was dead ahead now, and Carruthers found himself looking at the ravaged side of the *Marlborough*, with the *Epee* visible just above her. The colony fleet was gathering, grouping their ships to pool their fire in an overwhelming volley aimed at the center of the alien ship. As far as he knew it was the fleet's ship computers guiding this part of the battle. It seemed like a sound strategy, so he did nothing to override the computer.

He returned to his seat, watching the view from the forward cameras as lasers and rail gun rounds slammed into the alien. At the same time, thermal cannon fire lashed up from the planet below. One white streak after another scorched into the underside of the alien ship, destroying one or two or three of the little composite ships each time.

With every hit the alien's shields weakened. The rail gun rounds pouring in from the fleet flew straighter, and hit with more force. Finally the shield failed entirely and an inferno of destructive energy tore into the alien ship.

The survivors panicked. Ships broke apart and fled, hunted by laser beams and projectiles. The thermal cannons on the surface fired, obliterating the ships they hit. Carruthers watched one ship after another take a fatal hit, and suddenly there were no more targets.

Not a single alien craft had escaped.

He blinked, staring into his tactical display, hardly daring to believe it. Oh, a few ships might have slipped away in the chaos. Half a dozen, at the outside. Not enough to cause much of a problem. And he suspected the number was smaller.

He suspected it was zero.

"It's over," he said. "Merciful God in Heaven, it's over." He looked around the bridge, seeing the same startled relief on the faces of the others. "Jarvis. Plot an intercept course with the *Balisong*. It would be pretty rude to let them crash." They'd link with the other corvette, pull it up into a stable orbit, probably offload any nonessential crew. He switched the tactical display over to a damage report. He'd verify the status of the *Indefatigable* before he tried to give support to anyone else.

"Sir?"

He looked up. Chavda met his gaze, and he felt his stomach tighten as he saw the tension in her face. "What is it, Rekha?"

"It's not quite over." When he gave her a blank look she said, "That one big ship. The one that stopped decelerating?"

His relief evaporated. "Oh. Right."

"There's nothing on the tactical display," she said. "I think they're planetside."

He glanced to his right, where the bulk of Ariadne showed as a rusty bar along the bottom of the starboard window. *We won this part of the battle. But what's happening down there?*

# CHAPTER 11 – HARDY

When the Hive ships were close enough that Hardy could make out the component craft with his naked eyes, the first wave of missiles lashed out. Half a dozen missiles streaked forward, trailing lines of vapor, each targeting a different amalgamated ship. Each missile exploded just short of its target, hitting a sacrificial ship sent out as a shield. Hardy glanced over at the *Adamant*, wondering how many missiles it carried.

Not the several hundred they'd need to actually survive this battle.

"Fighters converge on Bravo," said a voice in his ear. His tactical display showed a label on each amalgamated ship, and a red circle appeared around the one marked 'Bravo'. When he looked up his implants painted a red circle around the corresponding ship. He saw motion in his peripheral vision as three more fighters advanced.

*I'm in the EDF fighter comms net*, he realized. He glanced back at the *Tomahawk. Well, they aren't giving me any contradictory orders.* He hit the *Bumblebee's* thrusters, keeping pace with the EDF fighters as they advanced on target Bravo.

"Missile in five," said the voice in his ear.

The other fighters opened fire about four seconds later, so Hardy joined in. He was close to Bravo, close enough that it terrified him. The massive ship seemed to be hurtling straight at him, engines blazing as it continued to decelerate. Laser beams splashed across the surface of the amalgamated ship, stopping just short of the hull, dissipated by an energy shield. Rail gun rounds poured in, a quadruple torrent from all four fighters, only to slow and turn as they neared the ship. Hardy watched in frustration as his rounds bounced from the alien hull and tumbled away, doing no harm.

"Missile away."

Instantly a smaller ship detached itself from the rest of the alien craft. The other fighters concentrated their fire on the lone ship, and Hardy joined in, seeing their strategy. The little ship, without the others boosting its shielding, took a vicious pounding from the four fighters. The hull began to shred, and the ship tumbled sideways.

An instant later, the missile flashed past. It missed the blocking ship by a handspan, then slammed into the big ship. Hardy squeezed his eyes shut against a flash of light, and opened them to see bits of wreckage rebounding from his cockpit windows.

After that, there were no more coordinated attacks. All the amalgamated alien ships broke apart and surged forward in a chaotic swarm. Hardy opened fire, destroying an advancing ship at a range of less than ten meters. Other ships blew apart around him as the fleet opened up. For a moment Hardy just flew straight, afraid to fly into the path of lasers and rail guns from the fleet.

Then a ship loomed beside him, three alien craft together, the heat weapon on the belly of the amalgamated ship glowing red. Hardy forgot about the danger of friendly fire as he twisted the *Bumblebee* sideways. No one had quite gotten around to giving him any Fourier shielding, a grievous oversight in his opinion. He had to trust to nimble flying and good luck to keep himself alive.

Something clanged against the nose of the *Bumblebee*, tearing a furrow in the skin of the fighter. A rail gun round, he decided. Friendly fire, but he was too busy to worry about it. More rounds hit the amalgamated ship chasing him. It must have been a volley from the *Theseus*, because the hole that appeared in the middle craft was as big as Hardy's head. The other two ships broke away, leaving their crippled companion to float among the wreckage.

For several seconds that felt like hours Hardy twisted and dove in the thick of the swarm. Then he found himself in empty space. He and the other fighters weren't a priority, he saw.

Only the *Cassandra* mattered.

The aliens closed on the big gunship. A few Hive ships came too close to the top of the tower and were shattered as another rock erupted out.

Hardy turned the *Bumblebee* and headed for the action. Alien ships coalesced in front of him, darting in close and turning their heat weapons on the tower. He saw an EDF fighter strafe an amalgamated ship, doing little damage.

The *Theseus* loomed suddenly close, her nose pointed straight at the amalgamated ship as it began to melt the side of the *Cassandra*. A storm of ballistic rounds erupted from the converted freighter, and the amalgamated ship seemed to fly apart.

"Bloody hell!" A woman swore in Hardy's ear, and he saw an EDF fighter twist away from the barrage, the end of one wing a jagged, splintered mess. "Let's go with the secondary target. We're not doing any good here, and we're not going to live long enough to find a target."

"Roger," said a man, and another fighter pulled out of the cloud of metal. Hardy watched them race away from the battle, wondering if he should follow.

An alarm blared in his ears. He'd been scorched in passing by a laser. A moment later, the *Bumblebee* rocked as three or four rail gun rounds banged into her nose.

"To hell with this," Hardy muttered. He hauled on the stick, feeling the ship vibrate as his nav thrusters swung him around. The one alien attack had bubbled some of the paint on his starboard side, but all the real damage was coming from friendly fire.

He pointed the nose of the *Bumblebee* at the tails of the two retreating fighters and goosed the engine.

*I wonder where we're headed?* The EDF pilot had said she had a 'secondary target', and that, Hardy decided, was good enough for him.

As he raced into the darkness he glanced back at the battle. Most of the aliens were swarming the *Cassandra*, but a few ships were going after corvettes as well. He saw one ship drop in close to the *Theseus*, then break apart and scatter as the *Theseus* swung around, bringing her aft guns to bear. For an instant he considered turning back, trying to help. But the little alien ships, although they evaded the *Theseus'* main battery, were disintegrating, ripped up by lasers and ballistic rounds. The *Bumblebee* wouldn't last a minute in that maelstrom.

*And how long will I last, without a fleet to go back to?*

A yellow pulse glowed on his tactical screen. A rock had just gone past, a kilometer or so to starboard. A moment later he saw another flash. The *Cassandra*, despite the way she was being mobbed, was still firing.

*Your 'secondary target' had better be worthwhile*, he silently told the fighters ahead of him. *It's probably the last thing we're going to do.*

The battle raged on behind him as the three fighters raced into the dark.

# CHAPTER 12 – HAMMETT

ark against the side of the *Cassandra*. We need to be able to shoot those things without hitting her."

Eddie gave Hammett a quick, frightened glance over his shoulder, then turned to his controls. The *Theseus* was close to the aft end of the elongated ship. As they moved closer, the absurdly long structure of the *Cassandra* wobbled and shook through the front windows in vertigo-inducing swoops.

The *Cassandra* was essentially a massive gun with an eight-hundred-meter barrel. A dozen holes gaped along the length of that barrel, showing twisted metal struts still glowing with heat. The gun still worked, though. Hammett caught a flicker of motion as the armature retracted from the forward end of the ship, ready to fire another round.

He wondered briefly if it had all been worth it,

then dismissed the thought. Of course it had. They were doing real damage here today. Crippling the Hive, if he was any judge. If even one ship could escape to bring word back to Earth about the location of the alien nest, humanity might be able to return before the aliens could recover.

They might wipe the Hive out completely.

In the meantime, every shot the *Cassandra* managed to fire was a victory. He felt a vibration through the deck plates as the *Theseus* bumped against the *Cassandra*. Many of the smaller gun turrets could be aimed, but the big guns, the nine rail guns pointing forward and the nine pointing aft, could not. They pointed wherever the ship pointed.

And now, they pointed along the ravaged hull of the *Cassandra*.

A Hive ship swooped in a hundred meters or so ahead. It noticed the *Theseus* and jerked back, then moved sideways, coming in close to the hull of the *Cassandra* well off to one side. Eddie and Hal got busy without waiting for orders, working the ship's nav thrusters with the skill of virtuoso pianists. The *Theseus* drifted sideways, staying close enough to the *Cassandra* that the two hulls bumped several times.

The forward rail guns began to fire as the *Theseus* lined itself up with its target. From Hammett's position this close to the hull of the *Cassandra* the EDF ship looked like a long silver plain stretching away before him. The alien ship was a strange lumpy balloon floating just above the plain. Silver gave way to red just beneath the balloon as the heat weapon burned into the *Cassandra's* hull.

The balloon began to shred as massive rounds tore into it. It drifted sideways, but Eddie and Hal kept the *Theseus* drifting along with it. Round after round hit the alien vessel, and at last it came apart. Component ships banged into the hull of the *Cassandra*. Others spun away, tumbling into space.

Into the midst of that wreckage came a corvette, one of the EDF ships, lasers and rail guns blasting. The hull of the corvette was strange, lumpy with parasitic shapes. Limpet ships, Hammett realized. He'd encountered them on the *Alexander*, where they had torn through the hull to put commandoes into the corridors of his ship.

That was months ago. Now, the aliens knew so much more about human ships and technology. What horrors would they be unleashing inside that corvette?

Even as the thought formed, the corvette lost control. A nav thruster flared on the port side and the corvette collided with the *Cassandra*. The two hulls scraped together, and then the corvette bounced away, tumbling end over end.

"Oh, my God." That was Vicente Ramona, eyes glued to the window, hands locked to the arms of his chair in a deathgrip. He spoke again, more softly this time. "Oh, my God."

*I need to get him off my bridge. It's not like we need him for communications, not on this side of the Gate.*

Before Hammett could order the boy to go, Hal twisted in his seat. "What do we do, Admiral?"

"We keep on fighting," Hammett said grimly.

"But – shouldn't we help them?" Hal made a helpless gesture toward the corvette. "Try to dock with them? Get survivors?"

*Dock with them? Like hell. I'm not letting alien commandoes on board.* "We fight," Hammett repeated. "We keep the *Cassandra* firing."

Hal locked eyes with him for a moment longer, then turned away. The *Theseus* drifted sideways, circling the hull of the *Cassandra*, looking for more Hive ships.

It didn't take long to find some. The next attack was close to the forward end of the ship, almost half a kilometer distant. Eddie and Hal lined the *Theseus* up as best they could, and the ship began another barrage. It was hard to see if the rail guns were even hitting their target.

"Lieutenant Nicholson says they're getting low on ammunition," Eddie announced. "He says they're below ten percent of the big stuff."

"Acknowledged," said Hammett. *What do I do when the ammunition runs out?* He shrugged to himself. *Keep on improvising, I guess. This battle can't last much longer.*

As if to punctuate the thought, the forward end of the *Cassandra* blew apart in a storm of flying steel. At first Hammett thought it was the alien ship, maybe struck by another missile. He could see the alien moving away from the wreckage, though, still largely intact. He gaped through the window, then said, "What the hell just happened?"

"I think it's the armature," Sanjari said. "Something blocked the track, or the track twisted. When the armature reached the blockage ..." She mimed an explosion with her hands, then looked at her screen. "I'm pretty sure the armature shot out the end and kept going."

Hammett imagined the metal cup, separated from its cargo of stone, sailing through the void and striking one last blow against the Hive base. "Is there any chance the *Cassandra* is still firing?"

Sanjari, eyes on her display screen, said, "None at all, Sir."

*Then it's time to think about survival. About getting home. Getting a message back to Earth.* He tapped his tactical display screen. "Let's see if they're going to give us any breathing room."

The aliens, though, showed no sign of withdrawing. Instead they shifted the focus of their attack from the *Cassandra* to the surviving corvettes. They'd made several ineffective attacks on the *Theseus*. Now, it seemed, they were saving her for last.

"Let's get out there and do some damage," Hammett said. "Eddie, bring her-"

"Wait," said Hal. "We're getting a request from the *Cassandra*. Their engines are dead. They want to come aboard."

"Tell them to get a move on," Hammett snapped. "Vicente." He gestured at the nose of the *Theseus*. "Go to the airlock. Help the survivors get onboard. Then get them settled."

The boy gave him a jerky nod and hurried from the bridge.

"Be careful," Hammett yelled after him. "Your mother will kill me if you get hurt."

The only answer was the clomp of Vicente's boots as he hurried forward. Hammett sighed, feeling the weight of his rank pressing down on him. *He's just a boy. If I can't keep him safe ...*

And then there was nothing to do but wait. The *Theseus* held its position, ignored by the alien swarm, as crew streamed out of a hatch in the side of the *Cassandra*, sailed through fifteen meters of hard vacuum, and piled into the lock at the aft of the converted freighter. Hammett, fidgeting with impatience, watched the first few refugees through the feed from a camera above the lock. Then he turned his attention to the battle raging around them.

Hal tilted his head, then slid his hands through the opening in the front of his helmet, reaching back to plug his ears. He listened, then murmured a response. In theory, communications were supposed to go through Sanjari. Eddie and Hal were the ones with working implants, though.

"Admiral," Hal said. "There's more survivors on the *Cassandra*. It's the bridge crew, and they're trapped. They want someone to come for them with a laser cutter."

Hammett stared at Hal for a long moment, heartily wishing he'd never decided to become an officer. This was the kind of decision that would never, ever stop haunting him.

But it had to be done.

"No. We can't wait. If they can't reach our airlock, they aren't coming aboard. We have to go."

Hal's face twisted like he was going to be sick. He nodded, though, and turned away, murmuring again. His hands reached for the thruster controls in front of him – and then froze.

He swiveled his chair around. "Admiral? You're not going to like this."

## CHAPTER 13 – VICENTE

Vicente left the bridge on legs that wobbled and shook. Panic nibbled at his brain, telling him to break into a run. He gave in and ran, galloping down the catwalk, and arrived panting a moment later at the aft airlock. He entered the lock, feeling his weight decrease, and waited while the lock began to cycle.

Metallic clangs echoed through the little metal chamber, loud at first, then muffled as his suit detected the drop in pressure and the faceplate on his helmet closed. The first refugees had arrived, and were banging frantically on the outside of the lock.

*I forgot to close my faceplate. Stupid, stupid, stupid. The next mistake may kill me. I've got to pay attention. I have to get things right. I could die. Oh God, I could die.*

The outer hatch slid open, mercifully interrupting his gibbering thoughts. Figures in vac suits pulled themselves in, shoving Vicente aside in their haste. Five or six people entered the lock, almost filling it. Vicente was reaching for the 'door close' button when another survivor grabbed the edge of the hatch and pulled herself in.

Vicente forced himself forward, pushing past Spacecom sailors until he could see outside. The *Cassandra* was like a glittering road beneath him. He could see another handful of survivors gathering on the side of a rectangular structure almost directly below him. As he watched, the first of them began to kick off, soaring toward the airlock.

They wouldn't all fit. Vicente pulled his head in and slapped a fat yellow button on the wall. The hatch closed, air rushed in, and the inner door opened.

More frantic banging started on the outer hatch. Vicente sighed, doing his best to ignore it, as the first batch of survivors hurried onto the catwalk. The inner hatch slid shut and the lock began to cycle.

A hand closed on Vicente's arm, and he jumped. One of the refugees was still in the lock, a short young woman who stared into his face with dark eyes that burned with intensity. "The captain is trapped," she said.

"The captain?"

"It's the whole bridge crew," she said. She had both hands locked around his forearm, and she was squeezing. "They can't get out. Someone needs to rescue them."

The outer hatch opened and more refugees poured in. Vicente endured another jostling, then stuck his head out the hatch.

Nothing moved on the surface of the *Cassandra*.

He closed the hatch, waited while the refugees trouped into the *Theseus*, then turned his attention back to the girl.

"I need tools," she said. "A laser cutter. Maybe a pry bar. And maybe some help."

He stared at her, wondering if he should call the Admiral. Then something clicked in his memory. "I saw toolkits," he said. He stepped out of the airlock. "Here they are!"

Bulky lockers lined the bulkhead just inside the lock. The lockers held vac suits and emergency vac sacks, a full set of firefighting gear, and a couple of boxes simply labelled "Tools". He dropped the toolboxes on the catwalk, and they each opened one.

Each box held a tool belt. The belts had laser cutters and small pry bars, which was all Vicente cared about. He strapped on a belt and headed back into the lock. The girl followed him, strapping on her own belt.

As the lock cycled he wondered if he should call the admiral. The man was busy, though. He was an admiral, after all. *I'll be proactive. I know what needs to be done, after all.* Shrugging to himself and hoping he was doing the right thing, Vicente grabbed a safety handle and leaned outside as the outer hatch slid open.

His body moved past the limits of the force

field that gave the ship its artificial gravity. He felt a moment of giddy vertigo that faded as he grabbed a handle on the outside of the ship and drew his entire body out. The *Cassandra* looked terrifyingly far away, and he gulped, wondering how he would find the courage to let go of the *Theseus*.

Then the girl sailed past him, arms stretched out ahead of her, soaring toward the crippled ship. Vicente took a deep breath, braced his feet against the hull of the *Theseus*, and kicked off.

He wanted to scream from a mix of terror and exhilaration. Only the suit radio kept him silent. He worked in vac suits all the time, but zero gravity was mostly a new experience. He couldn't decide if he was falling or flying, soaring toward his target or plunging hopelessly out of control. The side of the ship came closer, moving at alarming speed, and he wondered if he'd kicked off too hard.

Then his body banged into a thick steel girder and he bounced away. He grabbed for the girder, missed by a few centimeters, and watched helplessly as the ship moved farther out of reach. For a moment he thought he was a dead man, doomed to tumble endlessly through the void.

His hands were already moving, though, guided by some part of his mind that had been paying more attention than he realized. The toolbelt had canisters of compressed air on either hip, little propulsion systems for situations just like this. He pointed his head at the ship, his feet into deep space, and fired a tiny squirt of air from both canisters.

He floated forward, ever so slowly, scared to use the canisters again. After several seconds he got a hand on the girder and looked around.

"This way." The girl's voice was impatient but directionless. He finally spotted her behind him, clipping a safety line to a handle on the outside of a spherical lump just forward of the ship's engines. He started toward her, pulling himself along the lattice of girders that formed the biggest part of the ship.

When he reached her he spent a moment fumbling at his belt, looking for a safety line. He had just clipped the hair-thin cable in place beside hers on a safety handle when he heard Hal's voice over his implants. "Vicente! What are you doing? You need to get back here right now."

For a moment Vicente froze. The girl's booted foot was in front of his face, and his eyes tracked upward, from her leg to the toolbelt to her helmeted head, which was peering through a small steelglass window. A couple of people stared out from the inside, helmeted heads together, gloved hands pressed against the pane.

"Vicente, do you hear me? The admiral is furious. You need to get back here now."

He looked through the window. A man and a woman looked back at him. He couldn't seem much through their helmets, but their eyes were unnaturally wide. "I can't leave yet," he said to Hal. "There's people trapped. I have to help them."

"No, no, Vicente. You need to get back here

now. The admiral's going to leave without you."

Returning to the *Theseus* was impossible, of course. Perhaps if the call had come a minute earlier he could have done it, but not now. Not with those desperate, frightened faces staring out at him. He said, "I'll be as quick as I can." Then he grabbed a laser cutter from his belt, pulled himself up beside the girl, and got to work.

A metal flap covered the edge of the steelglass pane on all four sides. He started cutting away the flap, then muttered a curse as he realized just how long it was going to take.

"Make two cuts," said the girl. "Then bend the flap back." She was working on the far side of the window, making a finger-long cut at one end of the metal flap on her side. Vicente nodded and copied her.

When he had a cut on each end of the flap he jammed a pry bar between the flap and the steelglass and tried to bend flap back. The metal gave slowly, and he cursed again, wondering if the *Theseus* had left yet. He was too scared to look.

The girl poked his shoulder. "Switch sides," she said.

He looked up. She had made a third cut, in the middle of the metal flap. He switched places with her, jammed his pry bar into place, and started to heave.

With the flap of metal cut in half the bending was easier. It took a minute or so, but he got both pieces of the flap bent back until he could see a thick rubber gasket covering the edge of the glass. He played his laser cutter over the gaskets, which burned away was gratifying speed. He could see the edge of the steelglass, covered in bits of charred rubber.

By that time the girl was done cutting the flap on the opposite side of the window. She moved around, rotating clockwise, and he took her place.

He was heaving on the pry bar when he saw movement reflected in the steelglass. At the same time, the man on the other side of the window opened his mouth. Apparently the suit radios had found a channel to share, because Vicente heard him cry, "Behind you!"

Vicente turned, expecting to see the *Theseus* racing away, abandoning them. The freighter was still there, but a small alien ship was looping around the hall and plunging toward him.

He jerked back, letting go of the pry bar, and fumbled for his laser cutter. It was, after all, just a powerful hand-held laser. He pointed this pitiful weapon at the alien ship and pressed the button.

The beam was invisible in the vacuum of space, and if it had any effect on the alien ship he couldn't see it. He couldn't even see a red dot. The ship dropped toward him, so fast he wondered if it meant to crush them with its hull.

The first rail gun round flashed past between him and the alien. It rebounded from a strut, ricocheted, and missed Vicente by less than a meter. He didn't see it exactly – it was a blur of motion, barely registering – but a divot appeared in the strut. He stared at the dent in the metal, his heart galloping madly, but there was no time to process what had happened.

The alien ship shook, then came apart in a burst of tearing metal. Chunks of wreckage spewed out, battering the *Cassandra* in eerie silence. A chunk the size of a chair came right at Vicente, and he threw an arm up to protect himself.

The impact was less than he expected, a gentle tap against his right forearm. He fell back, felt the girl's hand on his shoulder steadying him, and watched the piece of wreckage tumble away.

His screaming nerves told him to stay frozen in place while his brain caught up. Instead, he turned his back on the *Theseus* and the remains of the alien. His pry bar floated forgotten in the void beside him, and he grabbed it and went back to work.

The second set of flaps was bent back in moments. By that time the girl was done cutting the third flap, and she joined him with a pry bar of her own as he went to work bending back the third set of flaps. They didn't bother with the remaining side, just burned away the rubber seal across from the remaining flap and worked their pry bars around the edge of the steelglass.

The trapped crew joined in, pushing from the inside, and the edge of the steelglass pane began to lift. Vicente let go of his pry bar, grabbed the edge of the pane with both hands, braced his feet against the hull, and heaved.

For an endless time nothing happened. When the window gave way it moved all at once, and Vicente found himself flying outward as his legs abruptly straightened. The safety line tightened and swung him around in an arc until he banged into the struts on the far side.

By the time he got himself oriented and unclipped, a dozen or more Spacecom sailors were soaring toward the hull of the *Theseus*. Vicente lined himself up, took one last look around, and kicked off.

He was barely in the lock, the hatch still closing behind him, when the *Theseus* began to move.

# CHAPTER 14 – HAMMETT

There," said Hammett. "Fifteen degrees to port and almost thirty degrees up. That's the *Tomahawk*." The corvette was ringed by three amalgamated ships, all of them trying to melt through her hull. "Let's give her a hand." He didn't hold out much hope for the survival of the *Theseus*, but the *Tomahawk* might yet win free. The corvette could generate wormholes, and she held the survivors of the *Gideon* as well. "Signal Kaur," he said to Sanjari. "Tell her to get out of here if she can."

Sanjari nodded and murmured into the microphone set in her console. Hammett turned his attention back to the ships ahead.

Two of the alien ships were achieving little, their heat weapons dispersing across the corvette's Fourier shielding. The third ship, though, had found a vulnerable spot between the engines. Hammett could see a red glow coming from the corvette's hull. "There!" he cried. "The aft end of the *Tomahawk*. That's your target."

Hal nodded absently, nudging the nav thruster controls. Eddie worked the main thrusters, sending the *Theseus* gliding forward. The ship opened fire at point-blank range, and a barrage of metal and stone erupted from the forward rail guns.

The alien ship tilted and spun, and Hammett found himself staring into the maw of the heat weapon. It glowed like a furnace, and he had to fight the urge to throw up a protective hand in front of his face. The alien was a good hundred meters away, after all, though the distance was closing rapidly.

A second volley tore into the Hive ship, and the heat weapon began to cool. Several small ships broke away, and the *Theseus* tilted as the pilots tried to bring her to bear on another alien. The *Theseus* had too much velocity, though, and it drifted past the *Tomahawk* without getting off another volley.

There were plenty of other targets. Amalgamated ships filled the sky. They clustered like ticks around the engines of the *Adamant*. As Hammett watched, one of the destroyer's main engines flared brightly, then died. An EDF corvette swept across the tail of the *Adamant*, firing an ineffective barrage. Then the corvette twisted away, frantically dodging its own pair of pursuing ships.

Hammett started to point, but Eddie and Hal were already reacting. The *Theseus* came up alongside the corvette, the nose of the *Theseus* tilted sideways and up, and Hammett felt a hint of vibration as the aft battery fired.

"We're losing this fight, Admiral."

Hammett glanced at Sanjari. She looked perfectly calm, her eyes glued to her displays. He said, "We'll get through it."

She shook her head. "We're the only ship that can even touch them when they're clumped together like that, and we're almost out of ammo."

She was right, of course, but saying as much wasn't helpful. Hammett felt his irritation flare. "Well, what the hell would you suggest?"

"Running, of course."

He blinked. "Running? Where?" He gestured at the windows. "There's nowhere to run."

"There are, let me see, three functioning Gates in this system," she said calmly. "They aren't even very far away."

He watched as the *Theseus* bore down on an alien ship, fired a barrage, then pursued the alien as it fled. His attention was on Sanjari's words, though.

"If we run, we need to do it now," she said. "While some of these corvettes still have working engines."

He wanted time, even a few seconds to weigh his options, consider the consequences. But she was right. Every second that passed put the ragged remainder of the fleet in terrible danger. And if a wormhole-capable corvette couldn't escape, there was no point in any of them escaping.

"Signal the fleet," he said to Sanjari. "Tell them we're leaving. Eddie. Get us out of here."

Eddie glanced back, and Sanjari said, "Forty-five degrees starboard and a bit down."

Only three ships made it clear of the scene of battle. The *Theseus* led the way, with the *Tomahawk* following on one side and the EDF corvette *Sgian Dubh* on the other. Behind them the pocked hulks of the *Adamant* and the *Cassandra* floated among the wreckage of the other corvettes, the supply ship, and uncountable Hive ships.

Most of the alien fleet gave chase. Seven amalgamated ships remained; two of them had taken damage, and paused to link up before joining the pursuit. Each corvette had a Hive ship close on its tail, almost within range of its heat weapon. The other four Hive ships trailed after.

"We can't decelerate when we get close to the Gate," Sanjari said. "They'll be all over us."

Hammett shrugged. "One crisis at a time, please." He checked his display. "Everyone's travelling in a perfectly straight line. That means we should be able to line up the aft battery."

"I'm on it," said Eddie, and began to work his controls. Slowly, delicately, the converted freighter began to drift sideways.

"Hal," said Hammett. "How's our ammunition holding up?"

Hal tilted his head, accessing his implants, then murmured something. He turned. "We have forty-seven rounds left for the big guns. About a hundred and thirty rounds of mixed sizes for the other guns."

Hammett shook his head, wincing. The *Theseus* was almost toothless. "Tell the crew to unload the forward guns. We'll only be firing backward for a while." *Five shots from each gun. We'll have to make them count.* To Eddie he said, "Line us up carefully. We can't afford to miss."

"We're gaining slightly," Sanjari said. "Maybe shooting soon is best." She looked at her screens. "The *Sgian Dubh* is the fastest. She's holding back to stay even with us. The *Tomahawk* is going almost full-out. The *Theseus* is the slowest pony we've got in this race. Still a hair faster than the aliens, though."

Hammett stood and turned, staring back through the aft windows. The glass had taken more damage during the battle. There was hardly a spot bigger than his hand without cracks in it. It was holding for the moment, though.

The largest alien ship, formed from two amalgamated ships that had linked, was slowly overtaking the other aliens. *They could catch us,* he realized. *If they formed up into two or three huge ships, pooled their thrust, they could overtake us.*

Either the aliens were afraid of a missile strike, or they were willing to let the humans escape. *And why shouldn't they be? We can sting them a bit if they catch us. If they chase us away, we won't be any danger to them at all. We're the shattered remnants. We don't matter.*

Hal said, "Are we going to make it, Admiral?"

Sanjari spoke before he could answer. "The Gate is almost edge-on to us. We'll have to decelerate at least a little. They'll be all over us. It's going to be ugly."

Eddie added, "And they'll follow us through, won't they?"

"Maybe they will," Hammett said. "Time will tell." He'd have to destroy the Gate once they were through. It would minimize pursuit, and it would keep the aliens fragmented.

"Where will we end up?" Hal said, his voice plaintive.

"I don't know," Hammett admitted. "In a few minutes, though, we're going to find out."

# CHAPTER 15 – HARDY

The Gate was a white triangle gleaming at the edge of Hardy's display. Five red squares made a ragged line in front of the Gate, alien ships poised to block incoming missiles. On the other side of the screen a green star represented the *Bumblebee*, with green circles on either side showing him the EDF fighters that accompanied him.

He was tail-on to the Gate, decelerating hard. Nothing showed through the cockpit window but empty space and the distant, tiny shape of the alien settlement. The battle he'd fled was invisible, even the *Adamant* and the enormous length of the *Cassandra* made impossibly small by distance. He asked himself for the thousandth time if he should have stayed, and told himself yet again that it didn't matter.

He'd made his choice. He looked at the five red squares on his display. It wasn't as if he was taking the easy way out.

"Five on three," he muttered. "It won't be so bad."

"It'll be bad enough," said a woman's crisp voice in his ear. "This is Lieutenant Spellman. Who am I speaking to?"

*Whoops. I should have realized I'd be broadcasting.* "I'm Ken Hardy."

"Welcome to the scrap, Hardy. Thanks for coming with us."

"Sure," he said.

"I'm Sam Dante," said a deep bass voice. "That's me on your port side."

"Hi, Sam."

"We'll engage the enemy first," Spellman said. "Try to get some quick kills. But the Gate is our priority. We're here to destroy it. Understand?"

Hardy said, "Yes," and Dante rumbled agreement.

"Ram the Gate if you have to," Spellman went on. "Survival's not a big priority here. I don't think any of us will be seeing Earth again."

A cold silence fell, and Hardy shivered.

"Hey, Hardy," Dante said. "I'm glad we get to fight on the same side. I wasn't looking forward to fighting against you guys, you know what I mean?"

"I do," Hardy said.

"All right," Spellman interrupted. "Enough chatter. The music's starting; let's show these turds how to dance."

Hardy glanced at his display. He was almost to the Gate, with a relative velocity below a hundred kilometers per hour. He brought the nose of the *Bumblebee* whipping around, battle lust rising in him like a hot wave as the Hive ships moved forward to meet them.

An alien came at him straight on. He poured fire into it, then jerked the ship sideways to whip past. The Hive ship dodged in the same direction, and he struck the ship a glancing blow. His helmeted head slammed against the side of the cockpit, he saw bursts of light, and then all he could see was stars. He shook his head, disoriented, then brought the nose of the *Bumblebee* around.

Two Hive ships were converging, with a third about to join them. Hardy, knowing that a group of three would be all but impervious to the fighters, pointed the nose of the *Bumblebee* at the third ship and opened fire. He hosed it from end to end with lasers and rail gun rounds, and instead of merging with the other two, the third ship rebounded and tumbled away. Hardy whooped as he shot past.

He was sweeping around for another pass when he glimpsed the Gate to his left. There was no time to consider his options. He jerked the control stick sideways and the *Bumblebee* slewed around. He had to oversteer and give the main thrusters a squirt to soak up his sideways velocity. Then he lined up on the Gate and charged in.

Closer and closer it loomed. Several times, Hardy started to squeeze his triggers. Each time, though, he hesitated. The Gate, he realized, was bigger than he'd thought. Much bigger. Each time he thought he was practically on top of it he was wrong. It was bigger and farther away than he suspected. Somewhere behind him Spellman and Dante were fighting for their lives, but perhaps he was buying them a reprieve. The aliens were here to protect the Gate, after all. Odds were, they'd break off the dogfight and chase him.

He was too busy – and too frightened – to look.

Finally the buzz of a proximity alarm told him he was at point-blank range. He hit his braking thrusters and opened up with lasers and rail guns. He was almost perfectly edge-on to the giant triangle, so that it loomed like a pillar with a pyramid at the top and bottom. Shot after shot slammed into the side of the pillar and bounced away.

Another buzzer sounded, similar to the proximity alarm but deeper in tone. It meant a larger ship was approaching. Hardy, without time to blink, much less look around, shoved the thought to the back of his mind and concentrated on firing. The pillar, maddeningly, showed no damage.

Then, as he was about to veer off, a crack appeared. Gritting his teeth, Hardy made himself hold the ship steady. *Ram the Gate if you have to.* An endless second passed, the Gate expanding in his view as the distance closed. Round after round hit the side of the Gate, a chunk of the outer covering broke away, and one final round hit home, striking inside the structure of the pillar.

Hardy hauled desperately on his control stick and stomped on the left foot pedal, triggering the port-side nav thrusters. The nose of the *Bumblebee* turned, but the ship was still hurtling toward the Gate at a terrifying speed. He fired the main engine, felt an instant of thrust pushing against his back, and then the tail of the ship banged into the side of the Gate.

The *Bumblebee* spun madly, and Hardy could do nothing but clutch the sides of the cockpit, helplessly dizzy. The ship's computer would notice the spin and stabilize him in a moment.

Except most of the autonomous systems had been ripped out when the fighter was reconditioned for manual control. Almost everything that couldn't be relied on to work after an EMP strike had been removed, replaced with pedals and handles and buttons. He spent a moment spinning, trying to decide if he was going clockwise or counter-clockwise. Then, fighting a tremendous centrifugal force that made his arm feel as heavy as a small freighter, he stretched out a hand, wrapped it around the control stick, and dragged the stick to the left.

For most of thirty seconds he clung to the stick, eyes squeezed shut, waiting for the ride to end. He thought he felt consciousness slipping away, but realized it was, in fact, the centrifugal force becoming less. When he merely felt drunk instead of insane he forced his eyelids open.

The stars swung past, but slowly. He let go of the stick, took a deep breath, then began working the stick and pedals, bringing the ship under control. When the stars stopped moving he looked down at his display screen.

The Gate was dead astern, along with several small ships and something new, a large vessel, closing quickly.

He brought the *Bumblebee* around. A hole gaped in the side of one pillar of the Gate, and the glow was gone from the three pyramids. Disabled, he decided. It would be better to smash it completely, but all travel was shut down, and that was good enough for now.

A hundred meters or so from the Gate he saw the two EDF fighters, one pretty much stationary relative to the Gate, the other drifting along, turning slowly end over end. Both ships were burned and mangled. A couple of Hive ships floated nearby, lifeless hulks riddled with laser and impact holes.

Between them he could see an amalgamated ship, three little ships joined together. The amalgamated ship was heading toward the *Bumblebee*.

"Well, come on then," he snarled. "Let's see what you've got."

A couple of stars vanished from the sky beyond the approaching alien. He shifted his gaze. A behemoth was coming up from behind, a massive alien craft. He could see a central shape, a design he'd never seen before, one big ship maybe half the size of a corvette. Half a dozen of the little Hive ships formed clusters on either side, like detachable engine pods. Hardy stared, his mouth going dry.

*Well, it's not like I thought I was going to live through this.* He let go of the control stick, clenched and unclenched a fist, then grabbed the stick again. "Come on, then. Let's do this."

A groan filled his ears. It was a deep voice, full of pain. The groan ended, and Dante spoke, sounding as if every word came at great cost. "One of us might as well get out of here, and it ain't gonna be me. Run, Hardy." Dante coughed. "RUN!"

One of the ruined EDF fighters came to life. Engine light flared behind it, and the fighter surged forward. It was moving for less than a second before it slammed into the three-ship amalgamation that was closing on the *Bumblebee*.

Hardy didn't wait to see what happened next. He accelerated hard, yanking sideways on the stick and stomping a foot pedal to sharpen his turn. He pointed the nose of the *Bumblebee* at deep space and flew for all he was worth.

It took thirty seconds or so to realize he was snarling, a primitive sound of frustration and terror and rage. His helmet mic would be picking up the sound and broadcasting it to ... possibly no one, he realized. But perhaps he was annoying the hell out of someone on an EDF corvette and blocking a channel someone needed to use. He made himself stop, then flew on into the dark, sobbing quietly.

He wanted to turn the *Bumblebee* around, charge back into the fray, hurt them for what they'd done to Spellman and Dante. He couldn't achieve a damned thing, though. Not against amalgamated ships.

If they were pursuing him, he decided, he'd turn around and ram them. Go out with a bang. He glanced down at his cockpit displays.

He was alone. A tap to the screen resized the display, and he saw alien ships clustered around the damaged Gate. They weren't pursuing him.

Hardy felt no relief. A few more minutes of life held little value for him, not when there was nowhere to run, no way to escape the system. Instead, he found himself wondering how he could inflict one last blow before he died.

"There were more Gates," he murmured, and tapped his screen again. "Let me see ..."

It didn't take long to find another white triangle. It wasn't even very far away. With any luck, there wouldn't be any alien ships guarding it. After all, the aliens could have intercepted the missiles from the *Adamant* anywhere along their path. They didn't have to go to the Gate itself.

He turned the *Bumblebee* and got it pointed at the next Gate, then shot an ugly glance over his shoulder at the Gate he'd just disabled and the Hive ships gathered around it. "You didn't chase me," he muttered. "That was a mistake. You'll regret it."

# CHAPTER 16 – HAMMETT

**F**ire!"

The word had barely left Hammett's lips when he saw the leading Hive ship tremble. It was the biggest craft, the one formed by two amalgamated ships joined together. The resulting misshapen blob twisted sideways, moving out of the path of a follow-up barrage. It lost speed as well, dropping behind the other Hive ships.

"Cease fire." The *Theseus* had only fired the one volley, but he wanted to make sure no enthusiastic gunner wasted more of their precious ammunition.

"Right, Sir," Hal said, then glanced over his shoulder at Hammett.

"Stop accelerating," Hammett said.

The background vibration of straining engines vanished. He felt as if he was going to pitch forward out of his seat as the pressure of acceleration disappeared. Hammett watched his screen as the Hive ships began to overtake the *Theseus*. They quickly stopped accelerating, though, and he saw the glow of thrusters as they braked slightly. He grinned. *They're scared of us. They think it's a trap.*

Both corvettes stopped accelerating as well. They drifted ahead, moving just a bit faster than the *Theseus*, until they braked one at a time.

"What now, Admiral?"

Hammett looked at Eddie. "See if you can line us up for another shot."

Both pilots nodded and set to work. It quickly became obvious, though, that the aliens understood the restrictions of the big guns. Each time the *Theseus* came close to lining up on a Hive ship, the alien would edge out of the way.

"We'll save our ammunition," Hammett decided. "Get ready to bring us about and decelerate." They were well past half way to the Gate. They'd be moving very quickly when they arrived. "Signal the corvettes."

"They report ready," Sanjari said.

"Bring us around, Eddie. Maximum burn. Slow us down."

The ship spun on its axis, and Hammett felt the press of acceleration return. Deceleration, technically, but it felt the same. The corvettes matched the *Theseus* almost perfectly, and the alien ships followed suit an instant later. For a moment the amalgamated ship closest to the *Tomahawk* overshot the corvette, and Hal moved the *Theseus* closer, trying for a point-blank volley. The alien braked hard, falling back until it was even with the next alien ship, perhaps sixty meters behind the two corvettes.

"Looks like they're satisfied with running us out of the neighborhood," Sanjari said. "I don't think they want a fight if they can avoid one."

*They just need to dither for a few moments longer.* Hammett checked his screens. The Gate was coming up fast. The *Theseus* was losing velocity quickly, but ...

"You two will have to do some sharp flying," he said to the pilots. "We need to thread a needle at high velocity."

Neither man responded, but he saw Eddie's shoulders move ever so slightly as the muscles tightened.

"You can do it," Hammett said softly. "You've been flying this thing for years, after all. I wouldn't be trying this if I didn't have complete confidence in both of you."

Sanjari's head moved in the corner of his eye, and he glanced at her. She was looking at him, one eyebrow up, the expression on her face saying, *I know you're so full of crap.* He grinned and shrugged. Eddie and Hal were pretty good, and the odds of them getting the ship successfully through the Gate were ... probably better than even, he decided.

"We need to spread out a bit," Eddie said. "Otherwise we'll crash into each other as we go through."

"I'll signal the *Tomahawk*," Sanjari said, and lifted a handset.

"We'll go through last," said Hammett.

"Right," said Eddie. "I'm swinging wide."

The *Theseus* slid sideways, and the engine flare vanished from the trio of alien ships. They seemed to leap forward, converging on the corvettes. Two ships attacked the *Tomahawk*. The third went for the *Sgian Dubh*.

"Damn it," said Hammett, "we have to get back-"

The corvettes were already reacting, though, twisting left, then sharp right to hurtle straight at the Gate. Eddie and Hal worked the helm controls together and the *Theseus* turned, roaring at a column of metal that changed as they approached, becoming a triangle. Hammett caught a quick glimpse of a corvette flashing through the opening and vanishing. Then the triangle seemed to leap at him, and his hands clutched reflexively at the arms of the chair. The Gate went by so quickly that he honestly couldn't tell if they'd missed it or not.

He twisted around in his chair, then stood and turned in a circle. Empty space surrounded the ship on every side. Then the nose of the ship tilted upward and he saw a star, a vast orb of dark and angry red that filled a good forty degrees of arc through the front window.

"I guess we made it through," Sanjari said.

"Yes," said Hammett, peering through the windows. "But where in hell are those corvettes?" He shook his head. "For that matter, where's the Gate?"

He sat back down, tapping his display screen.

Sanjari spoke before he could orient himself. "The Gate's a hundred kilometers that way." She pointed at the deck. "And receding. We came through with quite a lot of sideways velocity."

Hammett's screen showed him a white triangle, rapidly moving away, and a green circle, moving more slowly. There was no sign of alien activity.

"It's the *Sgian Dubh*," Sanjari said. She looked at Hammett, her face bleak. "The *Tomahawk* didn't make it."

"No." He wasn't sure if he'd spoken the word aloud. It had the sound of a scream in his mind. *No, it can't be true. Not the* Tomahawk. *Not Kaur, and the rest of the crew. And Captain Harrington and everyone from the* Gideon *as well.*

*Not the last, best shot we had at getting home.*

"The *Sgian Dubh*," he said. "Does it have ..."

"A wormhole generator?" Sanjari asked. "No."

He wanted to bellow, to bury his face in his hands, to pound the arms of his chair in grief and frustration. His decades of experience were asserting themselves, though, and his voice was even as he issued orders. "Eddie. Match velocities with the *Sgian Dubh*. Hal, get them on the radio. Tell them we're going back to the Gate. And ask them for a status report."

As both men busied themselves at their consoles, Sanjari murmured, "What do we do now, Sir?"

"We destroy the Gate," he said. "Then we take a good look around and try to figure out where we are. After that ... we'll see."

# CHAPTER 17 – KAUR

Meena Kaur watched the alien Gate flash past and swore. It was a good curse, too, one thoroughly unbecoming an officer, and she felt her cheeks getting warm. She was suddenly aware of Captain Harrington standing behind her, could almost feel the woman's eyes boring into her back. *She's been a captain for ten years. She must think I'm ...*

Embarrassment was a good distraction from her rising panic, and she felt her dismay recede. *Gotta focus on where I am now, not where I wanted to be. Gotta focus on solutions.*

The bridge crew looked thoroughly rattled. That was her first priority, then. She had to calm them down, and that meant keeping them busy, even if she had nothing useful for them to do.

"Benson. Get our nose pointed at that Gate. Keep us lined up. I want us moving in the right direction the instant we get the engines back.

Ramirez. Scan for communication traffic. I want to know if there's anyone else alive in this system." Both men looked down at their consoles, and her gaze swept the bridge. "Tolstoy."

The young man standing against the port windows stiffened.

"Run down to the engine room. See what's going on, see if you can help. Organize volunteers from the *Gideon* if it will help. If Geibelhaus doesn't need you, come back here and give me a report. Go."

Tolstoy nodded and dashed from the bridge.

"Touhami. What's happening at the Gate? Are we being pursued? Did they all follow the *Theseus* through the Gate?"

Touhami didn't speak, just stared at her, his hands gripping the edge of the console in front of him.

"Touhami," she said again.

All he did was stare. She'd never seen his eyes so wide or his face so pale. He looked stricken, a good man who'd been pushed too far for too long and had reached a point where he couldn't cope. She knew exactly how he felt. She was about a millimeter from joining him in shocked catatonia.

Kaur opened her mouth to say something soothing, then froze. If they survived this, he'd live with the memory of this day for the rest of his life, and she sensed that gentleness on her part would embarrass him deeply. If she told him it was all right and relieved him of duty, it would give him a burden of shame he'd never recover from.

She sneered, instead.

"Whassa matter, Hammy?" She kept her voice hard, sarcastic. "You need me to come over there and give you a hug? Maybe pat you on the head, tell you mama's gonna keep you safe?"

In her peripheral vision she saw Benson and Ramirez gaping at her. She ignored them, keeping her attention on Touhami.

His face went from white to red in an instant, and his hands released the edge of the console. "No." He bit the word off like he was biting through nails. "Ma'am."

"Well, then, scan the area around the Gate. Tell me what the enemy is doing."

He glared at her, then gave her a jerky nod and turned to his console. "Aye aye, Ma'am." He lifted his handset and started calling the ship's spotters.

The handset was too bulky to fit inside his helmet, which put the earpiece several centimeters from his ear and the mouthpiece the same distance from his mouth. It was a design flaw, and Kaur made a mental note to take it up with Spacecom. She had to remind herself she wasn't with Spacecom anymore. Nor was she likely to make it back to Ariadne, or Earth.

*One crisis at a time.* She glanced at the tac screen on her console. It was just a decoration now, set at an angle so she couldn't even use it to hold up a cup of coffee. How she yearned for functioning electronics! And working implants.

She'd be able to-

Touhami said, "We're not being pursued. By the look of it they overshot the Gate by a few kilometers and went back. They're gathering around the Gate now."

*And do I hope those ships start disappearing?* Part of her did, she realized. *And why shouldn't I? I want to live. And I've got two crews to think of. It's not just me.*

The clatter of feet drew her attention to the bridge entrance. Tolstoy appeared, looking as if he'd run the whole way from the engine room. "The engines are in pretty bad shape," he said, puffing a bit. "Mr. Geibelhaus says he can probably give you about ten percent thrust, both sides. Or sixty percent thrust on the port side only."

That would be useful if she wanted to tear around in tight circles. Otherwise, not so much.

"He's got some engineering staff from the *Gideon* already helping out," Tolstoy continued. "It's getting pretty crowded down there." He glanced over his shoulder. "It's pretty crowded everywhere, actually."

Kaur nodded impatiently.

"Anyway, he says the engines could be fixed in a full shipyard. Out here, well ..." Tolstoy shrugged.

"I'll need you to be more specific," Kaur said dryly.

Tolstoy squirmed ever so slightly. "Well, he was kind of busy, as you might imagine. But an engineer from the *Gideon* talked to me. He says

the side of the engine casing has a hole in it, and there's damage to the distribution coupling. The casing is fixable. The coupling isn't. Without a new one he says we'll never get above fifty percent balanced."

"All right," Kaur said, then added grudgingly, "Good work."

"Oh!" said Tolstoy.

She waited.

"He says the wormhole generator is bug- er, he says it's malfunctioning. But he thinks the hardware is probably okay. He'll have to re-run the wires to the generator."

Kaur nodded. The engines were aft, and the wormhole generator was in the nose of the ship. If the wires in between were damaged, it would be a relatively minor fix. But the generator used a fantastic amount of power. She'd never get it working without something close to full engine power.

And the only source of replacement couplings was the wreckage of the other corvettes, back in the heart of the asteroid field. Back where the Hive had torn the entire fleet apart. Well, one crisis at a time. "Benson."

"Yes, Ma'am?"

"Are we pointed at that Gate?"

"Yes, Ma'am."

The Gate and the lingering Hive ships were in the same direction as the asteroid field and the remains of the fleet. Every instinct she had told her to keep on fleeing, but there was nothing for her in the deep dark, and nothing for the people who relied on her, except a slow death of starvation.

And if they were going to die – it looked like a certainty, barring some kind of miracle – they might as well die harassing the Hive.

"Tolstoy."

He straightened up.

"Head back to Engineering. Tell Mr. Geibelhaus to give me what thrust he can, as soon as he pleases. It's not urgent. Make sure he understands that. But I want to get us moving."

Tolstoy nodded. "Understood, Ma'am." He hurried out.

Kaur took a deep breath, then let it out slowly. *Give me strength. If all I can do is die here far from home, let me die with some grace and dignity. And let me blow up one more Hive ship before I go.*

"Touhami," she said.

"Yes, Ma'am." He looked sullen, like he would be a long time forgiving her. Well, that was all right. He'd deal with it by busting his ass to be the perfect officer, to show her she'd been wrong. She could live with that.

So could he.

"What's the status of our weapons?"

His head tilted, the habits of a lifetime making him try to check his implants. Then he closed his eyes, thinking. "One working laser battery. All the rail guns are offline. There's a team working on the port gun, though. They hope to have it working soon." He lifted his hands in a half-shrug. "They weren't able to be more precise."

When did he have time to get an update on

gun repairs? She let the surprise show on her face, hoping he'd realize he'd impressed her. "Thank you, Mr. Touhami. We need to-"

A light flashed on his console, and she paused while he lifted the handset. "The enemy ships are moving," he said. He murmured briefly into the handset, then put it down. "Most of them are retreating toward the settlement. Four ships are coming this way, though."

She felt a surge of irrational relief. They were pulling back! She would have to follow them, though. She had no choice but to continue on to the battlefield. Without proper engines there was simply nowhere else to go.

First, though, she had to deal with the small matter of four approaching ships.

"Captain Harrington," she snapped.

"Yes, Captain."

Harrington sounded perfectly calm, which irritated Kaur no end. Kaur twisted around in her chair. Harrington stood behind her, hands clasped behind her back, looking serene and unruffled. *She's not judging you, Meena. She lost her ship, after all. You still have yours, if barely. You're still the captain here.*

"If you please, Captain, could you find me some of your crew? I could use three or four people to run errands."

Harrington was moving before Kaur stopped speaking. She stepped through the bridge entrance, then stopped, her back still visible in the doorway. The corridor outside must have been crowded with refugees, because Harrington was back a moment later, four sailors following her.

"Check both ventral laser turrets," Kaur said, not bothering with introductions. "The one in the nose is fine. I need to know if there's any hope of field-repairing the others. Check all the rail guns as well. Assist in repairs if you can. We're about to need weapons very badly."

The sailors dispersed, and Kaur stared at the front of the bridge, feeling her pulse pound, wondering what in space she was supposed to do next.

"You're doing fine." The words, almost a whisper, came from directly behind her. From Harrington, who was speaking too softly for anyone else to hear. It caught Kaur by surprise, sliding some of the weight from her shoulders. She didn't acknowledge the other captain, didn't turn around. But she felt ... better.

The engines started with an audible hum, and the ship trembled. Benson said, "We're still moving away from the Gate, Ma'am. We should reach matching velocities in, let me see, four minutes and a bit. After that we'll start moving closer."

"Right," said Kaur. "Touhami. Status on those approaching ships."

"They were five minutes away when the engines started, Captain. That's assuming they started decelerating in another minute. Now that we're braking they'll reach us sooner." A light flashed, he picked up his handset, listened for a moment, then turned. "They're braking, Ma'am.

It's too soon to tell when they'll reach us."

Another curse of dealing with fried electronics. A good tactical computer would have told them to the second. "We'll save our ammunition," she said. The ship had plenty of power, though. "Tell the laser crew to fire at will. They might get lucky."

Touhami nodded and grabbed his handset.

A sailor from the *Gideon* stepped onto the bridge. It was a young woman, not one of the four Harrington had recruited, but she seemed to have been pressed into service. She looked faintly familiar. *Specialist Moore,* Kaur thought. *Fiona, or Phoebe. Something like that.*

"Captain." Moore glanced at Harrington, then addressed herself to Kaur. "The starboard rail gun is beyond repair. Heat has twisted the frame of the ship. The rails are bent now. The gun can't be repaired without full spacedock facilities. Maybe not even then."

Kaur winced. *Oh, my poor ship.*

"The belly guns are even worse," Moore continued. "We're transferring rounds to the port gun. We estimate between eight hundred and a thousand rounds. All ballistic. You've used up the exploding rounds."

"Thank you, Specialist." *Eight hundred rounds. Not a lot. But with only one gun firing, it'll last twice as long ...* "Any word on the progress of repairs?"

Moore brightened. "The gun fires now, Ma'am. Not quickly, but it shoots. We fired off a test round. They've stripped out the loader and magazine. Should take about ten minutes to straighten out some bends." She grimaced. "It makes a right mess when the gun jams. It's all fixable, though. We're using parts from the starboard gun. You've got a firing rate of about two rounds a second right now. We've got people lined up to hand-feed the gun if you need it. In ten minutes you'll have full rate of fire."

"All right," said Kaur. "Can they use you at the gun?"

Moore's face fell. "Not really, Captain. It's getting pretty crowded there." She looked around the bridge. "It's pretty crowded everywhere but here."

The bridge was as full as Kaur had ever seen it, barring the brief moment when she'd briefed the four sailors from the Gideon. The rest of the ship had to be a real snarl. "Stick around, then," she said. "I might need a runner."

"Aye aye, Ma'am." Moore stepped to the back bulkhead where she stood beside Harrington.

"Captain," Touhami said, twisting around in his chair. He had a handset pressed close to his ear. "More data on the approaching ships." Seeing that he had her attention, he said, "The first four ships are limpets."

Cold washed across her skin. 'Limpet' was the name Spacecom gave the ship that had attached itself to the hull of the *Alexander*. Limpets were bigger than the smallest alien ships. None had been captured, but the best guess put them around the size of a three-ship cluster. One laser and one rail gun would be hard pressed to destroy a limpet, never mind four of them.

The second problem was, the *Alexander's* limpet had burrowed through the hull and put commandoes aboard the cruiser. There had been fighting in the corridors.

There had been deaths.

That was before the Hive learned about fighting humanity. This attack would be worse. How, she wouldn't know until they struck. But worse.

"Moore. Tell the rail gun crew we're facing four targets. They should manage their ammunition accordingly."

Moore acknowledged the order and dashed away, leaving Kaur to brood in silence. The limpets would be fast, hard to hit. They'd be able to soak up a depressing amount of damage, too. Even if she could destroy all four – a long shot at best – did she dare use up the last of her ammunition?

She imagined aliens burrowing through the hull of the *Tomahawk* with explosives, or something worse. She didn't dare hold back.

"Wait a minute," she said, abstract concerns about ammunition suddenly forgotten. She stared at Touhami. "Did you say, 'The first four ships?'"

He bobbed his head. "Yes, Ma'am. There's a fighter out there, too." When she didn't speak he clarified. "It's one of ours. Either the *Bumblebee* or one of the EDF fighters. It just came flying in from one side." He illustrated with a wave of his hand. "I don't know where it came from."

Kaur shook her head. *What else is going to pop up?* Well, they were flying toward an enemy Gate. Anything at all might come through from the other side. She wondered if she should blow the Gate, assuming she ever reached it. She didn't want to strand the *Theseus* and the *Sgian Dubh* – but whatever was on the other side could hardly be worse than what was here.

It was an alien transport hub, she decided. She'd destroy it if she could.

"Ramirez. Contact that fighter if you can."

"Aye aye, Ma'am."

"Captain, could you pass the word? Everyone needs to hang on."

"I'm on it," said Harrington.

"All right, Benson," Kaur said. "The gunners will do what they can, but the rest is up to you. Keep those things off my hull."

# CHAPTER 18 – JANICE

The truck rolled along a rough-graded road, moving rapidly enough that whole vehicle vibrated, setting Janice Ling's already frayed nerves on edge. A colony with limited resources and not too many vehicles had never tried too hard to lay down smooth, perfect pavement. Janice sat on the truck bed, soldiers crowded in on either side of her, sighed, and resigned herself to enduring the vibration.

"Bump coming up," said the man across from her. The name strip on his chest said 'Chiweto'. She'd never spoken to him before.

"What?" The word was barely out of Janice's mouth when the truck bed dropped away beneath her, then slammed into her buttocks with force enough to make her grunt. Her head hit the side of the box, the helmet taking most of the force.

Chiweto grinned apologetically. "The

irrigation splashes on the road here. Erodes it. Don't worry, though. It's smooth for the next ten, fifteen K."

She looked around. The truck box held two rows of soldiers, backs against the sides of the box, feet almost touching along the center line. There were eight people in the box, with the sides of the box rising high all around. She could see a dark blue rectangle of sky above, and that was it. The countryside was completely invisible. "How do you know where we are?"

"Huh?" Chiweto blinked at her. "What do you mean?"

"You know where the bumps in the road are. You know it's smooth for the next while. How could you possibly know that?"

He smiled. "Oh, I take this road every day. Into town and back out again. Or I did, before the invasion." The smile faded.

"But how do you know where we are?"

That made him frown in concentration. "Well, I saw the oaks." He gestured at the air above and behind Janice's head. "And the road curves a bit. There's a little bump when you pass the Smith driveway. And then, about a minute later, you hit the washed-out spot." He shrugged. "Simple, really."

"Right," she said grumpily. "Simple." It was difficult not to glare at Chiweto. Her bad mood wasn't his fault, after all. He hadn't done anything wrong. He was just another soldier.

Same as her.

That, she realized, was at the heart of her

discontent. She was a journalist. It was how she thought of herself. It was who she was. Except now, she wasn't. Now she wore a green uniform and light body armor, the same as the soldiers around her. She carried a rifle, and had a radio clipped around her ear. It didn't feel like her.

She was a refugee from Earth, with a skill set no one wanted in a beleaguered colony. For a short time she'd been able to get by on charity. The colonists saw her as an extension of the Navy force she'd travelled with, and it was in their nature to share with someone in need.

That charity wouldn't last forever, though. When the call had gone out for volunteers to join the new Colonial Forces, she hadn't hesitated long before signing up.

After all, she had nothing else useful to do.

All the way through her short, intense training period she'd felt like an outsider. She didn't fit among the Navy personnel who did most of the training, or with the handful of veterans among the colonists who'd pitched in to help train the recruits. She certainly wasn't a colonist. On some level she'd thought of it all as temporary. She had a bedroom in a villa that she shared with a sailor from Earth and a colonist from a distant farm. It had the feel of a short-term billet, not a home.

As she went through the training she'd been filing away all kinds of details in case she wanted to write about the whole experience. She'd been thinking of it as an assignment. Gathering background for an awesome story. Deep down inside she thought of herself as a journalist travelling with the real soldiers.

Except she had no journalistic career to return to. Nowhere to file a story. Nowhere to live, to be, except Ariadne. She was a colonist now, whether she liked it or not.

She shifted her rifle from one side to the other, careful to keep the barrel pointed up. Controlling where the gun was pointed, remaining constantly aware of the muzzle direction, was second nature to her now. She was a decent shot, and she had a solid grasp of small-unit tactics. She was no seasoned veteran, but she was a competent soldier now. She was as good as anyone in the back of this truck.

And now, she was on her first real assignment. Alien ships had touched down in the countryside, and CF troops were heading out to see what was going on. The idea should have excited her. After all, she was finally going to put all that training to work. She could understand if it were to terrify her instead.

She felt some fear, true, but her main reaction was surliness. *It's because I'm a soldier. I really am. I'm going out to face the aliens, and I actually know what I'm doing.*

*I'm not a reporter anymore. I'm a private. This isn't a story. I'm not getting background. I'm doing my job.*

Janice sighed and closed her eyes. *This wasn't supposed to be my job.*

"We're passing my place now," Chiweto said. Janice opened her eyes. He was staring past her, like he was trying to look through the truck box.

He wore an expression of such wistfulness that Janice felt her own grumpiness fade.

*I don't get to be a reporter. Boo hoo, poor me. Look how I've suffered during the alien invasion.* She looked up and down the truck box. *Do you think any of them wanted this job?*

Well, most of the soldiers were men, and men were funny creatures. The young ones looked eager, excited. Even some of the older men had a look in their eyes sometimes, like they were getting a second chance at the dreams of their youth.

But still, not being lunatics, who among them would choose to go rolling into battle in the back of a truck when they could be building a colony, building lives?

She'd chatted with Knute, the man at her left. He was in his fifties, and he'd spent his adult life carving a farm out of a terraformed wasteland. Leaving when the aliens came had just about broken his heart. He'd stand with the rest of them, never flinching, but all he really wanted was to get back to his farm and see what was left.

*Okay,* Janice decided. *Pity party's over. It's time to think about what comes next. You've seen aliens before, so there's no excuse for panicking if one pops up in front of you today.* She closed her eyes again and ran through a weapons drill in her mind. *Lift the rifle. Stock against your shoulder. Cheek just touching the breech. Look past the sights, eyes on the target. Quick one-two-three on the trigger, pause, evaluate. Then fire again.*

The truck braked, her body tilted toward the

cab, and Janice's pulse quickened. *Are we there? Is it about to begin?* All that happened, though, was that the truck turned and started bumping its way along a much rougher surface. *We're crossing farmland now. It can't be much farther.*

Her body tilted the other way, and she found herself leaning against Knute, his rifle between them, the stock digging into her hip. They bounced and swayed as the truck climbed a gentle slope. After an endless time the truck stopped. There was a breathless moment of silence, then the sound of cab doors opening and closing.

Janice drew her legs in, preparing to rise. Chiweto and some of the others did the same, but Knute didn't move. She glanced at him, and he shrugged.

A man near the tailgate rose to one knee, waited for thirty long seconds, then sat back down, looking flustered. And the doors to the cab creaked. The truck bed rocked ever so slightly as the driver and sergeant climbed back in. The doors slammed, and the truck resumed moving.

Janice said, "Maybe it'll be a while before-"

The truck stopped, and she heard the thump of feet outside. The tailgate dropped and the sergeant, a blocky woman in her forties, glared in at them. "Let's go, kids! Move it, move it! This isn't a holiday outing."

Soldiers scrambled out of the box, and Janice followed. The truck stood just below the crest of a low hill. The driver was setting up a telescope on a tripod, just low enough to keep himself from being skylined. "Spread out," said the sergeant. "Look sharp. Buggers touched down somewhere near here. And stay off the bloody horizon."

Janice headed across the hillside, staying at the same altitude, checking to make sure her head wouldn't block the telescope. The ground underfoot was in furrows with dead plants poking up in tidy, withered rows. She had no idea what grew here, if this was a crop that had been harvested or young plants that had died from neglect when the farmers died or fled.

To the east the crater wall loomed, made flat and featureless by distance. The crest of the hill blocked her view to the north. To the south and west she saw rolling farmland and patches of scruffy trees. Several hectares of timber had been harvested, leaving an orderly grid of round stumps. She wondered idly if more trees would be planted there.

"Nothing so far, Sarge," the driver said.

"All right. Head around the hilltop and look north. We'll leave the truck where it-"

Light flashed white in the corner of Janice's eye, someone screamed, and she dove forward, landing on her elbows and stomach in the dirt. The stalks of dead plants poked at her. She stared at the side of her left hand, where a plant had scratched her and drawn blood.

She smelled ozone, burnt earth, burnt flesh. Instinct made her roll sideways, downhill. After one complete rotation she came up on one knee, rifle ready, and looked around.

A black line scored the hillside just above the

indentation where she'd thrown herself flat. She saw a trough half the width of her body, with charred plants and crisp-looking soil. She followed the trough with her eyes and saw a soldier named Hansen, sprawled on his back, his back arched and his body twisted in agony. He was dead, his torso burned most of the way through.

Janice's gaze moved back along the trough, and she shivered. She'd thrown herself flat an instant before some terrible heat weapon had swept across the hillside. She'd dropped out of the kill zone without a second to spare.

The truck erupted in flame, and Janice turned her head in time to glimpse a white-hot line in the air. The weapon was somewhere behind her, south, down the hill. It fired again, sweeping across the hillside, and caught another soldier. The beam swept up, raking the soldier from toes to head in the blink of an eye. Janice couldn't tell who it was, couldn't even tell if it was a man or a woman, as the blackened remains of the soldier dropped to the ground.

She sprang up, running for the top of the hill. There was no time to think, no time for strategy. The weapon was behind her. The crest of the hill meant safety.

Soldiers took cover behind the remains of the truck, braving the heat of the burning vehicle for the protection it provided. The sergeant laid her rifle over the hood and fired, and a man stood at the back of the truck, firing wildly into the distance. It was enough to attract the attention of the alien gunner, and flames engulfed the remains of the truck as Janice lumbered over the top of the hill.

*Just a few more steps. Almost safe. I'm almost over the top. But I'm skylined. I'm the most visible person on the hill right now. I'm a perfect target. I-*

She threw herself flat. Terror hit her then, and she lay for a long moment, panting furiously, her limbs frozen. Was she safe? Was she over the horizon, hidden? Or were the soles of her feet plainly visible from the alien's hiding place? Was it lining up a shot even now?

Janice jerked herself sideways, rolling, then squirmed forward on her elbows and the insides of her knees. Wriggling along was nightmarishly slow, but she couldn't bring herself to rise any higher. On and on she squirmed, until a glance backward showed her nothing but dirt and dead plants.

She rose then and ran, hunched forward, until she was well below the top of the hill. Then she stopped, panting, and looked around.

She was alone, and that scared her badly. Then a shape rose from the dirt almost at her feet. She almost fired, and Chiweto threw a hand up, palm out. "Hey!"

"Sorry." She pointed her rifle at the sky, then lowered it a few degrees at the sound of running feet.

Another soldier rounded the hill. It was Mark Stewart, still in his teens, a boy who'd annoyed her all through her training by easily running faster, shooting straighter, lifting more, and generally outperforming her. He was white-faced and frightened now, the rifle in his hands vibrating. He stopped in front of her, and she reached out a hand, tilting the barrel of the rifle sideways so it no longer pointed at her chest.

"Dead," Stewart said. "Oh, my God. They're dead." The rifle barrel began to drift back toward her chest.

She wrapped one hand around the barrel, keeping it pointed at the sky. With her other hand she poked his shoulder where his body armor ended. He seemed oblivious to both actions, staring around with wide eyes. She wasn't sure he could even see her or Chiweto.

"Stewart." She poked him again. When he didn't respond she slapped him, hard.

That got his attention. His eyes focused, he stared at her, and a look of hurt indignation filled his face. He touched his cheek. "Hey!"

"Welcome back," she told him, and gestured at the far side of the hill. "Is anyone else alive?"

That put his eyes back out of focus. "The sarge is dead!" Janice lifted her slapping hand, and he leaned away. "Stop that."

"Is anyone else alive?"

His brow furrowed. "No," he said. Then his face crumpled. "Oh, God ..." Then, as her hand started to rise, "Stop hitting me!" His gaze shifted. "Why are you holding my gun barrel?"

She let go. "We need to get out of here."

"Where will we go?" The voice was Chiweto's, and he sounded wonderfully calm. Both men were looking at her, she realized, waiting for her to make a decision.

*But you're the men! You're supposed to be good at this army stuff. And you live here. Why are you looking at me?*

*Because Stewart's just a kid, and even Chiweto's at least five years younger than me. And he's never been anywhere. And they both really want what I want. For someone else to take charge and tell them what to do.*

She turned her back on them, looking north. Her heart thumped urgently, telling her to get moving, start running. But that heat beam, whatever it was, had come from a long way off. It would take time for the aliens to reach the hilltop. She could take a moment to figure out where the hell she was running to.

The ground before her fell away in wrinkles, as if one hill after another had been mashed together by the hand of an impatient giant. It made an endless expanse of crests and ridges, none of them very high. There was very little flat ground. Instead of orderly crops this side of the hill was planted with a lot of waist-high bushes, each decorated in tiny leaves.

They would make terrible cover.

On a knob of land surrounded by a rippling ravine she saw a farmyard. The house was made of timber, and she shivered as she imagined how it would burn when the heat weapon touched it.

The barn, though, was made of stone. It was squat and solid, with walls that looked reassuringly thick from Janice's vantage point on the hillside. The barn was small, too. Small enough that three people ought to be able to defend it.

There was no sign of life in the farmyard. No one to help them with their defense. No innocent civilians to be caught up in the coming battle.

"There," said Janice, pointing. "We'll hold them off in that barn." And she took her rifle in a two-handed grip and started to run.

# CHAPTER 19 – HARDY

The *Bumblebee* plunged through the void, pursuing four Hive limpet ships toward the battered *Tomahawk*. The little fighter was moving in a straight line, and it would take at least a minute to close with the enemy, so Hardy unsealed his gloves one at a time.

His fingers shook, making the simple chore surprisingly difficult. Fear was getting to him, which surprised him. He thought he'd already accepted his death. One more dogfight – fought on borrowed time – should be nothing. But when he tilted his glove, a trickle of sweat poured out to pool on his thigh. He was sweating and panting for breath as if he'd been outside running alongside the *Bumblebee* instead of sitting in the cockpit.

"Knock it off, Hardy," he murmured, low enough that he hoped the microphone in his helmet wouldn't pick it up. "Fear's in your head.

Fear's a choice. Set it aside and concentrate on shooting these yahoos."

Fear, however, declined to be set aside. His muscles kept locking up as some primitive corner of his brain told him to hide by freezing in place. Again and again he had to fight himself for control, calling on lessons he dimly recalled from his earliest days of pilot training. *Focus on your breathing. In and out. Alter it slightly. Breathe in a bit slower, hold it for a second. In through the nose, out through the mouth. Since you can't help breathing anyway, it's the one part of you that won't freeze up.*

It worked, but it took a ridiculous amount of mental energy. *I'm a combat veteran, for the love of God. I'm supposed to be past things like this.*

He wiped his hands on his thighs, leaving shiny streaks on the fabric of his vac suit, then pulled his gloves back on one at a time and resealed them. By the time he finished that chore, the *Tomahawk* and the four limpet ships loomed uncomfortably close.

The battle began while he was a kilometer out and braking hard. The *Tomahawk* twisted and dodged, and he saw streams of small rail gun rounds rebound from the hulls of the limpet ships. Again and again the four ships tried to dart in close enough to latch onto the corvette. Each time, the *Tomahawk* managed to evade.

A rail gun fired a stream of projectiles, and four shots smacked into a limpet ship racing in. The ship continued to close, then crashed into the hull of the *Tomahawk* and bounced away, a cloud of shattered Fourier metal filling the void around it. The limpet ship drifted off, disabled, and an enthusiastic laser gunner burned a deep trench in the side of the alien before the battle moved on and left the limpet ship behind.

And then Hardy was in the thick of it. He found himself rushing a limpet ship nose to nose, and his nerves betrayed him. He fired too soon, wasting a long stream of rail gun rounds before he found his target. A dozen or so rounds slammed into the nose of the alien ship, bouncing away in every direction. A spent round hit the steelglass canopy in front of Hardy's nose, and he flinched, hauling on the stick as he did so. He shot past the limpet ship, then veered sideways and curved around the stern of the *Tomahawk*.

Another limpet ship – or possibly the same one; it was hard to keep oriented among the constantly shifting ships – loomed before him, and he braked, trying to line up a careful shot. Very little ammo remained in the *Bumblebee's* magazines. The alien was tail-on, and he was staring into the glow of the engines, finger tightening on the trigger attached to the control stick, when the ship jerked sideways. A chunk of hull burst outward and a rail gun round from the *Tomahawk* came sailing out, having gone right through the alien ship.

Hardy swore and hauled sideways on the stick, realizing too late that the *Tomahawk's* gunners were unlikely to fire again. After all, they'd destroyed the alien utterly. Besides, the

*Tomahawk* had already turned. Her rail guns were no longer pointed at him.

Hands shaking, he turned the *Bumblebee*, hating the jerky way the fighter moved. He was flying like a novice, like an amateur on the edge of panic. He sneered at himself, trying to find the calm that had enveloped him in the last battle.

It helped that the limpet ships were ignoring him, except to dodge his shots. Their attacks focused entirely on the *Tomahawk*. Of course, they'd turn on him next, once they'd dealt with the corvette. All he had to do was keep the corvette alive and he'd be fine.

Except that he'd die anyway. He was lost in enemy space with a damaged corvette and nowhere to run. He was going to die soon, and the weight of that knowledge was finally becoming more than he could bear.

A limpet ship darted in and pressed itself to the steelglass window on the port side of the *Tomahawk's* bridge. Vapor puffed out as the alien breached the window, and Hardy screamed, a raw sound of frustration and terror and fury. He pointed the nose of the *Bumblebee* at the alien and dove in, doing his best to hold the fighter steady, pouring rail gun rounds and firing his laser, focusing both weapons on one spot in the middle of the limpet ship.

The *Bumblebee* was no more than a dozen meters out when the rail gun hit empty. He inhaled and screamed again, determined to ram the fighter into the side of the enemy ship, steering straight for the bright red glow of his laser on the alien hull.

At the last possible instant the side of the limpet ship crumpled inward. Something burst inside the alien ship, chunks of hull burst outward, and Hardy stomped on the center pedal in the cockpit. Nav thrusters on the underside of the *Bumblebee* kicked the fighter upward, and he felt a shock of impact as he bumped the limpet ship in passing.

He brought the fighter around in a broad turn. The *Tomahawk*, he was relieved to see, was still moving, twisting and dodging to avoid the remaining limpet ship. The limpet from the side of the bridge was drifting away, trailing bits of wreckage. The port bridge window was a blackened mess, most of the steelglass gone, and Hardy saw a spiky shape go floating off into the void.

An alien commando.

The remaining alien made a run at the belly of the corvette. The *Tomahawk* spun along its axis, and the hull banged into the limpet ship in the last instant before it would have landed. More Fourier metal shattered and flew off, and the alien tumbled for a moment, then steadied itself.

It quickly moved in for another attack.

And Hardy's fear vanished. He experienced a glorious moment of clarity where the adrenalin in his blood sped up his thoughts, his reflexes, without overwhelming him. He could see exactly what was about to happen.

And he could see exactly how to prevent it.

He pointed the nose of the *Bumblebee* at a

spot between the limpet ship and the hull of the *Tomahawk*. His instincts told him he'd get there just before the two ships came together, so he aimed the fighter at just the right spot, and then he accelerated hard.

The *Bumblebee* shot forward, gaining speed with every split second, racing toward the hull of the corvette. Just when he thought he'd miscalculated and he was going to slam into the *Tomahawk*, the limpet ship dropped into place in front of him.

He didn't even feel the impact.

# CHAPTER 20 – HAMMETT

The cargo hold of the *Theseus* was an absolute mess.

Hammett sat on the staircase that led up to the bridge. He was about three meters above the deck, high enough to see over the heads of the crowd that jammed the converted freighter. People had climbed onto the rail gun tubes to escape the crush, and sat along the top three gun barrels. Now, the gaps between the barrels were rapidly filling with supplies from the *Sgian Dubh*.

They were abandoning the corvette. The *Sgian Dubh* had taken terrible damage in the last few moments before she darted through the Gate. Her crew were stripping the ship, removing everything that could be of use. That included every scrap of food and drop of water. It could be a very long trip home, after all.

A weary lieutenant in a Spacecom uniform

came plodding up the steps. He leaned against the railing beside Hammett and said, "We've got a little bit of ballistic ammunition for you. We've fired all the explosive stuff."

"All right," said Hammett.

"The captain wants me to ask you for more storage space." By the embarrassed look on the lieutenant's face, he already knew it was a ridiculous request.

"We aren't hiding any empty cupboards, Lieutenant. You'll have to do the best you can."

The lieutenant nodded and straightened up. He started to turn away, then paused. "Thanks for taking us on board."

"Sure."

"Whatever happens ..." The lieutenant hesitated, then shook his head and returned to the teeming chaos below.

*Whatever happens? That means he thinks something might happen. Something I'll find unpleasant.* Hammett stood and leaned over the railing, searching the throng below for a familiar face. All he could see was helmets, some blue, some green. Finally he just shouted, "Hey, you!"

A figure in a green helmet looked all around.

"Up here," said Hammett, and she tilted her head back. He recognized a young colonist named O'Reilly, her pale face framed by red hair. "Come up to the bridge. Bring three or four people with you. Colonists only," he added.

O'Reilly nodded, then tapped a couple of people on the shoulder. She spoke with them briefly, then pushed herself into the crowd, trying to work her way to the bottom of the staircase.

"O'Reilly!" Hammett shouted. When she looked up he said, "Climb straight up. It'll be faster."

She nodded, made her way to a support post holding up the staircase, and swarmed her way upward, clumsy in her vac suit. Hammett helped her over the railing, and she turned to help the men who climbed up behind her. Five colonists in total made the climb.

"Does everyone have a sidearm?" Hammett said, and they all nodded. "Good. You're in charge of bridge security. Hold the staircase as long as you can, but if you start taking serious fire, retreat into the bridge and lock the door."

O'Reilly stared at him, wide-eyed. "Are you expecting trouble from the other crews?"

"I think it's a good possibility," Hammett told her. "We'll try negotiation first. Don't be in too much of a hurry to draw a gun. But we'll hold the bridge, no matter what. Understood?"

Five people nodded solemnly.

"Good." He jerked a thumb toward the top of the staircase. "Your post is up there."

They clomped up the steps, and he turned back to the crowded deck. Where there had been a chaotic sea of milling bodies, patterns were emerging. He could see clusters of color, blue and green helmets clumping together as people joined their crewmates. They were segregating themselves instinctively, which was a crying shame.

A ripple of motion caught his eye, a knot of three or four people forcing its way through the crowd, moving toward him. The knot was blue and red, an EDF officer with some Spacecom personnel. The knot grew as two more people joined the group, one in a blue helmet and one in red. After that they formed a triangle, the Spacecom personnel in a wedge with the EDF officers behind them.

Hammett watched as the wedge drove its way forward, people cursing or grunting as they were forced aside, others creating a swirl of motion as they filled the empty space behind the wedge.

By the time the group reached the base of the stairs, Hammett could make out rank markings. All the Spacecom personnel were officers. He couldn't read the EDF rank markings, and he didn't care. The EDF officers would be full of importance and low on competence.

They climbed toward Hammett, and he moved to the middle of the staircase, planting his hands on his hips. They would have to stand a couple of steps down and look up at him if they wanted to talk to him. It was a petty psychological advantage, but he would take what he could get.

He recognized some of the Spacecom officers. The woman on the left was Commander Lauren Fortescue. She had "Cassandra" stenciled on her shoulder. The others were from the *Sgian Dubh*. There was a very young lieutenant who looked familiar, though Hammett couldn't remember his name. The craggy blond man almost Hammett's age was Max Steinfeld, captain of the *Sgian Dubh*.

Another lieutenant stood beside Steinfeld, a petite black woman Hammett had never seen before.

As soon as the Spacecom officers stopped, a couple of EDF officers pushed their way through the line. Vac suits tended to make every body look the same, but both of them were clearly overweight. The man opened his mouth, then glanced uncertainly at the woman and closed it.

She had none of his diffidence. She stopped one step below Hammett, glared up at him, and said, "I expect full cooperation, do you understand me?"

"I'm Admiral Richard Hammett," he said mildly. "Welcome aboard the *Theseus*. Who might you be?"

She stared at him, flustered, then said, "I'm General Friesen of the EDF. I'm in charge here. Now, I expect you to-"

"Who are they?" Hammett interrupted, gesturing at the other officers. He didn't care overmuch. He just wanted to interrupt the obnoxious woman.

She froze with her mouth open. Finally she indicated the man beside her. "This is Colonel Fuller." She turned, pointed at Steinfeld, and said, "This is, ah ..."

"Captain Steinfeld," Steinfeld said, sounding amused. "The Admiral and I are acquainted." He nodded to the black woman beside him. "Lieutenant Da Costa is my second in command. That's Lieutenant Remington, and Commander Fortescue, who commanded the *Cassandra*."

Hammett nodded politely.

"We'll be taking command of your ship," Friesen said. She pointed up the stairs. "Is the bridge this way?"

"My crew is under orders to shoot any non-colonial personnel who try to force their way onto the bridge," Hammett said. He kept his voice mild and his posture relaxed.

"Well, order them to stand down," Friesen snapped.

Hammett ignored her.

"Didn't you hear what I said?"

Behind her, the Spacecom officers looked distinctly embarrassed. They would back her play if they had to, Hammett decided. The key was not to force them into a corner. "We're allies," he said. "Being allies has worked out well so far, don't you think? After all, I've now rescued the personnel from two different Spacecom vessels." Friesen opened her mouth to speak, and he interrupted her again. "We have all the enemies we need. I don't think we really need to fight among ourselves."

"There are lines of authority that need to be established first," she said. "The EDF has authority over all Spacecom vessels."

Hammett sighed. "Where do you think you are?" He gestured around him. "Does this look like a Spacecom vessel?"

By the look on her face, the thought hadn't even occurred to her. She looked left and right, then said, "It's a vessel."

"A Colonial Forces vessel," Hammett said. "If

you insist on being in charge, you'll have to go back onboard the *Sgian Dubh*."

She scowled, standing there with her mouth open and her head tilted back, clearly searching for just the right scathing response.

"I'm glad you've all come to speak with me," Hammett said. "We need to discuss strategy. It's a conversation every experienced naval officer should participate in."

He couldn't tell if Friesen recognized the snub, but Colonel Fuller flushed.

"We'll decide what to do," said Friesen. "We don't need your input."

"He's the commander of the ship we're on," Steinfeld said, sounding a mite impatient. "He's also got experience fighting the Hive. We could use his input."

Friesen whirled to face him, but didn't seem to know what to say.

"As I see it," said Hammett, "the first order of business is to figure out where we are. How far are we from Earth, or any point on the Gate network?" He gestured behind him at the bridge. "Our scanners and navigation software aren't the best. This ship was designed as a short-haul freighter." He looked at Steinfeld. "Have you been able to get our location?"

The captain shook his head. "We were working on it when we lost power to the ship's computer."

Hammett whistled. The corvette was in desperate straits indeed if the main computer had lost power. "Okay, I guess we're doing it the hard way."

"We're going to head immediately for Earth," Friesen announced. She pointed a stubby gloved finger at Hammett. "You will comply immediately, or you will be placed in the brig."

The *Theseus*, of course, had no brig. Nor did it have a wormhole generator, which meant the trip home would take decades at least. He mentioned neither of these facts. "Would you like to tell me which direction Earth is?" he said.

Friesen gaped at him.

"Why don't we go up to the bridge," he said, keeping exasperation from his voice with a mammoth act of will. "We'll figure out where we are. Then, when you actually know what direction you want to go, you can make all the silly ultimatums you want." He leaned toward her, not quite hiding a sneer. "Okay?"

When she didn't respond he straightened, turned, and said, "This way, if you please."

O'Reilly stood with her people in a cluster at the top of the stairs. Hammett said, "Stand down for the moment. This bunch can come onto the bridge with me. No one else, though."

She nodded, and the guards edged backward onto the catwalk leading to the nose of the ship. Hammett was tempted to bring a couple of guards onto the bridge with him, but there simply wasn't room. He doubted he'd get all of his 'guests' into the tiny bridge at once.

He entered the bridge, then took his seat. Friesen, Fuller, and Steinfeld filled the back of the bridge. Vicente had never returned to the bridge, and Fuller sat at his station, which made enough room for Fortescue to squeeze in. The lieutenants gave up and waited outside.

"Have we made any progress on determining our position?" Hammett asked.

Hal turned in his seat. "I haven't found it in the atlas yet," he said, "but there's a fairly distinctive nebula just aft of us."

Hammett looked backward, and could see nothing but a row of vac suits. All four visitors gaped out through the aft windows. "Your windows are in terrible condition," Steinfeld said. "You should think about steelglass."

*You should think about shutting up.* "Does anyone recognize it?"

To his surprise, someone did. Fortescue said, "I think it's the Ballerina."

"Doesn't look like a ballerina to me," said Friesen.

"Aha," said Hal. He was looking at a red blur on his screen. "The Ballerina nebula. It's totally looks like a girl in a tutu from the other side." He rotated the image in his display. "Yup, that's it, all right." He glanced over his shoulder. "Good catch."

Fortescue inclined her head.

"We're quite close if we can see it with the naked eye," Hal said. "I think that star must be XC195." There was a long pause. "Oh, that's not good." He turned again in his chair, his face mournful. "We're a good two hundred light-years from home."

A long, uncomfortable silence fell over the

bridge.

"Well, we can still make it," said Friesen. She patted her ample stomach. "Food might be getting a little thin by the time we get back, but some of us might even benefit from that." She looked at Hammett. "How far can this tub of yours jump?"

"It can't jump," Hammett said. "We can reach the nearest Gate in about five hundred years."

That made her eyes pop. "Well, what are we going to do?" Friesen looked from one officer to another, anger and fear twisting her features. "We can't just stay here!"

*There isn't any point in asking, you fool. There aren't any suggestions to be made. We're trapped here, and demanding solutions from your officers isn't going to-*

"Well," said Fortescue.

Every person on the bridge turned to look at her.

"The *Manatee* was carrying a Gate," she said. "In case the colonists disabled the Gate we came through." She gave Hammett an apologetic shrug. "We thought you might do that, Admiral."

Hammett barely heard her, his mind racing with the possibilities. The supply ship had a Gate! If the Gate could be deployed, it would link to the matching Gate near the Earth. Would it work that way? He wished he knew more about trans-dimensional physics. Was the other Gate attuned somehow to the Naxos system?

"What good does that do us?" said Friesen. "The *Manatee* is destroyed."

"Maybe," said Fortescue. "All we know for sure is that it was disabled."

"But it's back with all those aliens!" Friesen sputtered. "There were hundreds of them!"

A babble of voices broke out. Hammett spoke over all of them, drowning everyone out. "Commander." He looked at Fortescue. "Do you know what will happen if the Gate is deployed from here?"

"Well, how can it be deployed?" snapped Friesen. "It's surrounded by-"

Hammett gave her a hard look, and she went silent.

"It'll connect," Fortescue said. "It will take a while. Several hours, because of the distance. But it will connect."

Earth, connected directly to the Hive. A nightmare scenario even a short time ago, but now? With the Hive scattered, their settlement in ruins?

They would never be more ripe for attack.

"That's it, then," Hammett said. "We have to get back to the *Manatee*. We have to open that Gate."

Friesen started to argue, but Eddie was already reaching for the controls. Hal tilted his head to activate his implants, and murmured for a moment, then said, "They're disconnecting the *Sgian Dubh* now."

"Good," said Hammett. "Clear the bridge, please."

"Now, look here," said Friesen.

"No, Linda." It was Colonel Fuller who spoke,

startling pretty much everyone. He rose from his seat and put a hand on Friesen's elbow. "Let the man do his job." He pushed her toward the exit.

Friesen planted her feet, resisting him. "But-"

Fuller looked at Hammett, gave him an apologetic smile, and said, "Admiral. I order you to fly us through the Gate and take us to the *Manatee*." He snapped his fingers in a parody of arrogance. "Now! That's an order!"

"Yes, Sir," said Hammett, smiling.

"Is that what you wanted?" Fuller said to Friesen. She didn't answer, but she let him push her toward the exit. The Spacecom officers, poker-faced, exited first to make room. A moment later, O'Reilly poked her head in.

"No more visitors," Hammett said.

"Right."

The stars moved as the ship swung around to point at the Gate, and Hammett felt a chill settle into his bones. *I can't believe we're going back into that meat grinder. God help us all.*

## CHAPTER 21 – JANICE

The barn burned.

Oh, the stone walls were fireproof enough. In fact, the mortared stone that Janice crouched behind was still cool to the touch, and she pressed her cheek to the rock, wicking away some of the heat.

She was hot, drenched in sweat, her hair plastered to her forehead beneath the rim of her helmet, her hands slick on the rifle she held. Part of it was fear, mixed with a visceral excitement she hadn't expected.

The rest was from the fire. The roof of the barn was in flames above her. It roared, an unsettling, greedy sound she did her best to ignore. She couldn't fight the fire, and she couldn't leave the barn. So she told herself the inferno two whole meters away was unimportant. She had enough to do playing soldier. She wasn't going to play fire chief too.

She knelt on one side of the barn's broad entrance. There'd been a door, but it lay in scorched chunks on the ground now. Chiweto knelt on the other side of the entrance, his face shiny with sweat. Stewart was behind her, watching through a small window in the back wall, making sure the aliens didn't come at them from that side.

Ahead of her, across a short yard covered in dead grass, the farmhouse burned. That fire was past its peak now. For a while the flames had shot a good twenty meters into the air. It was high enough she could almost hope someone had seen it, and was sending help.

Except the farmyard was nestled down among the wrinkles in the land, well below the tops of the surrounding hills and ridges. This part of the valley was pretty much depopulated. No one was going to see anything.

The radio clipped around her ear would let her talk to Chiweto and Stewart, and that was it. The long-range gear was in the truck, or in the sergeant's backpack.

Janice wouldn't be calling for help any time soon.

Chiweto tensed, and Janice raised her own rifle. She didn't look where he was looking, somewhere off to her left. Her field of fire was to the right. The aliens liked to move simultaneously, to keep the humans from concentrating their fire. Chiweto took aim, then fired a quick three-round burst.

Something came around the side of an

outbuilding, a spiky angular shape, and Janice fired three quick shots. The alien came across the yard toward her, and she fired another burst, then another. Chiweto shifted position, firing almost straight into the burning house. At least three aliens were on the move, then.

She unleashed another burst at the alien, saw the spark of a ricochet against an armored forelimb, and fired another burst as the alien changed direction. It fell back, skittering behind the outbuilding, and Janice indulged herself in a moment of quiet satisfaction.

Except that the aliens likely had a plan. They'd sent out a well-armored commando to keep her busy while other aliens advanced. Whatever their strategy was, she was doing little enough to slow them down.

The outbuilding, a shed of some sort, was a flimsy-looking structure of wood. Janice poured half a dozen shots through the walls, hoping to catch that commando by surprise. She had little chance of harming it, but if she could keep the alien hugging the ground it could only help.

A line of white light seared its way across her vision, splitting the air between her and Chiweto. A stone cracked, and Stewart cried out. Janice pulled back from the doorway as the beam swept left and right. It blackened the stones where she'd rested her cheek just moments before, then vanished.

She turned to the back of the barn and felt her heart lurch in her chest. Stewart was down. The brave boy who'd managed to survive the attack on the hillside was flat on his back, staring up at the ceiling.

They'd lost their best marksman, too.

Then Stewart sat up. He stared at the blackened line that now decorated the back wall of the barn, then stared at Janice and Chiweto.

"Get over here," she hissed, and gestured at a spot beside here. He leaped forward, reaching her side in two terrified bounds, and stood with his back to the wall.

"They're shooting through the fire," Chiweto said. "They're behind the house."

Which meant the three of them couldn't shoot back – not with any real hope of hitting anything – until the fire died down.

"They're beside the barn." Stewart's voice came out as a frightened whisper, barely audible above the grumbling of the flames. He curled the fingers of one hand, pointing behind him. "I hear them."

Chiweto started to lean out, rifle rising, then flinched back as the heat weapon once again played across the front of the barn. Janice pulled back too. *But that's what I'm supposed to do. They're providing cover fire. They fire the heat weapon blind to make us pull back, and then the alien outside-*

The line of white fire disappeared and she rose to her feet, stepping out into the doorway of the barn. She found herself facing an alien commando at point-blank range. He was just rounding the corner of the barn, no more than three meters away, and he sprang at her as she

177

started to fire.

There were no three-round bursts this time. She squeezed the trigger as fast as she could, firing shot after shot. The creature surged forward, those steel-clad forelimbs reached for her, and she hurled herself sideways. She landed hard on the floor of the barn, and Chiweto and Stewart poured a lethal barrage into the alien.

It fell twitching, dying in the middle of the barn floor, and both men ducked back into the corners. That was all the warning she got. The heat weapon was back, sizzling through the doorway. Janice lay beside the alien in the middle of the barn floor, completely exposed. She rolled onto her back, did her best to press herself into the dirt floor, and stared up, mesmerized, as the probing finger of white energy wobbled back and forth in the air above her.

The weapon stopped firing, Janice had a single moment of sweet relief, and then a fist-sized ember plunged from the burning roof, straight toward her face.

She shrieked and brought a hand up, batting at the lump of wood, feeling an instant of heat against the base of her thumb. The ember landed beside her, close enough that she could feel heat on the side of her neck. She rolled to her feet and sprang over to join Stewart beside the door.

"Your hair," he said, and slapped at the side of her jaw. Janice smelled burning hair and shrieked again, shifting the rifle to her left hand so she could bat at the side of her head with her right.

"Hold still, dammit. You're not helping." Stewart dropped his rifle, grabbed her by the collar with his left hand, and used his right hand to pinch out flames. Janice reached for the chin strap on her helmet, trying to open it one-handed.

"Better leave that on. There's more cinders falling."

As if to illustrate his point, a chunk of debris the size of a twin mattress plunged from the ceiling and engulfed the dead alien on the floor. The sound of the fire grew from a mumble to a roar as fresh air rushed in.

Stewart picked up his rifle. "If it keeps falling in little chunks, we might survive." A crackling sound came from directly above him, and he looked up. "Crap."

Janice was just starting to look up – not the best idea, since it exposed her face – when Stewart grabbed the edge of her armor just under her chin. A hard jerk brought her stumbling forward, and he hauled her across the open doorway to join Chiweto on the other side.

Janice said, "What the hell?"

The three of them were pressed close together in the corner beside the doorway. Stewart had to twist his head sideways to see past Janice's shoulder. "I thought that corner of the roof was going to-"

A rumble made Janice turn her head. She was just in time to see the far side of the roof collapse. The ends of burning beams tumbled down, creating a maelstrom all along the opposite wall. The spot where she'd been standing was completely engulfed in flames.

"I guess you're forgiven," she murmured.

Chiweto, looking straight up, said, "I think we'll be all right. The side should hold for a couple of minutes, unless something happens to-"

A concussion shook the ground, knocking Janice to her knees. A crack opened in the wall beside her, and she stared at it, trying to figure out what had just happened. Someone was shouting, but her overwhelmed mind couldn't process the words. Then hands grabbed her armor where it passed over the tops of her shoulders, and Stewart and Chiweto dragged her out of the barn.

The roof collapsed behind her. She didn't see it, but she heard a rumble, felt a wave of heat against the back of her neck, and watched clouds of sparks billow past her. She wanted to pat her hair at the back, make sure it wasn't burning, but holding onto her rifle seemed more important.

Directly in front of her, the house was almost fully consumed by flames. The aliens might already be able to see them through the sinking fire. She took a single step to the right, thinking to run around behind the barn, but Chiweto's arm stopped her.

"We need cover," she panted.

"Look," was all he said.

A line of shadow swept across the yard. Janice tilted her head back and gasped. A corvette filled the sky, hovering just a few meters above her head.

"Reinforcements are here," Chiweto said. "I guess we get to live."

# CHAPTER 22 – KAUR

Make a hole, people."

Kaur stalked through the corridors of the *Tomahawk*, wrestling with impatience as sailors pressed themselves against the bulkheads. There was simply nowhere for the refugees to go to be out of the way, and she fought the urge to snap at people who took too long to get out of her path.

It wasn't as if she was in a hurry, really. Sure, a sense of urgency clawed at her, but there would be nothing for her to do when she reached her destination. She had nothing to do on the bridge, either. The *Tomahawk* was coasting up to the enemy Gate, but they wouldn't arrive for a good ten minutes.

And when they got there? She shrugged inwardly. The long-term plan was to figure out which way human space was, find a way to fix the distribution coupling, and start the long, long journey home.

Not that they'd make it. Starvation would finish them off long before they reached a friendly Gate. Unless she chose a subset of the crew to live, and condemned the rest to starvation or suicide.

With cannibalism, a greater portion of the crew could survive. It was an ugly thought, but to dismiss it out of hand was to condemn more of the crew to a slow death. So she had to consider it.

"Why the hell did I ever want command?" she muttered.

"Ma'am?" said a sailor.

"Nothing."

She needed to pop through the Gate, she supposed. See what had become of the *Theseus* and the *Sgian Dubh*. See if the far side of the Gate was any closer to human space.

Then pick a side, destroy the Gate, and start the long, hopeless trek home.

At last she reached the door to the medical bay. It seemed wonderfully open at first glance, until she saw the bodies that covered the floor. Men and women stared up at her, faces tight with pain, or stoic, or filled with medicated bliss, or blank with unconsciousness. She paused for a moment, taking it all in. Then she worked her way forward, stepping carefully over arms and legs and torsos.

"What can I do for you, Captain?" Kaur didn't recognize the woman – she had to be the medical officer from the *Gideon* – but she spoke with the crisp authority of a doctor in her own environment.

"I'm looking for a pilot named Hardy. Probably your newest patient."

"He's back there." The doctor pointed at the back bulkhead. "Don't bother him." She turned away, kneeling to examine a young man on the floor.

Her utter disregard for the chain of command was ... startling. Almost refreshing, so long as it didn't spread. Kaur delivered a mocking salute to the back of the woman's head, then picked her way to the back wall.

Hardy was unconscious, breathing with the aid of a respirator mask and a stimulator pack clipped to his chest. His face was dreadfully pale, and dark bruises filled the hollows around his eyes. His vac suit was gone, and his uniform. A thin blanket covered him. He seemed thin and frail without his clothes, and Kaur felt her heart go out to him. She had no idea how badly he might be hurt, and she looked around for the doctor. But the doctor was clearly busy, and so was her own medical officer, who knelt in the far corner.

"They're ignoring you," she whispered to Hardy. "That's good, right? You must be out of danger."

*Or beyond help*, said a cold voice in her mind. She stretched a hand toward Hardy, then hesitated, afraid to touch him, afraid to disturb him. He looked so vulnerable under the blanket. He *was* vulnerable without a vac suit. If the ship lost atmosphere, he was a dead man.

In fact, every patient in the medical bay was unprotected. The doctors, too. Kaur's was the only vac suit in the bay. She thought about ordering the doctors at least to suit up, but how much clumsier would they be in gloves and thick sleeves?

*If I want them kept safe, I have to keep the hull intact. And I can't do that from here. I can't do anything from here. I'm wasting my time.* She stood, feeling her stomach twist. Hardy had crashed his fighter into a limpet ship to protect the *Tomahawk*, and it felt wrong to just walk away from him. But staying would do no good.

She worked her way across the floor, one careful step at a time. She was almost to the door when the speakers in her helmet came to life. "Captain to the bridge."

"Coming." She picked up her pace, reaching the doorway in two long strides. She glanced back, got a dirty look from the *Gideon's* doctor, and moved into the corridor. She was less patient now, shoving past sailors who were too slow getting out of her way. In another minute she reached the bridge.

An opaque emergency patch covered the port window where the limpet ship had made a breach. The whole bridge crew, though, was staring in the opposite direction. Kaur looked through the starboard window – and felt some of the weight slide from her shoulders.

There, not fifty meters away, was the *Theseus* in all its battered glory.

"The admiral would like to speak to you," said Jin.

Kaur dropped into her seat, then unsealed her helmet and dropped it into the rack. "Admiral. Kaur here."

"Captain." He sounded as calm as ever, as if they'd all spent the day having a picnic. "I'm delighted to find you still alive. What's the status of your ship?"

She explained the situation with the distribution coupling. "We've lost maybe twenty percent of our Fourier metal, and we lost our fighter. It's pretty crowded in here, too. Aside from that, we're good."

"Your wormhole generator is intact?"

"Yes, Sir."

"Excellent. I want you to go through the Gate. You'll find the *Sgian Dubh* on the other side. Take their coupling and install it, then come back through to this side. It's probably closer to home. Once you're through the Gate, I want you to open a wormhole and leave immediately. Don't even get your bearings first. Make a jump into deep space, get out into the middle of nowhere where they can't find you. Then figure out where you are, and get home."

"But-" Her objections rose in a lump, choking her, silencing her. She couldn't blurt out her calculations in front of the bridge crew. She couldn't fill their heads with thoughts of starvation, cannibalism, death. "Sir, I need to speak to you in person."

There was a long moment of silence. At last he

said, "Fine. I'll meet you in the nose."

By the time Kaur reached the airlock, the two ships were already docked together. She fidgeted, waiting for the lock to open, then stepped through and into the *Theseus*.

Hammett waited inside the lock, the hatch open behind him. A long catwalk stretched away behind him, extending along the top of the ship to the bridge. The catwalk was empty, and she wondered if she could send twenty or thirty people over. They could line up along the walkway and have more space than they had now.

"Would you like to come to the bridge, Captain?"

"I'd rather not, Sir." He nodded, and she said, "Most of us will die if you send us home."

"Staying here isn't exactly a safe option."

"Dying in battle is bad," she said. "Dying of starvation is worse. We're months from home. Not weeks. Not days."

Hammett frowned. "Still, I'd rather see a few of you survive than none of you. And if my mission fails, I need somebody to get back to Spacecom with the position of the Hive."

"Mission!" She pounced on the word. "What mission?" *It has to be a mission I can help with. Please, God, anything but slow starvation.*

"There's a Gate in the hold of the *Manatee*," he said reluctantly. "I'm going to try to get back to the wreck. I'll try to find the Gate and deploy it."

"That's a much better option," Kaur said. "But you'll need my help."

Hammett shook his head. "It's suicidal."

"So is going home the long way," she said. "At least your way lets us skip the cannibalism."

That made his eyebrows climb his forehead.

"You've got a shot at getting us directly home," she said. "And a shot at bringing reinforcements from Earth directly to the Hive's home system." She clutched his arm, then remembered herself and let go. "That's a priceless goal. It's worth gambling everything. This is no time to divide your forces, Admiral."

For a long moment they stood there, staring at one another. Finally he said, "I want you alive at the end of this, Meena."

"Not at the cost of eating my crew," she said. "That's a favor I don't need."

The silence stretched out. At last he nodded, a reluctant jerk of his head. "Fine. We'll put everything on one roll of the dice. Let's go see what's left of the *Manatee*."

# CHAPTER 23 – BLOCH

When the temperature dropped below minus 100, Wolfgang Bloch reluctantly decided to abandon the bridge. The decision wasn't easy. Getting his bridge crew to leave proved even more difficult.

Frost rimed the bulkheads and screens all around him. Frost coated his shoulders and chest, and flaked away from his arms as he pushed himself up from his chair. The ship's gravity was long since gone, and he kept a hand on the arm of his chair, then pulled himself across to the next station.

Remlinger was in her seat. She hadn't moved in quite a while. Frost made her faceplate opaque, and he wiped the worst of it away, then peered at her face. Her eyes were closed, and she didn't react to the jostling as he touched her helmet. He grabbed her shoulders, fearing the worst, and shook her. It took three good shakes, but at last, to his profound relief, her eyes opened.

She blinked, mumbled, then shook her head, took a deep breath, and squinted at him. "Commodore?"

Her voice over the suit radio was faint, but at least she recognized him. "Lieutenant," he said. "Nap time is over."

She nodded, and he let go of her shoulders. He floated over to the Communication station, stopped himself by grabbing the communication officer by the helmet, and slapped his hand against the man's faceplate until the man's arms came up, scraping at the coating of frost.

By this time Remlinger was up, pulling herself along toward the Operations station. She reached for Durand's shoulder, but Durand brought an arm up to stop her. "I'm awake," he said, his voice raspy. "I'm cold, but I'm awake."

In a minute or two the entire bridge crew was awake and listening. They'd put their suits in power conservation mode, which meant they were not quite hypothermic, but close to it. It gave the best odds for long-term survival, with the crew in a state close to hibernation, barely moving, barely breathing. But now, Bloch decided, it was time to take some action.

"It's been several hours," he said. "We haven't been boarded, and no one in the rest of the ship has contacted the bridge. We will wait no longer. We will go in search of our shipmates. We will go in search of air and warmth."

The ship was compartmentalized, with quite a

few redundant systems. There was an excellent chance that parts of the ship still held air. Main power was clearly down, but that didn't mean there was no power anywhere. That no one had contacted the bridge was disappointing, but there could still be other survivors, preoccupied with the immediate needs of survival.

He would wait no longer.

The hatch to the bridge was the first challenge. Before the Hive, bridge security was a token thing. Now, with entire ships' companies committing mutiny and joining the rebel colony, the loyalty of a crew could no longer be taken for granted. The new bridge hatch was armor-plated and firmly locked. Fortunately the locking mechanism was on the inside. Without power it still required tearing away a couple of big wall panels and cranking a wheel to pop the lock. After that, a couple of sailors hauled the hatch open by brute force.

The corridor beyond was empty, frost thick on the walls. Bloch tried to work out what that meant as he led the others along, rebounding from wall to wall, from ceiling to floor. *Things got cold, and then the ship attempted to repressurize this section, releasing moist air that formed frost as it cooled ...*

It didn't matter, and he pushed it from his mind. When he reached an intersection he headed aft. The key systems – engines, the missile bay, Medical – were all well aft of the bridge. There was light enough to see, coming from the self-contained lights embedded in the ceiling. He was glad the days of completely centralized ship's power were long in the past.

He didn't see any direct signs of damage, which wasn't surprising. The bridge was in the well-protected center line of the ship, a good ten meters from the hull in every direction. He stayed on the same deck as he worked his way aft. It was quite a shock when the deck plates in front of his face ended and he found himself staring at stars and drifting chunks of rock.

He rotated his body. A piece of the ceiling was gone, giving him a view of a dark room above. Below, he could see the jagged edges of three decks. The enemy had carved a vast pit in the belly of the *Adamant*. The damage chilled him, and he caught the torn edge of a ceiling panel, dragging himself along, wanting to get past this terrible wound in his ship.

"Oh, my God."

He didn't know who had spoken, and he didn't care. "We're not here to sight-see," he barked. "Keep moving." He sounded obnoxious, he knew. That was fine. If the crew was busy resenting him they wouldn't be thinking about the devastation around them, or wondering when the aliens would come back.

They would come back. Of that Bloch had no doubt. The Hive was regrouping, or rescuing survivors in their ravaged settlement. Or they were patiently waiting for these battered human interlopers to die. But eventually they would come back to the *Adamant*. They would eradicate any life that remained, and cut up the ship for scrap to use in the repair of their home.

And Bloch, if he was honest with himself, knew he wouldn't put up much of a fight. He was leading a pitiful handful of refugees through the crippled remains of a ship. There wasn't a whole lot he could do.

But the *Adamant* had a missile bay well-stocked with explosive warheads. Those warheads could be detonated by hand, if it came right down to it. The aliens would find less salvage than they expected when they returned. And maybe take a few more casualties.

A body floated just beyond the devastated section, a man, judging by the bulk of his torso. His legs were missing, and the inside of his faceplate was dark with frozen blood. Bloch pushed the remains up against the ceiling panels and kept going.

No one spoke as they passed the body and followed him.

Bloch moved an appalling distance through the ship, the bridge crew trailing along behind him, before he finally found a sealed hatch. He pressed his palm against the flat panel, knowing he had no chance of feeling warmth if it was there but unable to resist trying. Then he pushed himself back, getting his bearings.

Medical was directly above him. Kitchen stores to starboard, crew quarters to port. The kitchen was on the other side of this hatch, with the enlisted mess just beyond. The crew quarters would be his best bet, he decided. They were heavily compartmentalized. Emergency doors were set at intervals as short as five meters in some places.

"This way." He led his band of followers a few meters aft, then into a cross corridor. He found a closed hatch, opened it, and moved through, saying, "Last one in seals the hatch."

The next hatch wouldn't open. He pulled apart a bulkhead, found the override handle, and twisted it. There was no way to be sure the section of corridor he was in was airtight, but he couldn't advance without taking chances.

The hatch slid open a finger's width, and a rush of air pushed him back. Hands against his back and shoulders stopped him, and he waited while the air pressure equalized. Frost formed on every surface, and he had to scrub his faceplate clear.

"Somebody get that hatch." He waited while a couple of sailors grabbed the edge of the hatch and heaved it open. They moved aside and he led the way into the next compartment.

Crew cabins lined the corridor. The cabin doors were closed, and he ignored them. At this range any survivors would hear him on their suit radios. There was no need to search the cabins.

The next hatch opened as he approached, and light flooded the corridor. He checked the status panel on the sleeve of his suit. The temperature was chilly but tolerable, and he retracted his faceplate.

The air, dry and cold, smelled of burned plastic and dust. He wrinkled his nose, sneezed once, and pulled himself forward. He was in a cross-corridor, and he drifted forward, moving toward the kitchen. As he went, he found himself sinking toward the deck plates. By the time he reached the next hatch he was taking long, bounding steps in about ten percent of a gee.

Again the hatch slid open as he approached. He stepped through and found himself facing a knot of figures gathered beside the main ovens. There were five of them, all in vac suits with faceplates retracted, armed with a mix of kitchen knives and handguns. They hastily lowered their weapons as they recognized him.

The air was noticeably warmer here, and the gravity was stronger, almost fifty percent. Bloch felt some of his pessimism slide away. The ship was still dead in space, but it felt more like a ship now, less like a hulk. It felt like an inventory, something to work with, not a place to huddle in the dark while he waited to die.

A woman with a single thin rank stripe across her chest stepped to the front of the little group, glanced at the bridge crew gathering behind Bloch, and wiped the palms of her gloves on her hips in an unconscious nervous gesture. "There's about twenty of us," she said. "We haven't seen the others, but we hear them." She touched the side of her helmet. "Two men are in the sun room. They say the enemy ships all pulled back."

The sun room was a small lounge for off-duty personnel. Located on the top deck at the starboard side, it featured a wall and ceiling of steelglass. It would make an excellent observation post.

"There are some others in the engine room," she said. "They're trying to get main power back on. They aren't very optimistic, though."

Bloch activated his implants. The menu across his retina showed only embedded data sources, and no communications at all. He turned on his suit microphone instead. "This is Commodore Bloch. Your vacation ends now. We'll be repairing as much of the ship as we can, concentrating on weapons and movement. We will also be preparing to repel boarders. We'll begin with a roll call. Who's in the sun room?"

"Specialist Davis and Technician Murtaugh," said a man's crisp voice.

"Engine room," said Bloch. "Report."

There were four technicians in the engine room, plus three wounded, all of them unconscious.

"Who else have we got?" Bloch demanded. "Anyone else?"

"This is Doctor Parker," came a rasping voice. "I'm in the medical bay, and I'm trapped. I've been trying to get the door open for a while now. I've got three wounded in medical pods. It's just the four of us in here."

"Anyone else?" said Bloch. "No?"

Silence.

"Specialist Davis. Report. What have you seen?"

"Some of our ships made a run for it at the end of the battle, Sir. Most of the enemy gave chase, and they never came back. There were a few Hive ships prowling around. They burned off the starboard laser turret. We haven't seen them in a couple of hours, though."

"Good," said Bloch. "What else?"

"There's a lot of wreckage outside. I can see the *Sai* and the *Cassandra*." He was silent for a moment. "There's no sign of life on either one."

"All right. Anything else I should know?"

"There's lots of alien wreckage, too. We hit them bad, Sir."

Bloch turned his attention to the engine room. The technicians were unanimous in their verdict that the engines and main power were beyond salvage, at least without a dockyard.

"Forget about that, then," Bloch said. "One of you get up to Medical and get the doctor out. Put your wounded into pods. The rest of you, meet me in the missile bay. We're not quite done fighting."

There was a process for manually launching missiles, though he'd never imagined he'd have to use it. The missiles themselves were complex self-contained machines that could fire up their engines and steer toward targets, once they were free of the confines of the missile bay. Spacecom's engineers had planned for an eventuality like this one, where a ship was crippled with unfired missiles. The bay even came equipped with a tiny airlock designed for expelling missiles into space one at a time.

Bloch supervised a couple of technicians as they pushed a missile out through the airlock. The only survivors with the authority to access the missiles through their implants were Bloch and Remlinger. He ordered her back to the kitchen to make sure they couldn't both be killed by one enemy strike, then called up the missile on his implants.

He found himself staring at the outside of the hull through a tiny camera in the missile's nose. He ran through the menu, checking his options. If he'd ever been trained on the particulars of directly controlling a missile he'd entirely forgotten it. The menu was quite simple, though. He could scan, choose targets, and activate the missile. That was it.

Getting the rest of the missiles out through the little airlock would be labor-intensive but not complicated. He called the kitchen crew to the missile bay, put a technician in charge, and led the rest of the technicians into the corridor.

"Get me some maneuverability," he said. "We're all boxed in by rocks and wreckage. I need to be able to see what's going on. I need to be able to move."

Twenty minutes later he had an improvised bridge set up in the engine room. Zimmerman, his helmsman, held a data pad that gave him control over half a dozen maneuvering thrusters. Movement would be slow and clumsy, but the ship would move.

Tomlin stood nearby, managing communications through his implants. At the moment he had nothing to do. Rearden, his Operations officer, was assisting Zimmerman. She had her eyes closed as she watched the view through a camera on the hull of the *Adamant*.

"I think we're ready, Sir," said Zimmerman.

Bloch was opening his mouth to reply when Rearden said, "Ship!" Bloch looked at her. She didn't open her eyes, but she said, "A ship just went past my camera. Very close. I couldn't identify it."

"Alien or friendly?" Bloch demanded.

She shrugged, eyes still closed. "I just saw a blur, Sir."

"Could you tell if it was-"

"Commodore," a voice interrupted. "This is Davis. There's a ship on our starboard side. I think it's trying to dock with Airlock Seven. Sir, it's the *Theseus*."

*Better than the aliens,* Bloch thought. *Still, not exactly friendly.* "Tomlin. Contact the *Theseus*. Tell them to use Airlock Six." That would put the rebel ship even with the kitchen. With luck they'd be able to dock without wasting any more air.

Bloch paused a moment, thinking. What were the names of those sailors in the kitchens? Which ones had sidearms? "Harvard. Kim. Meet me in the kitchen. We're going to greet some guests."

# CHAPTER 24 – HAMMETT

Hammett stood at the port window on the bridge of the *Theseus*, staring out through the battered glass at the shambles that remained of the alien settlement. He could make out a distant glint of engines as a last few ships retreated from the asteroid field. Most of the Hive ships had already pulled back to the settlement by the time he came back through the alien Gate. The few who'd remained had trickled away as the *Theseus* and the *Tomahawk* approached. Now, the human invaders had the entire asteroid field to themselves.

The aliens were busy, though he couldn't make out what they were doing. Ships bustled around the wreckage of the settlement, reminding him of ants in a disturbed anthill. He felt something close to remorse as he looked at all he'd helped to destroy. This had been something glorious. Something grand, something

humanity could have learned from.

Now, it was a shattered ruin.

*We had no choice. We truly didn't. It seems like an incredible opportunity in the abstract, and no doubt future generations will condemn us for squandering all the possibilities that come with First Contact.*

*But we had no choice.*

A flare of light caught his eye. It was the reflected shine of an engine somewhere behind him, distorted and blurred by the glass. The *Adamant* had a runabout, and a team of rescued crew from the *Cassandra* had gotten it flying. Now the *Tomahawk* and the runabout were working together, combing through the wrecked ships, looking for survivors.

It made Hammett's skin crawl. He was waiting for the Hive to turn its attention back to these impudent human trespassers. The alien response was just a matter of time, and when it came, it would be violent. They were only ignoring the humans because the humans appeared to be no immediate threat.

Soon, the threat would become obvious. And the aliens would react.

When the next attack came, Hammett wanted both of his remaining ships ready. He longed to order the *Tomahawk* to join the *Theseus* in the tense job of watching the enemy. But it was not so easy to order a ship to break off rescue work.

They'd found pockets of survivors on three different ships so far, including the *Manatee*. Every rescue seemed to buoy morale, but it filled

Hammett with unease. What good did it do to gather rescued crews together in the ships that were about form the front line against the alien counter-attack? Sailors trapped in disabled ships might actually be better off than the people being rescued.

It was two hours since the *Theseus* had docked with the *Adamant* long enough for a difficult meeting with Bloch. Two hours, and the Gate was still being unpacked. Getting at the thing had proved to be a monstrous task. Dozens of crew from the *Theseus* and *Tomahawk* were taking part, and incidentally relieving the crowding on both ships. It had taken most of an hour just to force open the supply ship's big cargo doors. After that they'd set to work offloading cargo. He didn't know if they'd reached the massive Gate components yet, never mind starting to assemble it all.

The plan was to stick the Gate pieces right onto the side of an asteroid. Arriving ships would seem to spring from the rock itself. It would make the Gate impossible to attack from behind.

Hammett didn't care. He just wanted the whole nerve-wracking process to be over.

"Admiral? Geibelhaus here."

Hammett swallowed. It was the moment he'd been dreading and yearning for.

"The Gate's live, Sir. They powered it up about a minute ago."

It would take hours for the Gate to connect to its counterpart in the Sol system. Long, terrible hours while he waited for the aliens to notice a

massive power surge and react.

"Thank you, Lieutenant. Get everyone back aboard one ship or the other as fast as you reasonably can."

"Aye aye, Sir."

Through the window the alien ships continued to scurry and flit. So far, they weren't reacting.

So far.

A metallic clatter, muted by distance and the muffling effect of his helmet, told him the runabout was docking with the *Theseus*. The *Tomahawk* would be picking people up directly from the Gate site. Hammett stared out the window and silently fretted, wondering how long it would take to get everyone safely inside a hull.

'Safely' being a relative term, of course.

"Admiral."

He glanced at Sanjari.

"I've got a new blip on my screen. It came out of nowhere, just this side of the settlement. I think it's smaller ships coming together. They just got big enough for the scanners to detect."

Hammett nodded, did his best to ignore the lump of ice forming in his stomach, and worked the radio controls on the sleeve of his suit. "Hammett to *Tomahawk*."

"*Tomahawk*. This is Captain Kaur."

"Captain, we're seeing a large enemy ship close to the settlement."

"I'll get a telescope on it," she said. "Stand by." It took most of five minutes, but at last she said,

"Our best count is between fifteen and twenty ships, with more joining every few minutes."

"Keep an eye on it," he said. "Keep me advised. And don't let anyone else go outside."

"Aye aye."

After that there was nothing to do but wait. The minutes crawled past and he stared into the void, trying hopelessly to pick out the growing alien craft with his naked eyes. *If it gets big enough to see at this range, you're a dead man, Richard.*

Slowly an ache in his lower back began to intrude on his consciousness. He blinked and was startled to find that his eyes stung. He shifted, felt stiff muscles protest, and rolled his head from side to side. His neck was painfully tight. *How long have I been standing here without moving?* He turned around, walked to his chair, and sat down. When he leaned forward his back cracked loudly enough that Eddie twisted around in his chair.

*Okay, this is stupid.* Staring out the window didn't help. He closed his eyes and leaned back in his chair, waiting for the hot, gritty sensation on his eyeballs to recede. Only when his mind started to drift did he open his eyes and lift his head. *Did I just almost fall asleep?* He smothered a yawn and tried to remember how long he'd been on duty. *If I'm this exhausted, what shape is the rest of the crew in?*

"Admiral?" It was Kaur over the suit radio.

"Yes, Captain, go ahead."

"I'd like to send some people over to the

*Manatee* and try to salvage some food and water. I'll need every scrap I can get if I end up going home the long way."

He shook his head. Kaur couldn't see it, but it helped clear his mind. "No. We're betting the whole farm on this one. You won't be jumping out of here. You're going home by Gate, or you're dying here today."

"Aye aye," she said, sounding dispirited.

She'd planted the thought of food in his mind, though, and it wouldn't leave. His stomach rumbled, and he tried to remember how long it had been since he'd eaten. "Sanjari. Any developments out there?"

"The big ship still isn't moving," she said. "It just sits there and keeps getting bigger." She gave him a bleak grin. "I wish they'd hurry up."

"I think we can take rotating breaks," he said. "Who wants to hit the galley first?"

"The galley's full of crew from the *Cassandra*," she said. "I'd rather take my break here, where there's a bit of elbow room." She patted her stomach. "I wouldn't mind grabbing something to eat and coming back, though."

Before he could answer, a metallic clang echoed through the ship.

"That runabout pilot must be getting tired," she said. There was a note of tension in her voice, though. She had to be thinking the same thing he was: that they weren't expecting the runabout. And there was no way to be absolutely sure there were no aliens closer than the habitat.

"I'll go check it out," Sanjari said. She rose

from her seat, checked the pistol on her hip, then left the bridge.

He heard her voice on the radio a minute later, sounding more cheerful than she had in hours. "Did you order a pizza, Admiral?"

She was back on the bridge soon after, her arms loaded with square packages that steamed and emitted delicious odors. "Bento boxes," she said, beaming. "The kitchen crew on the *Adamant* got bored and decided to start making lunches." She moved around the bridge distributing packages, then took her own seat. "For EDF goons, they're not so bad."

Hammett forgot the war for the next several minutes, trusting Sanjari and Kaur to keep half an eye on the enemy. He took off his helmet and gloves and gave his attention entirely to the food. The box contained a tray with cubes of vat chicken awash in a spicy gravy. There were sliced carrots and bread and a big lump of something sweet that tasted more or less like pineapple. He tried to simultaneously savor every morsel and gobble it all down. He didn't look up until the tray was spotless.

"All right," Hal said, putting his own tray down. "I'm ready for anything now."

"That ship is on the move," Sanjari said, setting her own box aside. "Coming this way."

"Don't fixate on it," Hammett said. "For all we know there's a couple of limpet ships hiding in the rocks waiting to use this thing as a distraction." He stood, crossed to the waste receptacle in the corner, and discarded his box.

"Spread the word. Everyone holds their fire until I give the order." The last thing he needed was an excited gunner wasting the last of their precious ammunition.

"They're coming slowly," Sanjari said. "I estimate at least half an hour before they reach us."

Hammett nodded, sitting back down and pulling on his gloves. "Considerate of them." Not that it would be enough. They needed hours, not minutes, to open the Gate.

*I have nothing to do for half an hour but sit here and second-guess my decisions.* He shook his head, amused at himself, and closed his eyes. He spent a minute or two just meditating, clearing his mind as best he could. Then he ran through everything that had happened since he came through the first alien Gate, everything he knew about this system and the ships in it. He didn't pressure himself to think of new strategies. He just gave his subconscious room to work. If there was something he'd forgotten, something he was overlooking, his brain would deliver it up to him if he gave it a chance.

"The enemy ship is braking, Sir."

Hammett opened his eyes, startled to find that a quarter of an hour had passed. He checked his screen. The *Tomahawk* was in position directly above the *Theseus*. Even the *Adamant* had lumbered out of the thickest part of the asteroid field. The destroyer was directly below the *Theseus*, positioned crossways. She had two working laser turrets, both on her starboard side, so she was side-on to the enemy.

"Hammett." Bloch's voice, peremptory and abrasive, came over the suit radio in a curt bark. "When they get within a kilometer I want you to advance. Engage them at close range and destroy any suicide ships that separate from the main body. I'll be firing missiles."

The urge to refuse him was strong, but the man's rudeness was a poor reason to discount a strategy out of hand. Hammett made himself consider the idea. Any action at all – anything to disrupt the enemy's strategy – was preferable to staying still and doing nothing. And if a missile got through, it would certainly help.

"Okay," he said.

The alien ship was visible to the naked eye now. It was big. Frighteningly big. He stared at it as it grew slowly in front of the *Theseus*, feeling his blood pressure climb.

He looked past the ship to the shambles that remained of the settlement. *Okay, Hammett. It's a big, scary ship. But it's all they've got. They're desperate. It only looks overwhelming because they know there's no point in holding anything back.*

*Of course, we're desperate too. We're betting everything, and our everything is a whole hell of a lot smaller than theirs. I've doomed us all. I've-*

"Well," said Eddie, "it's a nice big target, isn't it?" He turned in his chair, giving Hammett and Sanjari a strained grin. "We shouldn't have any trouble hitting it."

Hammett laughed. The laugh caught him by

surprise, draining away enough of his panic that clear thought returned. "Get ready, Eddie," he said. "We'll advance when they're a kilometer out."

Eddie nodded, keeping any doubts to himself.

"Lieutenant." Hammett turned to Sanjari. "Contact Captain Kaur. Ask her to advance with us."

Sanjari nodded.

"We smashed their home," Hammett said. "We blew their fleet to shreds. We beat them. And now we're going to do it again."

That brought nods from the bridge crew. No one pointed out that the aliens had also bashed the hell out of the human fleet.

*This is it. The last real battle of the war. If we lose, there will be other battles, but we won't be around to fight them. If we win .... If we win, the war is truly over. There will be skirmishes after this, as Spacecom hunts down the remnants of the Hive. That's all.*

*So all we have to do is find a way to win this battle. We have to keep them away from that Gate for a few more hours.*

Bigger and bigger the alien ship loomed. It looked like a mountain of metal in front of the *Theseus*, and Eddie said, "They're getting pretty close, Admiral."

The enemy was close enough now that even the *Theseus'* outdated scanners could calculate the range. The ship was well inside the two-kilometer range and closing quickly. Hammett watched the numbers flash past on his screen.

Fourteen hundred meters. Twelve hundred.

*Oh, to hell with it. Close enough.* "Let's go, Eddie."

# CHAPTER 25 – KAUR

They're moving, Captain." Even as Touhami spoke the *Tomahawk* began to move as well, matching the progress of the converted freighter. This had the effect of making the alien ship, already distressingly large, seem to grow at twice the rate.

Kaur kept her hands still with an effort, though she desperately wanted to fidget. *Why did I talk Hammett out of sending me home? That was stupid. Suicidally stupid. We could have made it. We could have found a way.*

She and Touhami had tactical displays of a sort, small screens strapped to the dead tac displays at their stations. The screens showed the feed from a camera freshly glued to the nose of the corvette. A sailor had found a box labeled 'Security Cam System' among the detritus in the hold of the *Manatee* and brought it back to the *Tomahawk*.

The Tomahawk moved closer and closer to the alien ship, until Kaur found herself wanting to lean back in her chair. She could see nothing but a few rocks through the remaining window. Touhami, a handset pressed to the side of his head, fed her a steady stream of reports from the corvette's spotters. The alien ship was a hundred meters dead ahead and still closing. The *Adamant* was aft, maintaining its position. The *Theseus* was directly below the corvette, and still moving forward.

The alien ship completely filled her screen. It looked enormous, and dangerously close. *What the hell is Hammett doing? We're going to collide in a moment.*

"Ships are separating," said Touhami.

"Lasers firing," said Jin at almost the same instant. No one was trying to directly supervise the gun crews. They had their orders.

Kaur watched on her screen as a handful of small ships broke away from the monster alien craft. They were barely clear of the main ship when the *Theseus* fired a volley from her forward rail guns. Two of the little alien ships vanished, ripped apart by rail gun fire. Another spun to the side, badly damaged. The *Tomahawk's* gun crews poured fire into a third ship, and it staggered.

Then, barely a second after the ships began to separate, the first missile struck. It hit a damaged ship, and Kaur cursed under her breath. The little alien ship was disabled, but the missile had come in too fast. The suicide ship was still in the way, and the missile exploded several meters short of the main ship. She clenched her fists, fighting back a frustrated scream.

And then the rest of the missiles struck.

They arrived in a storm of flame and death, one missile after another slamming into the front of the alien behemoth and exploding. More individual ships tried to break away from the main body and intercept the arriving storm, and the *Theseus* fired another volley. The missiles were coming in too fast now for the aliens to respond, and the ships on the front edge were the ones hit worst by the missile barrage. By the time half a dozen missiles had struck the aliens were no longer even trying to intercept.

Perhaps a dozen more missiles hit. They were coming in too fast for Kaur to count. A single Hive ship darted in from the side and intercepted a missile before it could strike the main ship.

The rest of the volley made it through.

"Their shields are down," Touhami cried. "Do we hit them now?"

"With everything we've got," Kaur said. Her magazines were full, courtesy of the *Manatee*.

He nodded and bawled orders into a handset. Kaur leaned forward in her seat, wishing she had a proper tactical display and undamaged scanners. Or a forward-facing window. She watched the blurry display on her screen as the *Theseus* fired one volley after another. They must have emptied the magazines for the forward rail guns, because the ship pivoted, swapping ends. Then it set to work with the aft battery, slamming massive stone-and-steel rounds into the alien ship.

"The Hive ship's breaking apart," Touhami said, and Kaur held her breath. She wanted to imagine the alien disintegrating, so ravaged by missile strikes that it was utterly destroyed. She knew the modular nature of the enemy too well, though.

"It's breaking into chunks," said Touhami, confirming her worst fears. "Five of them, looks like. No, six. Looks like their shields are working again."

Six juggernauts. Even in her most optimistic scenario, missile and rail gun fire might have disabled or destroyed perhaps a third of the enemy vessel. Fifteen to twenty percent was more likely. That left, what? A dozen ships in each of six amalgamated craft? More?

They would be able to ignore laser fire, and the *Tomahawk's* puny railguns would hit like spitballs. Three ships would come for the *Tomahawk*, she decided, and three for the *Theseus*. When both ships were disabled – in two or three minutes, probably – the aliens would swarm over the hull of the *Adamant* and eliminate the few maneuvering thrusters and laser turrets that remained.

And then they'd have all the time they needed to destroy the Gate utterly.

"Get ready to move," she said. "As soon as they come for us we'll evade. We'll keep running and shooting until ..." Her voice trailed off when she realized she didn't have an ending for that sentence. Not one she'd say out loud to her crew, anyway.

"They're spreading out," Touhami said, his voice shrill. "Two to starboard. Two to port and down. Two to port and up. They're surrounding us!"

"Main thrust on my mark," said Kaur.

"The ships on the starboard side are pulling back," Touhami said.

"We'll go port and up, then," Kaur snapped.

"The ships port and down are pulling back too," said Touhami. There was a pause as he listened intently to his handset. Then he turned to look at her. "All six ships are pulling back."

*What the hell? They have us! We're finished. Out of missiles, out of big rail gun rounds. We've got nothing left but lasers and small-bore ammo. We can't touch them.*

*But they don't know, do they? They know we've smashed their home. They know we've smashed their fleet. They ran us off, but we came back. And why would we come back if we weren't ready for a fight to the death?*

*They're demoralized, and they're scared. They think we're ready to destroy them.*

"Advance," said Kaur. "Slowly. But advance. Signal the *Theseus*. Tell them to advance with us." She paused. "Be polite. But tell Hammett to keep up."

She was aware of Ramirez in her peripheral vision, giving her a stricken look. He lifted his handset, though, and spoke.

The main engines hummed softly as the *Tomahawk* advanced, and Touhami, his voice full of wonder, said, "The enemy is increasing speed, Captain. They're running away!"

She nodded as if it was what she'd expected all along. "Reduce thrust."

Momentum carried the *Tomahawk* forward, but there was no more acceleration. The distance to the alien ships grew as the Hive fleet picked up speed. When Benson estimated the range at five hundred kilometers Kaur said, "Reverse thrust. We'll stop here."

The navigational thrusters in the nose of the ship burned until the *Tomahawk* was stationary relative to the asteroid field behind them. Up ahead, the aliens continued to retreat toward their habitat.

*I should leave now*, Kaur thought. *Before that Gate opens. I should offload all the Spacecom personnel. Maybe take on a few colonials from the* Theseus. *Maybe not, though. I don't want to be overcrowded for such a long trip.*

*I can take a little time to visit the disabled corvettes, or the* Manatee. *Load up on food and water. Maybe some more ammunition, in case we run into trouble on the way home. I've got at least an hour, maybe a couple of hours before that Gate opens. Even longer, if it takes Spacecom a while to decide it's safe to come through. I won't have to surrender to an Earth fleet. I can go directly to Naxos.*

*I can go home.*

She wasn't sure when the colony had become 'home' to her. It was, though. She was in temporary quarters in Harlequin. She'd barely seen her room, spending most of her time on the *Tomahawk*. But she knew she was welcome on Ariadne. She wouldn't go so far as to say that she belonged, not yet. But there was a place for her on Ariadne, and it was hers.

The idea that she might finish her days in a cell on Earth was bad enough. The thought that she might never see the colony again, though, gave her a surprisingly strong pang. Still, she realized she was going to have to take that chance. If she opened up a wormhole it might be the encouragement the aliens needed to renew their attack. She and Hammett were running a massive bluff, and if the aliens chose to call it ...

So she would stay put, looking fearless, and wait for the Gate to open. And then she'd face her fate, whatever it turned out to be.

# CHAPTER 26 – HAMMETT

Hammett was on the *Tomahawk* when the Gate finally connected to the Sol system. The *Tomahawk* and *Theseus* were docked nose to nose, and he'd crossed over to shower and change into a fresh uniform. He didn't know whose cabin he used, but with the ship crammed with refugees, no one could be too possessive about space.

He changed, then checked his appearance in the mirror in the cabin's tiny head. He looked tired, but respectable. The green uniform no longer looked so strange.

Yawning, he trudged back into the cabin's main room. His vac suit waited, folded neatly on a chair beside the bunk. He stared at the bunk, mightily tempted to stretch out. It would hardly be fair. He wasn't the only crewman hoping to take a shower, after all.

Still, just a few minutes wouldn't hurt …

A muffled buzz woke him. He peered around, bleary and disoriented. Sanjari's voice, tinny and echoing, came from the helmet on the chair. He sat up, yawned wide enough to hurt his jaw muscles, and grabbed the helmet. Feeling a bit ridiculous, he plopped the helmet on his head.

"This is Lieutenant Sanjari, calling Admiral Hammett."

"I'm here, Lieutenant." His voice sounded gravelly, and he cleared his throat. *How long was I sleeping?*

"The Gate is connected," she said. "The first ships are coming through."

A mix of dread and relief washed over him. "Any reaction from the Hive?"

"Not so far, Sir."

"I'll be right there."

He took off the helmet, then bundled up his vac suit. He wouldn't put the suit on, he decided. Not unless the aliens reacted strongly. He didn't care to be arrested in a Spacecom-issued vac suit. He'd wear his new uniform to his doom.

"Speaking of uniforms," he muttered, and gathered up the sweaty, wrinkled clothes he'd been wearing since the ship left Ariadne. He had a locker aboard the *Theseus*. He would stow everything on his way to the bridge.

When the hatch to the cabin slid open he heard a buzz of nervous conversation from the corridor outside. He stepped out, and a wave of silence worked its way down the corridor. Sailors pressed themselves against the bulkheads to make room, and he nodded his thanks.

"Good luck, Admiral," said a technician.

"Don't take any crap from the EDF," a specialist chimed in.

The comments kept coming as he walked. "You did the right thing, Sir." "You stood up for what's right. They can't take that away." "You'll still be the admiral, no matter what they do to you."

That last one was hardly encouraging. Hammett nodded to the sergeant who'd spoken, then stepped through the twin airlocks and onto the *Theseus*.

The catwalk along the spine of the ship was crowded with people in vac suits. A young colonist stepped in front of him, pulled the vac suit and uniform from his hands, and said, "Let me get that, Admiral." She turned her back before he could protest and led the way, barking, "Make a path! Admiral coming through."

A middle-aged man in a blue helmet gave Hammett an embarrassed look as he pressed himself back against the railing. Beside him, Lieutenant Parker saluted. A colonist barely out of his teens said, "We won't let them arrest you, Sir."

"I want no resistance," Hammett snapped. "The fighting's over. There's going to be no violence between human beings. Is that clear?"

The boy scowled, but he nodded. "Yes, Sir."

Hammett continued along the catwalk. A couple of Spacecom sailors wouldn't quite meet his eyes. A woman his own age, her cheek tattoos marking her as a colonist, clapped him on the shoulder and said, "It'll be fine, Admiral."

He passed a dozen more people before he reached the galley. None of the colonists let him pass without an encouraging comment. It was all entirely inappropriate for enlisted personnel speaking to an officer. It was also heartfelt, and Hammett loved them for it. His colonists didn't have the training and indoctrination of Spacecom personnel. They got by with only the best parts of the military tradition – courage, basic skills, and a boundless supply of loyalty and generosity.

He'd long since stopped being embarrassed by his new green uniform. Now, for the first time, he was fiercely proud of it.

"Miss."

The woman in front of him stopped and turned.

Hammett gestured at the hatch to the galley. "I've got a locker in there."

"I'll find it, Sir," she said, and ducked through the hatch. He heard her greet several people, then demand to know where the admiral's locker was.

He moved past the galley. O'Reilly and a couple of colonists still guarded the entrance to the bridge. "I want you to stand down," he told her. "I expect we'll be boarded soon by Spacecom personnel. I don't want you firing on anything with two arms and two legs."

She nodded her understanding. "I don't mind staying here, though." She looked at the others. "None of us do."

"They'll send marines first," Hammett said. "The marines are going to be ridiculously well-armed, and wound up tighter than guitar strings. I don't want them provoked." When O'Reilly opened her mouth he said, "You standing there with a gun on your hip might just be provocation enough. Let's not tempt fate."

Her face drooped. "All right, Admiral." She headed for the stairs, gesturing to the others. "Let's go, guys."

Hammett watched them go, wondering what would happen to them. He would protect them as best he could, but he doubted he'd be able to do much. Sighing, he turned and entered the bridge.

Sanjari looked up. Like him, she'd changed and taken off her vac suit. "The *Hannibal* just came through," she said. "Couple of corvettes, too. All three ships are heading this way." She gestured with her thumb.

Hammett turned, looking in the direction she indicated. The starboard window was a mess, and he wondered uneasily if it was likely to burst. Dying one room over from his vac suit because he wanted to look good would be really stupid.

It would save a lot of hassle, though.

It took a moment to spot the *Hannibal*. The cruiser's dark blue paint blended with the darkness of space and lost itself among the cracks and splinters in the glass. As the ship advanced, though, it moved into an undamaged section of the window and he saw it clearly.

He was admiring the cruiser's lines and thinking of the *Alexander* when a flash of light on the side of the cruiser caught his attention. The light source shot toward him, and he opened his mouth to shout, far too late to give an effective warning.

An explosion lit the void just ahead of the *Theseus*, and Hammett said, "Missile!"

Eddie flinched back from the explosion, shouted, "What the hell!" and twisted around in his chair. His face was a mask of bewildered outrage. "Why in hell are they shooting at us?"

Hammett dropped into his chair, full of weary anger. "It was a warning shot. They'd have hit us if they wanted to." *So this is the way it's going to be. Not even a radio call first. No negotiation. No acknowledgement of what happened here. Just a missile, exploding dangerously close.* "Raise the *Hannibal*," he said to Sanjari. "Tell them we surrender."

# CHAPTER 27 – BLOCH

Commodore Bloch looked down at the Earth and brooded.

He stood in the Starlight Lounge, a long room with one steelglass wall just forward of the *Hannibal's* bridge. The room was a lounge reserved for officers. He'd posted a marine at the door with instructions to turn away anyone Bloch hadn't personally summoned. He didn't much care if it displeased Colonel Laycraft, the *Hannibal's* commanding officer. After what Bloch had been through, he was damned well going to claim every perk of rank that came his way.

Looking down on the Earth usually soothed him. It reminded him why he wore the uniform, why he'd chosen his career. Things usually seemed so clear when he could gaze down on his home planet from above.

Today, that clarity eluded him.

Directly across from him, at a range of less

than a kilometer, the *Theseus* sat like a battered jewel displayed on black velvet. He supposed the converted freighter was ugly, if viewed objectively. The little ship had achieved so much, though, that it seemed elegant and grand to his eyes. The hull was dented, there were long swaths where the tendrils of Fourier metal had broken away, but still she looked ... heroic.

A shuttle was docked to her nose, giving the ship a lopsided look. As Bloch watched, the shuttle separated and left. Another shuttle promptly took its place. The colonists were being loaded aboard the *Theseus*. They would be sent home.

Not the former Spacecom personnel who had mutinied. They would stay here to face judgment. It was only right, but somehow it didn't *feel* right. Bloch frowned at the ship, thinking about his duty, his orders, and whether the two were the same thing.

The door to the lounge hissed open and a square of light appeared, reflected in the steelglass before him. He turned.

It was Hammett, with a marine guard on either side. He wore the rumpled green uniform of the Colonial Forces. Every last one of the prisoners, offered a prison jumpsuit, had opted to keep their ridiculous uniforms.

"You're dismissed," Bloch said to the marines. The guards left, and Hammett ambled over to stand beside the Commodore. He looked perfectly relaxed, as if he were strolling through his own apartment. Well, Bloch would expect no less from a man with thirty years of naval experience.

"We're releasing the colonists," Bloch said, nodding toward the *Theseus*. "They've broken interstellar law, but the Statsminister wanted to make a gesture of goodwill."

"The man's a paragon," Hammett said dryly.

Bloch bit back a sharp retort. The next part of the conversation was going to be difficult, but after everything Hammett had done, the very least he deserved was the truth. "I thought about letting you go."

Hammett turned to look at him.

"I thought about transferring you to the *Theseus*," Bloch said. "I figured at worst I might get a reprimand. With everything that's happened in the last day, though, I thought I'd get away with it."

Hammett didn't speak, just looked at him.

"I decided I couldn't do it." Bloch turned his gaze back to the *Theseus*, chagrined to realize this confession was easier without meeting Hammett's gaze. "My duty was clear. You had to stand trial for mutiny."

If any part of his monologue had an effect on Hammett, it's didn't show.

"Then I got this," Bloch said. He reached in his pocket for a data pad, frustrated by the clumsiness of the technology, wondering how Hammett and his people coped without working implants. He thumbed the pad to life and held it up where Hammett could see the screen. He played the video clip he'd received an hour before.

"General Bloch." The tiny figure of Jeff Acton looked haggard and tired on the little screen. "You've done excellent work. I congratulate you." Acton leaned forward, planting his forearms on a cluttered desk. "I understand you captured Hammett." Acton grimaced. "I wish you'd killed him. That would make things easier." He stared into the camera for a moment. "I want you to release him." He made a smoothing gesture with his hand. "Keep it quiet. Unofficial. If anyone asks, you're not sure where he ended up."

Bloch, who had watched the clip three times already, felt again the mix of shock and cold numbness he'd felt three times before.

"The situation down here is ... politically delicate," Acton said. "I need to look strong. I can't turn Hammett loose. But he's a symbol. A lot of people are going to rally behind him." Acton's face changed, fury and frustration shining through. It lasted only a moment.

"It would be better if he was gone," Acton went on. "Far away. Off in his distant colony where everyone can forget about him. So get him on board that ship that's going to Naxos. There won't be an investigation. I'll keep it out of the press."

*I'll keep it out of the press. My God. He actually said that.*

Acton's face twisted. "Either that, or he can have a fatal accident. I'm good with that too."

Bloch stopped the video. "He doesn't know I recorded that. I won't go public with it, either, so don't ask." He glanced at Hammett, and had to fight the urge to squirm.

"I've made a decision, Richard. I didn't consult you." He took a deep breath and made himself look directly at the other man. "I don't like you. I don't agree with the decisions you've made. You developed a swelled head. You let delusions of grandeur warp your judgment." He shook his head. "My God, man! You mutinied in the middle of a war! We don't always agree with the politicians who call the shots – Lord knows, I never liked that Saretsky woman – but we do our duty, and we remember our vows."

Hammett's shoulders moved in the tiniest of shrugs.

Bloch sighed. "You're a fool. But you thought you were doing your duty, didn't you? Your view of what your duty was, was twisted – but you never flinched from it. You did what you thought was right, and to hell with the consequences."

He stared into Hammett's unblinking brown eyes, wishing the man would react in some way. "I decided that my first impulse was the correct one," Bloch said. "It is my duty to deliver you to Earth to stand trial. If your trial disrupts a 'politically delicate' situation, well, maybe the situation needs disrupting. It'll be rough on you." *Now there's a bit of understatement.* "But I asked myself what you would want me to do if I asked you. And I think you would do what you always do. You would ignore your own well-being and do what you think is right."

Hammett's eyebrows rose.

"We're transferring you to Port Kodiak within the hour. After that, it's out of my hands."

"I see," said Hammett.

"You fought well," said Bloch. "I'm honored to have fought beside you." He was surprised to find that he meant it. "Good luck." He held out his hand, and Hammett shook it. "I'll see you at your trial."

## CHAPTER 28 – HAMMETT

The shuttle ride from Port Kodiak to Hawking was always harrowing. It was more of a shuttle drop than a shuttle ride, since the station was in a geosynchronous orbit almost directly over the city. Hammett, his wrists cuffed before him, ignored the marines who guarded him and pressed his face to the window, watching as the shuttle plunged into a layer of cloud. The cloud broke and he saw the Baja Peninsula below him, growing rapidly as the shuttle hurtled downward.

The city expanded, turning from a rough-looking dark patch on the peninsula to a circular grid of streets. By the time he could make out individual buildings he knew what the shuttle's destination was. Spacecom headquarters, the grand, solemn building which had once been the Naval Academy.

It was fitting, he decided, that it would all end

here in the place where it had begun. It gave things a pleasing symmetry, a sense that he had come full circle. In those same marble halls where he'd learned to be an officer he would be judged and sentenced, and likely executed.

He regretted nothing.

Deceleration pushed him deeper into his seat, and walls rose around the shuttle as it descended into the yard beside the headquarters building. Hammett felt the hint of a bump as the shuttle touched down. Then the shuttle's hatch lowered and sunlight flooded in.

He tried to move slowly as he crossed the yard. It might be his very last exposure to sunlight, after all. Hawking had its own special smell, arid and mostly sterile with a hint of brine from the distant ocean and the faintest trace of perfume from carefully tended flowers. It took him back to his days as a cadet, when every day was a fresh adventure, duty was as clear as a highway stretching out before him, and he was sure he'd have a glorious career. Hammett smiled in spite of himself, though the smile faded when they led him inside.

The marines turned him over to a squad of military police, cheerless men and women who scanned him, gave him a prisoner's jumpsuit, and directed him to a booth where he could change.

"I'd rather keep my uniform," he said without much hope.

"You can change, or you can be stripped. It's your choice."

Hammett changed into the jumpsuit.

A young military policeman with a lieutenant's stripe and all the emotion of a vending machine gestured him into a chair in a tiny office and read out a long, preposterous list of charges. He led with treason and mutiny, but there were dozens more, ranging from insubordination to cowardice to misappropriation of Spacecom property. When he was done he pushed a thick document across the desk and said, "Sign each page."

Hammett stared at him.

The lieutenant leaned forward. "Sign. Each. Page."

"No."

"Sign it, or you'll be made to sign it."

That made Hammett laugh out loud. "And how are you going to do that? Get a couple of goons to hold my fingers? Press them against the pen?" He leaned back in his chair. "That sounds thoroughly entertaining. Why don't you go ahead and do that?"

The young man's eyebrows drew together. "There are serious consequences to noncooperation."

Hammett laughed again. "You know what I've been charged with. They'll find me guilty, too. What consequences could you possibly threaten me with?"

The lieutenant changed tack. "Being stubborn can only make things worse for you. It's a simple enough request. Is there a reason you won't cooperate?"

"Pure contrariness," Hammett said cheerfully.

He gestured at the document. "I don't care about your paperwork. What would my signature mean? Absolutely nothing, that's what. It's pointless bureaucracy. I've put up with rules and bullshit from the military for thirty years." He spread his hands. "Now? I don't have to." He lowered his hands and stopped smiling. "And you can't make me."

The two men locked gazes for thirty seconds or so. The lieutenant was both an officer and a cop, and he was good at stern glares. Hammett, though, was in a whole different league, and eventually the kid realized it. His fingers moved as he accessed his implants, and a couple of MPs came in.

"Put him in a holding cell."

The cell was tiny, but big enough to contain a bunk. Hammett stretched out and sank immediately into a long-overdue sleep. He woke with a military policeman shaking his shoulder. "Sir. Captain Hammett. Wake up, Sir."

"That's Admiral Hammett." Hammett sat up and yawned. "What's going on?"

"You're being moved, Sir."

It was only when he reached the ground floor and the guards on either side turned toward the main entrance that Hammett realized he was being moved to another building. "Where we going?" Spacecom didn't have any other planetside facilities.

"We're taking a car, Sir," said the guard on his left. Which wasn't much of an answer, Hammett reflected. *I guess I'll find out soon enough.* He let the guards guide him toward the massive front doors. The doors were closed, which struck Hammett as odd. They were ponderous doors, grand-looking things, but a pain to move. They normally stood open during the day.

By the angle of the sunlight coming through the windows in the front wall, it was late morning in Hawking. The building was open, then. Was this some new security feature?

Half a dozen marine stood just inside the big doors, another new feature that made Hammett's eyebrows rise. Well, he'd been through a bloody mutiny on the *Alexander*. Perhaps a few extra marines around the premises made sense.

A strong-looking marine put a shoulder to one front door and pushed. The door swung open and a wall of sound washed in. Angry voices rose in a clamor, the words impossible to make out, the tone only too clear.

"I see people are happy you guys won the war," Hammett said.

His guards didn't answer, just kept advancing. A couple of marines stepped outside. There were more marines in front of the building, a dozen at least, standing shoulder to shoulder and facing a massive crowd of angry civilians.

Hammett saw people of every age, jammed together, shouting or shaking fists. Holographic signs filled the air above with slogans like 'No EDF' and 'Free The Press'. One sign said 'Remember Montreal', which struck Hammett as good advice. Protesters had died when a

Spacecom ship had fired a missile at protesters in Montreal. This crowd didn't seem worried, though.

Everyone wore white. Not from head to toe, but he saw white shirts and coats, or improvised head scarves made from strips of white cloth. Quite a few people covered their faces with white bandanas. It was, he supposed, the farthest thing from the black armbands of the EDF.

The crowd seemed to recognize Hammett. Angry shouts turned into a roar, and the crowd edged forward. The marines braced themselves, hands going to weapons belts.

A marine sergeant stopped Hammett and his escort in the doorway. He gestured behind them, and Hammett's guards reluctantly drew him back. The door swung shut, reducing the angry roar to a rumble.

"The car will never make it through the crowd," the sergeant said wearily. "You better take him to the Ira Hayes door. I'll call the driver."

They took him across the wide lobby, the noise of the crowd fading until their echoing footsteps were the only sound. They brought him down a long corridor Hammett had never explored, and came at last to a small side door with yet another marine guarding it. "Car's just pulling up," said the marine, and opened the door.

A dark blue ground car with military police markings rolled up, and strong hands pushed Hammett into the back seat. His guards sat on either side of him, not speaking, as the car rolled down a narrow alley and turned onto the broad street that fronted the building. A handful of people on the edge of the crowd saw the car and let out a shout. Someone threw a fist-sized object, and Hammett flinched back. Something splattered against the window beside him, and he spent a puzzled moment trying to figure out how the window had ended up covered in blood. Then he spotted seeds in the mess and understood. The protester had thrown a tomato.

The car turned and quickly left the protesters behind. The man on Hammett's left pressed a finger to one ear, listening, then murmured to the driver. By the sound of it, there were blockades and protests all over the city. The man did his best to guide the driver around the worst of it while Hammett sat and watched, trying to work out where they were headed.

At last they turned onto a wide boulevard, the median in the center decorated with stone planters boiling over with scarlet flowers. Directly ahead, Hammett could see a grand building decorated with pillars a good four meters across. A massive statue of Justice stood in front of the building, her skin green with the patina of aged copper.

"You're taking me to the courthouses?" Hammett said. "I thought I'd get a court martial."

The man on his right glanced at Hammett, then surprised him by speaking. "You're getting a civilian trial. Things are ... complicated."

"Complicated how?" Hammett demanded. "Is

this one of those 'politically sensitive' situations I've been hearing about?" When the guard didn't respond he said, "Or is it a security concern? Are they afraid the military might not stand for it if you hold my show trial at Spacecom?"

The guard gave him a look that was almost sympathetic. "You're asking questions that go way above my pay grade, Admiral. They just tell me where to pick you up and where to drop you off."

Hammett nodded.

"Look," said the man. "The word is, you've been out there fighting the good fight. I appreciate it. I respect it. I'm still going to deliver you to the courthouse, but I'm hoping you won't make things difficult, because I'm hoping to deliver you in good health."

Hammett couldn't quite smother a grin. "Fair enough," he said. "I'll behave."

The guard nodded. "And I'll do everything in my power to make sure you get there safely, with none of your rights violated."

"Uh-oh," said the driver.

Hammett looked forward, and felt his mouth go dry. Armed figures ran into the street ahead, men and women in the baggy tan uniforms of the United Worlds army. The uniform had changed since Hammett had seen it last; the sleeves had black EDF armbands. Each soldier, though, had tied a white rag around one arm. There were at least thirty of them, and they filled this side of the boulevard. Traffic slowed, and the guard to Hammett's left muttered a curse.

The car began to accelerate, and Hammett braced himself, sliding a bit lower in his seat, expecting gunfire. If the driver thought to ram his way through the line, though, it wasn't going to work. Too many cars were stopping ahead, forming a barrier of vehicles two or three deep. To the left was the center of the boulevard, an unbroken row of stone planters. The driver veered right instead. The way was blocked, though, by other cars rolling to a stop. The driver put the car in reverse, honked in frustration at the cars crowding up behind, and started to back up.

A squad of soldiers hurried forward, two groups of three, jogging between the rows of cars. They reached Hammett's car in moments, three on the left and three on the right. Any hope he might have had that the roadblock was a coincidence vanished when their weapons covered the car. They carried blast carbines, powerful weapons that would do devastating damage at close range.

"Stand down," said the guard on the left. None of them could have done much anyway; they were all unarmed, standard procedure for cops who went within arm's reach of prisoners. Both guards and the driver lifted their hands.

"Open the door," demanded a gruff voice outside.

The guards exchanged glances. "They won't hurt him," said the man on the right. "They're on his side."

"I'm not worried about him," his partner

retorted. "I'm worried about us."

"It's not like we can keep them out." The guard on the right reached over and popped his door open.

Strong hands caught the man and yanked him out of the car. A peremptory hand reached in through the door and gestured at Hammett.

"Go," said the guard on the left. "I doubt they'll hurt you."

Hammett nodded and slid over. He expected to be yanked out unceremoniously, but the soldiers surprised him by edging back to give him room. He climbed out and stood, trying to read the situation.

The roadblock was dissolving, soldiers advancing through the rows of vehicles to surround Hammett's car. Frightened drivers took the opportunity to race away, while vehicles behind Hammett's car did their best to edge backward.

The military policeman lay face-down on the tarmac. A soldier knelt with a knee in his back, the muzzle of her carbine almost touching the back of the man's head. She kept her eyes on the prisoner. Other soldiers scanned the vehicles around them, or watched windows and rooftops.

"This way, Sir," said a man with sergeant's stripes on his sleeves. "We've got a vehicle waiting."

"Release him," Hammett said, gesturing at the man on the ground.

The sergeant said, "I don't know if that's a good-"

Hammett didn't speak, just stared at the man.

"Right. Private, release the prisoner."

"Let him get back in his car," Hammett said. "Let the car go." He tried to make it sound like a suggestion – a strong suggestion – since the sergeant was under no obligation to obey his orders.

The sergeant sighed. "Do what the man said." Then, raising his voice, "Let's go, people! Pick up your feet!" He led the way toward the nearest sidewalk, Hammett following him, soldiers all around.

"This way." The sergeant stepped onto the sidewalk and started toward a gap between buildings.

Hammett stopped and planted his feet.

No one touched him. The soldiers around him stopped, consternation on their faces. Someone said, "Uh, Sarge?"

The sergeant glanced back, then stopped. "Admiral Hammett! We have to go."

"I need to know what's going on," Hammett said.

"Sure. Once we're out of the city we can answer all your questions." The sergeant made a curt gesture, his face showing the strained impatience of sergeants throughout history forced to deal with difficult officers.

Hammett shook his head. "I'm not going into an alley with a bunch of armed strangers until I know what's going on."

The sergeant stared at him for several long seconds, as if trying to will Hammett into motion through the sheer force of his own frustration. Then his shoulders slumped. "Give us a perimeter," he barked, and the other soldiers spread out, facing outward, blocking the sidewalk and the closest lane of the boulevard.

"We're the Third Company of the Baja Battalion," the sergeant said. "Well, most of us are from the Third Company. They called us in to contain demonstrators who were marching on Spacecom headquarters." The sergeant shook his head, a world of bleakness reflected in his eyes. "We squared off against the crowd, a couple blocks from the headquarters building. They were upset, but they weren't rioting. Just shouting, mostly. Blocking traffic."

Hammett nodded, his stomach getting queasy. He sensed this story wasn't going anywhere good.

"They ordered us to fire on the crowd," the sergeant said. "We all got the order directly." He tapped the side of his head. "Our lieutenant tried to argue. Said the crowd wasn't violent. Said we'd make things worse. Said it'd be a war crime. The colonel told her to fire into the crowd or she'd be hanged for cowardice."

The sergeant grimaced. "The colonel wasn't on site, of course. He was tucked away nice and safe in his office in Liberty Hall."

Hammett flinched in spite of himself. Liberty Hall was a grand faux-classical edifice in the heart of the city. It held displays honoring the casualties of the Outer Systems War, and a museum showing the history of Spacecom. There were administration offices too, overseeing pension funds and support services for veterans, but mostly the building was a monument to the heroes of the armed forces. Hammett had been there several times. It was a hushed, reverent space that gave him goosebumps every time.

Now, apparently, the EDF had moved in and claimed the place for their own. It felt blasphemous. It felt, somehow, worse than all the other excesses of the EDF. Seizing power was one thing. Hammett could understand the lust for power. Violating the sanctity of Liberty Hall, though? That was just wrong.

"The lieutenant said she'd personally shoot anyone who obeyed that order," the sergeant said. "Then she pushed her way into the crowd, and that was the last I saw of her." He gestured around at the other soldiers. "The rest of us deserted together. We've been trying to figure out what we can do. Then we heard about your arrest."

"So you decided to rescue me?"

The sergeant nodded.

Hammett sighed. "I appreciate the effort. I really do. But I want my day in court."

The sergeant gaped at him. "Sir, they'll kill you! They'll stand you up against a wall and shoot you."

"Maybe." Hammett shrugged wearily. "But I'll stir up a world of trouble in the meantime."

"But-" The sergeant looked utterly flabbergasted. "Sir, I don't think you've thought this through!"

"Let me put it this way," Hammett said. "Statsminister Acton sent a personal request to an EDF general, asking that I be discreetly released and sent back to Naxos." He spread his hands in a shrug. "If that's what Acton wants, then that's what I'm not going to do."

The sergeant stared at him for several long seconds. Finally he said, "All right. We'll escort you to the courthouse, then."

"You'll do no such thing," Hammett said sharply. "Armed men in uniforms, with white armbands? You people are a walking incitement to violence." He gestured around him. "So far, no one's getting shot. No idiots are starting firefights, with civilians in the background catching stray bullets. I won't have you fanning the flames."

The sergeant drooped a bit.

"Thank you," Hammett said. "I won't forget this. Now take your people and get out of the city. Get yourselves out of danger. Put yourselves somewhere where you won't trigger a battle in the streets."

"No, Sir," the sergeant said.

Hammett blinked.

"We won't leave the city. We're bivouacked in a warehouse near here. We'll stay out of sight if we can. But if someone starts massacring civilians, we'll step in." He stepped away from Hammett. "All right, people, move out." He paused long enough to say, "Good luck, Admiral." Then he led the rest of the company into the gap between buildings. In a moment Hammett was alone.

He looked around. Traffic was moving again, some people gawking at him as they passed, others carefully looking away. There was no pedestrian traffic, though he saw people peeping out from doorways. There was no sign of the Military Police ground car. He admired the courage of the rebel soldiers, but all they'd really managed to do was cost him his ride.

He sighed, turned toward the distant courthouse, and started to walk.

# CHAPTER 29 – HAMMETT

He had the sidewalk to himself for a block and a half. When he met his first pedestrian it was a woman in a hooded jacket, the hood pulled up to cover a white kerchief over her hair. She gave Hammett a furtive look and circled wide around him, heading away from the heart of the city.

For the next block he passed more and more people, until the sidewalk became downright crowded. The crowd thickened and spilled onto the street, the last of the vehicle traffic turning off on one last cross street. Half a block later Hammett came to a barricade of crates, made irrelevant by the press of bodies.

Nearly everyone wore white. Some waved broad white flags over their heads. One flag had "EDF" scrawled on it, with a circle around it and a line through the circle. Holo signs added to the visual clutter. "Hang Acton", said one sign. "Free

Carol White" said another. The name was faintly familiar. Hammett thought she was a journalist, a political commentator popular in the feeds.

The crowd was angry and excited, with more than a few people giving Hammett hostile, suspicious looks. The average civilian wouldn't know a prisoner's jumpsuit by sight. He didn't look like an authority figure exactly, but any sort of uniform would be suspect here.

Shouting voices filled the air, creating a tumult of sound that made everyone incomprehensible. He passed a knot of a dozen people or so, chanting some slogan in unison. A man three meters away was ranting into a microphone, his amplified voice drowning out the chanted slogan completely. Hammett couldn't understand that man either. All he got was an impression of static and rage.

It all struck him as senseless, and dangerous enough to be downright foolish. Somewhere on the far side of this mob there would be a line of cops or soldiers. These people were provoking a government that had shown itself capable of appalling violence. He thought of the deserting soldiers who'd intercepted his car. They'd been ordered to fire into a crowd just like this.

Not every company was going to desert when they got orders like that. All it needed was for one of these protestors – just one – to go a tiny bit too far. Some army recruit barely out of his teens, blood full of adrenalin and mind full of terror, would panic and start shooting.

This crowd would achieve nothing. They

weren't here with an achievable goal in mind, he realized. They were venting. Speaking not to be heard, but to have spoken. Giving voice to a frustrated outrage they could no longer contain. If Acton had any sense, he'd let the mob exhaust itself. The people would scream themselves hoarse and go home tired, telling themselves they'd done something at last.

Restraint, though, wasn't Acton's style. He was the strong man, the man who took action and got things done. He had an image to uphold, and uphold it he would. The crowd was pushing him. He'd push back.

Hard.

*This is going to get ugly. Bloody. And here I am, pushing my way deeper into the crowd. And why am I doing it? So I can get myself back under arrest, and stand trial for treason.*

*I must be brain-damaged.*

This was just Hawking. What was happening in places like Nova Roma?

The crowd thickened until the press of bodies made it impossible to tell that Hammett wore an official-looking jumpsuit and nothing white. He caught a glimpse of his own face hovering above the crowd with the slogan "Free Hammett", and grinned. *To think my training officer back at the Academy told me I'd never amount to anything.*

At last he neared the front of the crowd. Banks of forcefield generators made a perimeter around a cluster of buildings that included the courthouse, Liberty Hall, and some government offices. The public library was inside the perimeter, and Hammett felt a flash of annoyance. Riots and the very real danger of a massacre were bad enough, but denying people access to the library offended him on a primal level.

When the wall of backs and shoulders in front of him became impenetrable he stopped. The layer of people ahead was only three or four deep, but a couple of tall men and a few flags were enough to keep him from seeing anything.

He turned back, looking for a vantage point. He found a giant ceramic pot, the edges waist-high, containing a vine-enshrouded tree. A couple of people already balanced on the lip of the pot, but there was room for one more. Hammett scrambled up, wrapped an arm around the trunk, and turned his gaze toward the courthouse.

Instead of soldiers on the far side of the forcefield he saw city police. That was a relief. Things could still go horribly wrong, but the mindset of a policeman was different from the mindset of a soldier. Cops didn't think in terms of killing enemies.

He saw about two dozen cops arrayed in front of the courthouse, and a dozen police androids. The man-sized robots were strong and practically indestructible, and programmed not to use lethal force. They would show more restraint than their human counterparts.

The cops were badly outnumbered by the protestors, which might be a good thing, Hammett supposed. It might keep the cops safely behind their barricade and prevent an escalation. Unfortunately it would also make them afraid, and frightened people with guns were never a good thing.

*Maybe this will all end without bloodshed. Maybe Acton can be voted out of office without any more blood on his hands than he's already got. In the meantime, I'm clearly not getting into the courthouse through the front doors. Maybe if I circle around I can-*

A distant rumble made the pot vibrate under his feet and told him he was too late. The sound was directionless, but a ripple in the crowd drew his attention to the left. The crowd churned, some people pressing forward, others trying to retreat.

And Hammett saw the first robot.

This was something entirely different from the police androids. This was a robot built for serious crowd control, a rolling behemoth the size of a garbage truck with a V-shaped prow and ugly metal protrusions jutting from the top edge of the roof. Hammett recognized those protrusions.

Shockers.

"Last chance," said an amplified voice that echoed from the buildings all around. "You had your fun. Now go home. This won't be gentle."

Plenty of people were taking the advice of the disembodied voice, streaming away from the advancing robot. Others hurried in to take their place, though, bellowing slogans as if the robot would listen.

As the robot reached the first press of protestors the shockers came to life, firing fat arcing sparks into the crowd. Hammett heard screams, saw people fall. Shockers were painful, and momentarily disabling. Some people would have minor burns. Some would have damaged implants, though likely no one would lose all functionality like Hammett. Anyone with a heart condition, anyone elderly, was in real danger of dying.

Still the angry crowd pressed forward, and the robot ground to a halt, unwilling to run anyone down. But another robot was rolling up beside it. The shockers flashed on both machines and the crowd broke, people stumbling away.

Cops in insulated riot gear advanced between the machines. Two cops would grab a fallen protestor and drag the person back behind the robots. Immediately two more cops would dart forward. One protester after another vanished behind the robots, which began to advance again.

A hail of missiles sailed out of the crowd, rocks or bricks or bottles, Hammett couldn't tell. It wasn't like the bad old days when gasoline had been readily available. Nothing burned, nothing exploded. The cops drew back and let the robots take the brunt of the assault. All the while, the shockers flashed and protesters fell.

Another robot joined the line, and then another. Protesters poured down the streets in droves, fleeing the riot. Die-hard troublemakers gathered in clusters, waving flags and hurtling bottles, until the robots were almost within shocker range. Then the rioters fell back, dashing past Hammett's tree. A man paused almost close enough for Hammett to touch him, taking a lump of broken brick from a satchel across his back. The man drew his arm back to throw, then dropped limp on the sidewalk as a stun shot from some police sniper took him in the chest.

"Whoa," said a man clinging to the tree beside Hammett. "That's enough for me." He hopped down from the pot and joined the crowd fleeing down the boulevard. That left Hammett and a young woman atop the pot. She cupped her free hand around her mouth, screamed, "Fascists," glanced at Hammett, and shrugged. Then she dropped to the sidewalk and jogged away.

Hammett stayed where he was.

A couple of cops moved out ahead of the robots, heading for the stunned man beside Hammett's pot. A band of fifteen or twenty protesters charged at the two cops, who simply fell back to the line of robots. The protesters in front tried to stop out of range of the shockers, but their friends behind them pushed them forward. Only when half a dozen of the would-be attackers were on their knees writhing and screaming did the rest give up. They dragged some of their friends back, left three of them on the ground in front of the robots, and fled.

Hammett looked around in time to see a section of forcefield drop. Cops from the front of the courthouse moved forward, grabbing protesters who'd been disabled by the shockers. There was no more resistance. One woman circled around the advancing police, shouted a few insults, then threw down her flag and ran. No one bothered pursuing her.

"Hey, buddy."

Hammett turned. A couple of cops were putting cuffs on the stunned brick-thrower, who was just beginning to stir. Beside them, a tired-looking cop stared up at Hammett. "Why don't you beat it? Go on, get out of here."

"Thanks," said Hammett. "I'll stay."

The cop's gaze sharpened. He looked Hammett up and down, seeming to notice the jumpsuit for the first time.

"That's right," said Hammett. "I'm an escaped fugitive."

The cop looked startled but cautious. "What did you do?"

That made Hammett chuckle. "Depends on who you ask."

"Well, I'm not sure I care. Why don't you run along and be someone else's problem?"

"I'm Richard Hammett. Formerly of Spacecom."

The cop stared up at him for a long moment, then shook his head. "Like I don't have enough bloody paperwork. All right, buddy, you win. You're under arrest. Why don't you hop down so I can cuff you."

# CHAPTER 30 – BLOCH

It felt strange to be sitting outside the Statsminister's office, waiting to speak to the great man himself. Bloch caught himself touching the black sash across his chest, subconsciously reassuring himself of his rank, his right to be here. He made himself lower the hand to his lap.

Before the war he'd answered to the Spacecom Admiralty. Now, as a general in the EDF, he outranked those admirals. He supposed it was normal for someone of his new rank to confer directly with the Statsminister. Still, it seemed ... odd. Not quite right, as if the usual checks and balances were being sidestepped.

*I'm the checks and balances now. Instead of three or four admirals, it's me. It's the way things are now, so I'd better get used to it.*

No fewer than six marines guarded the door to Acton's office. Considering the layers of security he'd gone through to get this far, Bloch couldn't help thinking the marines were excessive. Acton had stirred up quite a lot of animosity, though, so perhaps his paranoia was warranted.

A marine tilted his head, a sure sign he was receiving a message. He looked at Bloch and said, "You can go in, General."

Bloch stood, nodded his thanks, and stepped toward the door as the marines parted to give him room. He gave the door a quick rap with his knuckles, then pushed it open.

Acton was alone, sitting behind an enormous, cluttered desk. The man looked a decade older than he had during his brief campaign. He flapped a hand at a plush guest chair, then turned his attention to a pad in his hands.

Bloch sat, telling himself sternly not to fidget. The trip to Europe felt like an enormous waste of time. It had taken almost two hours, time he could ill afford to lose. He had a simple proposal for sending some ships to relieve several distant colonies. He'd submitted the plan to Acton, expecting a quick message telling him it was approved.

Instead, the Statsminister had summoned him for a personal meeting.

At last Acton lowered his pad. "General. You want to send some ships to Calypso."

"Calypso by way of Tanos, Aries, and Deirdre," Bloch said. "Those colonies have been out of touch since the beginning of the war. If there are survivors, they'll need-"

"Out of the question." Acton glared at Bloch as if he'd just spat on the rich carpet. "You've seen what's going on here on Earth." He waved a hand, encompassing the Parliament Building, the surrounding government buildings, and all of Nova Roma. "I can't spare a single ship."

Bloch suppressed a sigh. "Sir, the protests are a civilian matter. The police should handle it, and if the police aren't enough, you have the army. You don't need spaceships."

"I need every resource I can get!" Acton's hand slapped the table, making the data pad jump. "The very government is at risk! Now, when humanity needs to stand united!"

Bloch said, "The colonies-"

"Damn the colonies!" Acton panted, then composed himself. "No, General. Your ships will stay here, defending the Earth. Defending the government. Is that clear?"

*Defending Jeff Acton personally, you mean.* Bloch suppressed the treasonous thought. "Yes, Sir."

"Good. Now, I called you here because I have a new assignment for you. You're a hero. You're the man who won a great victory against the Hive. You captured Hammett. People respect you."

In most people's minds, the capture of Hammett wasn't a point in his favor. Bloch kept the thought to himself.

"I'm sending you on a speaking tour," Acton continued. "You're going to visit every major city in the world. I want you to talk about the alien threat. Make it clear that we only won a battle, not the war. I need people to understand that the Hive is still a serious threat."

Bloch stared at the Statsminister, speechless. Bloch had read every report from the forces that had gone through the new Gate, and he was certain the Hive was no threat at all. The few aliens that remained were a pathetic remnant hiding in the shadows. Acton knew it, too.

"People trust you," Acton said. He leaned forward, his eyes intense. "Make them see the danger. Make them realize the aliens could come back at any moment."

Arguing would achieve nothing. Bloch just nodded, numb.

"Now, I'm going to want ships deployed above every major city that holds United Worlds government offices. We can't let these protests gain momentum. We need to crush them as quickly as they form. The safety of the world is at stake!"

Bloch kept nodding, letting the words roll over him. It wasn't an entirely bad plan. If Spacecom's ships were distributed around the planet, they'd be ready to react if a swarm of Hive ships suddenly dropped out of a wormhole. Acton seemed to have no comprehension of orbital physics – he seemed to think that ships could hover over cities indefinitely – but that was just details. Bloch would distribute his ships so that every major city could be reached in a matter of minutes. He would obey the spirit of his orders, and Acton would never know the difference.

Acton stood, and Bloch stood with him. "Let your people handle the details," Acton said. "I want you to focus on your speaking tour. That's the important thing."

Bloch nodded, mumbled, "Yes, Sir," one last time, and walked out of the office in a fog.

He trudged through the new security station set up in what had once been a reception area, then followed a curved hallway that circled the rotunda. To his left he saw open lawns dappled by late-afternoon sunshine. Before the war – before Acton – the lawn would have held escorted tour groups and children on school visits. Now, he saw a handful of marines on patrol, and that was it.

One level down from the main entrance he found a com lounge with encrypted connections. He took a seat and punched in a request for a link to Captain Hakka of the supply ship *Condor*. He had four ships standing by, the *Condor*, two corvettes, and a Jumper. Hakka was the only one busily laying in supplies, though. She needed to know immediately that she could stop. In fact, she faced a tiresome chore of returning delivered supplies to their warehouses. It would be a major headache. She deserved to hear the order – and his apology – in a live call.

"This is Lieutenant Chalmers," said a brisk voice. "The captain's pretty busy sorting supplies. She should be here in a minute or so."

"That's fine, Lieutenant. It's not an emergency."

He broke the connection and waited, considering what he would say. The wasted effort wasn't a big deal. This was the military, where every waste of time was really a drill in disguise. She'd probably prefer to be busy anyway.

She'd be disappointed to be denied a mission in deep space. Not that she'd complain.

But she might ask why. He didn't have to answer a subordinate's questions, of course. But the question stood.

Why, when tens of thousands of colonists might be in desperate need of aid, was Spacecom doing nothing?

Acton's answers were thin at best. The safety of the Earth would not be compromised by the absence of these four ships. No, the fleet had to stay here because the corvettes might be needed to protect the Statsminister from his electorate. And the Jumper and the supply ship had to stay as well, because the presence of more ships was reassuring to a desperate, self-centered man who was obsessed with personal power.

"It's not my fault," he whispered. "Not my decision. There's a chain of command. I must follow my orders."

The voice of his conscience told him he was taking a coward's way out. He faced that voice squarely, as he always faced challenges, threats, and sources of discomfort.

"I obey my orders," he murmured, then double-checked there were no live connections. The last thing he needed was to broadcast his soul-searching to Captain Hakka. "It's not a whim. It's not following the path of least resistance. It's duty. It's keeping my vows."

And it was true, too. The military served a vital function. The military maintained stability. It protected civilian populations. It made the world safe. But the military didn't function without a strong chain of command. You couldn't simply hand lethal weapons to thousands of people and say, each of you follow your own conscience.

The rigidity of the command structure could be vexing at times, but it was absolutely essential. He believed in freedom and democracy, in the right of every citizen to wield a vote as he saw fit. The right to wield a rail gun, though, or a warship with a bay full of missiles, was another matter entirely. When you put on the uniform you agreed to be part of the machine. You subverted your will because otherwise the machine couldn't function, could even become a menace to the very people it was intended to protect.

Soldiers carried out policy. They didn't set it. Leaders set policy. The government, the admiralty.

But the government, that vast monolithic entity of bureaucrats and elected representatives, had changed since the war began. To a huge extent the will of the government was now the will of one man. Parliament members spoke out or remained silent according to their personal convictions, but there was an unspoken understanding that criticism of the Statsminister was unpatriotic, and could invite the wrath of the EDF.

Where there had been government, now there was Acton.

And the admiralty, once so powerful, was now subordinate to the EDF. The admirals had become administrators.

The realization hit him with a jolt. *Where there used to be an admiralty, there's me.*

He looked at the terminal in front of him. Hakka would take his call at any moment. What would he tell her?

*I could tell her to carry on with her mission.*

The idea was seductive and repellent at the same time. It would soothe his conscience. The colonists in Calypso and every place in between would have their salvation. He would know that he had done the right thing.

*No. I can't disobey my orders. I will order Hakka to return the supplies she's gathered and stay in the Sol system. It's my duty.*

*Why is it my duty? If it's the wrong thing to do, how can it be my duty?*

*Because I have clear orders from the Statsminister himself. The chain of command …*

*The chain of command is broken. It doesn't work. I should consult the admiralty.*

*But the admiralty has been deposed. It's been replaced.*

*By me.*

Bloch squirmed in his seat, trying to avoid the treacherous, treasonous thought that was rising in the back of his mind.

*What if my duty is to behave as the admiralty would? To provide a check, a balance? To restrain the excesses of the Statsminister's office?*

*Don't sugar-coat it, Wolfgang. It's not the office. It's the Statsminister himself. The problem is not the government. The problem is one man.*

*Two men. I'm the other half of the problem. After all, I'm about to cancel a desperately-needed relief mission. And then I'm going to go on a speaking tour where I'll tell people lies about the aliens so they'll think they still need the EDF.*

*And I'll tell myself I'm doing my duty.*

A low buzzer sounded and an electronic voice said, "Connecting your call to the *SS Condor*."

"Commodore," said a woman's voice. "This is Captain Hakka. What can I do for you?" She sounded guarded. He'd told her when he gave her his orders that the mission didn't yet have final approval. He'd assured her there was very little chance the mission would be scrapped, but she had to be bracing herself, just in case.

"There's a slight change of plans, Captain." He took a deep breath. "I'm coming with you. I'll come up in a shuttle and rendezvous with the *Condor*, and we'll join the rest of the fleet at the Gate."

"Very well, Sir." She sounded surprised, but not displeased. "I'll prepare you a cabin."

"Thank you, Captain." He broke the connection, then sat in the quiet booth, letting the implications of his actions sink in.

Finally he keyed in another call, to his wife in

Germany. Hazen liked to know when he was going to be away from Earth for an extended period. She saw very little of him even when he was close to home, but he owed her the courtesy of a notification before heading someplace as distant as Calypso. She would be satisfied with a message, but he found himself wanting to hear her voice. Hazen was a rock in his life, an unvarying foundation he wanted to cling to now that everything else seemed to be shifting.

Once, this conversation would have been quite difficult. In the early years of their marriage she had railed against his frequent absences. There had been tears and shouting and cold silences. It had been a relief when she'd finally learned to accept the realities of his career.

Now, she would be brusquely polite. She'd thank him for letting her know, and she would get on with her day. He found himself perversely missing the old days, when their lives had seemed so deeply intertwined and every absence still felt like a betrayal. It would have been comforting to imagine her waiting in an agony of suspense for him to come back to her.

It took a while for the call to connect. The days when she would have run to take a call from him were long gone. At last, though, the console chimed and the electronic voice said, "The other party has requested a vid link. Will you accept?"

"Yes," he said, and composed his face in something like a smile.

A screen across from him flickered, then

showed Hazen's familiar face. He'd hoped for a hint of warmth. Instead, he saw impatience. "Wolfgang. Is everything all right?"

"I'm fine," he said. "I might be going on a trip to the outer colonies, though."

Her eyebrows rose. "I see."

He surprised himself by blurting, "Do you remember that time I left my gun on my desk?" He hadn't realized he was thinking about it, but the memory suddenly filled his mind, every detail crisp. It was twenty years in the past, on a rare visit home. He'd been in the house for half an hour, sitting in the dining room and chatting through the kitchen door with Hazen, who was preparing a turkey. She made a comment about enjoying family time away from his work, then gave a pointed glance at his uniform.

He took the hint, going into his office where he took off his gun, laid it on the desk, and turned to the safe. Before he could open the safe, though, Hazen had called him from the kitchen. "Wolf! Help me, please."

Instead of taking five seconds or so to strap on his gun belt, he left it and hurried through to the kitchen. He found his wife struggling to lift the heavy turkey from the oven. He wrapped a dishtowel around his hand, helped her with the turkey, paused to give her a kiss, then returned to the office.

He found his six-year-old son standing beside the desk, holding his pistol, pointing it at his daughter.

Bloch took the gun from the boy's hand,

ordered both children out of the office, and sat down, his whole body trembling. *Oh, my God. I left my sidearm within reach of my children.*

Even though nothing had happened, the incident had rattled him deeply. He was a professional military man with a conscientious nature. It was his identity. He was not the kind of fool who was careless with firearms.

And yet, he had done it.

"Wolf," said Hazen. She was using her stern parent's voice, the one she used when the children were being difficult. "I can't chat with you right now. I have friends over."

"You're busy," he said.

"It's not that." A troubled furrow appeared between her brows. "It's you."

He stared at her, baffled. "It's me?"

"Rosa's son was arrested last week. He was protesting in Nova Roma."

"But I didn't-"

"Mildred's daughter is in hiding. She posted some vids on the dark feeds. The EDF tried to arrest her."

"Fine," he said stiffly. "I won't embarrass you any further. Take care, Hazen."

He caught a flash of distress in her face as he cut the connection. He wanted to dwell on the image, to decide if he should feel vindicated or guilty, but he couldn't concentrate. For some reason the memory of that moment two decades earlier filled his mind. His weapon, in the hand of his son. A tragedy that almost happened, triggered by a moment of carelessness.

A moment of criminal negligence.

He drafted a quick message to Hakka. *I will not be accompanying you. Rendezvous with the rest of the fleet and proceed at best speed to Naxos, and from there to Deirdre and the rest of the colonies.*

The Parliament Building was a high-ceilinged, airy place, but he found it strangely stifling. He walked outside, but the wide lawns populated only by marines seemed just as oppressive. He used his implants to call a shuttle.

Only when he reached the bridge of the *Hannibal* did the strange trapped feeling fade. Colonel Laycraft was not pleased to see him, and made only a token effort to hide it. He'd have to remind her that the chain of command didn't end with her.

Captain Molson gave Bloch a sour glance, then ignored him. Molson's dark expression didn't change when he looked away, either. Well, the man had commanded the *Hannibal* for almost a decade. He could be forgiven a little bitterness at being made subordinate to the EDF.

"How many battle-ready ships are in orbit around Earth, or on the surface?" Bloch said.

"Eight, including us," said a lieutenant, and started to list them.

"Never mind that. Get me all seven captains."

Laycraft raised an eyebrow. "You want to talk to the captains?"

Bloch frowned, annoyed with himself for the lapse. "Get me the commanding officers."

She nodded and looked at her

communications officer.

There was a delay of several minutes before all seven officers were connected to the channel. When the last major signed in, Bloch spoke.

"We are changing position. Form up behind the *Hannibal* and wait for further instructions."

"Where are we going?" said a shrill voice.

Bloch smiled to himself. *Time to give everyone a refresher on military protocol.* "Who asked that question?"

The silence stretched out. Finally a hesitant voice said, "It was me. Colonel Beaulieu."

"When I ask you a question, Colonel, I expect a prompt response. Is that clear?"

"Yes, General." She sounded flustered, as if she was startled to find herself facing criticism.

*You'll get used to it by the time I'm done with you.* "I see you've belatedly remembered how to address a superior officer, Colonel. Don't make me remind you again. You won't get another warning."

Silence.

"Colonel?" he said coldly.

"Yes, General." By the sound of it she was speaking through gritted teeth. "Sorry, General."

*I'm not really getting through to her. Well, I'll save the rest of the lesson until I can speak to her in private.* It was never a good idea to humiliate an officer too much in front of the lower ranks. He'd blister her ears for her later.

"Form up behind the *Hannibal*," he repeated. "Don't make me wait."

The fleet gathered with impressive speed.

When all eight ships were together he turned to Laycraft and said, "Take us to the Gate to Naxos, Colonel."

She gaped at him. "We're going to Naxos?" When he glared she flushed and added, "Sir."

"No, Colonel. We're just going to the Gate. Now carry out your orders."

"Yes, Sir." She took a hesitant step toward the navigation console, as if she thought he meant for her to drive the ship herself. Then she smoothed her uniform blouse with her hands and said, "Helm. Gate Three."

The long-standing system of numbering Gates had broken down during the war, with Gates being destroyed and replaced, and a new Gate opened to the Hive home system. The helmsman knew what she wanted, though. Before long, the small fleet blockading the Gate appeared on Bloch's screen and began to grow.

When the two fleets hung motionless beside the Gate, Bloch addressed every ship in both fleets. "This is Commodore Bloch aboard the *Hannibal*. We will be discontinuing the blockade of the Gate and moving to L2. We won't use a wormhole, since we're in no hurry. It'll be a good chance for everyone to practice moving in formation."

Laycraft stared at him. "But what about the blockade, Sir?"

Bloch left the channel open as he answered. "The Naxos colony is not going to attack us through the Gate. If they do, we'll have plenty of time to respond from L2. If the Hive attacks us, it won't be through the Gate, so we serve no defensive purpose by staying here. Not that the Hive will attack us. The Hive has been destroyed. They are no longer a threat to humanity."

God, but it felt good to speak the truth.

Laycraft said, "But, Sir, what about ships trying to leave?"

"We will no longer prevent ships from leaving the Sol system." A knot in his guts seemed to let go when he said it. "Spacecom has no business preventing the citizens of the United Worlds from travelling as they see fit."

Colonel Laycraft looked shocked.

"We'll go to the Lagrange point and take up station there," he said. "We'll be close enough to respond if the Earth faces some outside threat. But, at a million-plus kilometers, we'll be far enough away that no one will be tempted to use the fleet inappropriately for dealing with non-military threats."

Molson glanced at him, the sour look finally gone from his face. The captain nodded, then looked away.

*I don't need your approval*, Bloch thought. But it warmed him just the same.

Acton would be furious. This day would bring consequences, serious ones. Nevertheless, Bloch felt strangely cheerful as he watched the Gate recede behind the fleet. He thought back to that terrible day when he'd left a loaded gun in reach of children, and smiled. *Not this time. I made a mistake, but once was bloody well enough. I won't repeat it.*

# STARSHIP THESEUS

# CHAPTER 31 – CARRUTHERS

Ship coming through!"

Carruthers, who'd been quietly reading a novel on a data pad, jerked his head up at the announcement. Cadet Kuzyk was at the tactical station, his eyes wide with alarm. "More ships now!"

"Transponders?" Carruthers said mildly. He'd already glanced at his own tactical screen, so he knew the answer. This was a training shift for Kuzyk, though, and he wanted the boy to go through all the steps.

"Spacecom ships," Kuzyk said. "Uh, there's the *Condor* and the *Semenko* ..."

"Just give me the ship classes," Carruthers said, his eyes on his own tactical screen. The *Indefatigable* sat a hundred thousand kilometers from the Gate, between the Gate and Ariadne. If the arriving fleet had hostile intentions he'd have plenty of time to react before they could get close enough to do any harm. Still, if the sewage hit the rotating blades he didn't want a moment's delay.

"One corvette," said Kuzyk, his voice losing its excited pitch. "A supply ship and a Jumper. Oh, and another corvette just came through."

"Sound General Quarters," said Carruthers, and the low hum of an alarm started. "Start charging the wormhole generator. And signal the Spacecom fleet."

Officers filed onto the bridge, and Kuzyk gratefully gave his seat up to an arriving lieutenant. Rigoberto Ramona took a seat close to the communications station, ready to send untranslatable messages to his siblings in orbit around Ariadne and on the ground.

The Spacecom fleet didn't deign to reply to their signal. A glowing wormhole mouth appeared just in front of the Jumper and the little fleet vanished, one ship at a time. The Jumper went last, the wormhole hanging alone in space for several more seconds before collapsing and disappearing.

*If they were coming for us they'd be here already*. "Scan Ariadne," Carruthers said. "Signal the fleet. I want to know where they came out."

No ships had popped into existence close to the colony, though. Carruthers had his people start a careful scan of the system, in case the Spacecom fleet had jumped away for some reason, only to jump back in and catch them by surprise. His instincts, though, told him the Naxos system wasn't under attack. After five minutes of vigilance he was almost certain.

"Stand down, people," he said. "Everyone who's not on an active-duty shift can go."

Kuzyk, hovering near the aft bulkhead, said, "But where did they go, Sir?"

"My guess is they're on their way to Deirdre." Carruthers shook his head. "Depending on what they find, they'll likely keep going down the chain." He ran through the list in his mind. Aries. Tanos. Calypso, the most distant colony in the United Worlds, isolated since the first contact with the Hive. Was anyone left alive in those colonies?

*And how long will it take us to find out the details? God, what I wouldn't give for access to the news.*

While he was deeply grateful there was no shooting war between the Naxos colony and Spacecom, Carruthers was intensely frustrated by the cold war. A working Gate connected Naxos and Sol, but almost no traffic went through. He was frankly scared to send a ship through the Gate. There was no guarantee that ship and crew would ever be allowed to return.

It was nine days since the *Theseus, Gideon*, and *Tomahawk* had left for deep space. A day after that, the *Theseus* had come through the Gate from Sol with a hold full of subdued colonists and the news that the Hive was all but destroyed. The war with the aliens was effectively over, but Hammett was in custody, along with every officer and sailor who'd deserted from Spacecom.

Since then, only one more ship had come

through the Gate, and it hadn't been able to give them much news. In fact, the new arrivals had known surprisingly little. The degree of censorship in the press back on Earth had Carruthers utterly flabbergasted.

Kuzyk sat once again at the tactical station. His eyes went to his screen and he stiffened. "Captain! Another ship." He peered at the screen. "It's called the *Aardvark*. It's a civilian cargo ship."

"Message coming in," said the communications officer.

"Well, that's a nice change of pace. Let's hear it."

A man's voice, scratchy and excited, came from the bridge speakers. "I repeat, we surrender. This is Captain Roget of the Galactic Cargo Services *Aardvark*, surrendering unconditionally to the mutineer fleet."

"Give me a channel," Carruthers said. When the communications officer nodded he said, "Try not to panic, Captain Roget. No one's shooting at you."

"Is this the mutineer fleet?"

"This is Captain Carruthers of the Colonial Forces," Carruthers said, controlling a rising irritation. "Why don't you tell me what brings you to Naxos?"

"I'm defecting," Roget said. "The whole crew is. We want away from Earth. Don't fire on us!"

"You're a hundred thousand kilometers away," Carruthers said wearily. "You're in no danger."

"Oh," said Roget, sounding flustered. "Right."

"What makes you think I'm going to fire on you, Roget?"

"Well," the man said defensively, "you destroyed the *Scepter*."

The *Scepter*, a tiny civilian courier ship, had come through six days earlier with a couple of pilots, a refugee journalist, and three ministers of the previous government, all of them outspoken critics of Acton. They'd been seeking sanctuary, and they'd had to dodge a Spacecom blockade to slip through the Gate.

"The *Scepter* and all its passengers are perfectly safe," Carruthers said. "We don't shoot down every ship that comes through."

"That's not what the feeds have been saying," Roget said.

Carruthers was abruptly tired of the foolish, timid man. "Well then, maybe you'd better go back through the Gate where you'll be safe from all these savage colonists."

"Sorry!" Roget bleated. "It's just ... Well, we've heard a lot of alarming stories."

"Start moving toward Ariadne," Carruthers said. "We'll match velocities when you get close. We'll escort you in."

"Okay," said Roget. "Moving now. Thank you."

They sat down together in a conference room in Colonial Forces headquarters. Carruthers barely managed to talk his way in. The room was packed. Janice Ling stood near the door, data pad in hand, suddenly a reporter again instead of a soldier. The reporter from the *Scepter* stood beside her. Captain Roget sat at one end of the long conference table, his first officer and purser on either side. Ron Faraday sat at the opposite end of the table, surrounded by movers and shakers in the colony, along with a handful of ships' captains.

"I don't know how much I can really tell you," Roget said, looking at the table. He had a way of glancing up briefly, quick flicks of his eyes before returning his gaze to the table. The size of the audience had him clearly intimidated. "News is pretty censored these days."

"What's going on with the war?" Ron said. "What's happened with the aliens?"

Roget shook his head. "Story keeps changing," he said. "One day it's a glorious victory. Every alien's dead, and it's all because of Acton." His lip curled. "Next day, the aliens are getting stronger and all that got destroyed was an outpost." The corners of his mouth twitched in a hint of a grin. "The word on the dark feeds is, he needs the aliens still alive. No aliens, you don't need an EDF. And the EDF is just about all he has left."

"Dark feeds," Ron said. "What's that?"

"Unofficial feeds," Roget said. "Illegal ones. They keep getting shut down, and more keep popping up." He shook his head. "You don't know how good the real news is until you spend some time watching the dark feeds. Lots of nonsense. Wild conspiracy theories. Crazy stuff. But it's all uncensored, and sometimes you get the truth." His eyes flicked around the room, then dropped again. "Big challenge is figuring out which bit is the truth in the ocean of crap."

"What do you know about our people?" Ron said. "Admiral Hammett and the other Spacecom people who joined the Colonial Forces?"

Roget frowned, thinking. "Well, the official story is, everyone from the colony got let go. The dark feeds say they all got executed, though."

"I'm not executed," said a woman to Ron's left. "Your dark feeds got that one wrong."

"Oh." Roget looked flustered for a moment. "Anyway, the Statsminister is saying Hammett and the others will all be executed." A collective gasp made him look up for an instant, startled. "Sorry. Well, he says there'll be a trial first. But he says they're all guilty and they'll hang."

Carruthers said, "When? When is this trial?"

Roget glanced at him, then looked down. "I don't know. I don't think there's a date set."

*Not that it matters*, Carruthers reflected bitterly. *It's not as if I can do something*.

Ron and a few of the others went on asking questions. Roget gave most of the answers, with his officers speaking up from time to time. They knew very little, as it turned out. The United Worlds government seemed not to have a policy for dealing with the breakaway colony, and the new arrivals knew nothing at all about specific friends or family members of the colonists. Carruthers tuned it out, brooding over the trouble Hammett and his people were in.

The word 'war' snapped his attention back to the meeting.

"I don't know," Roget was saying. "Some

people say to just hang on and wait for Acton to call an election. I mean, it's supposed to be, what? Another two and a half years until we vote again, right? So it's too soon to say he's not going to step down." Roget grimaced. "He sure won't be re-elected. I can tell you that much."

"So people are just going to wait?" Ron demanded.

"Well, maybe," said Roget. "They're getting pretty mad about the press. Montreal almost started a civil war, and then a lot of people got killed in the riots. The government says it's their fault. But there's vids on the dark feeds." His face darkened. "The military's been shooting people who were trying to run away."

"Is there anything like an organized resistance?" Ron demanded.

Roget shrugged. "There's stories on the dark feeds. But like I said." His shrug deepened. "A lot of it's crap. I just don't know."

*Civil war.* Carruthers shivered. Would it really come to that? How savage would Acton be in suppressing a popular revolt?

What portion of Spacecom and the army would follow orders? What portion would rebel?

"I don't know what's going to happen on Earth," Roget said, "but I'm sure glad I got out. I couldn't believe it when they lifted the blockade. We thought maybe it was mines or something. But when we saw that Spacecom fleet go through, we figured maybe it was safe. Safer than staying, anyway. So we ran for it." He looked up, and for the first time managed to hold Ron's gaze for more than a moment. "Pretty soon, we might be looking back on the war with the aliens as the good old days."

Eventually the meeting broke up. Carruthers paced the lawn outside, his thoughts churning. He looked up when he caught sight of a familiar figure in the corner of his eye. Janice Ling strolled over and joined him.

"Did you record the meeting?" he said.

"Yes." She looked up at him. "Why?"

"There's something ..." He shrugged. "I don't know. He said something important, but I can't figure out what it was."

"Impending executions?" she said grimly. "Risk of civil war?"

He shook his head.

"Then maybe it's the fact the blockade is down."

*Of course.* He stared at her. "He really did say that, didn't he? The Gate is unwatched on their side."

She nodded. "That's what he said."

*It doesn't matter. Going through would still be really stupid.* He looked around at the stone buildings and tidy rows of trees that surrounded him, and the looming bulk of the crater wall in the background. *When did this place start to feel like home?* Strangely enough, though, it did. If he left the colony and couldn't return, he'd regret it.

For instance, if he flew into Spacecom-controlled space and got himself chucked into a cell right beside Hammett.

"You're thinking about going back to Earth,

aren't you?" Janice said.

"It would be pretty stupid," he replied.

She nodded. "But if you go, I'm coming too."

He raised an eyebrow.

"If I can get on these 'dark feeds', I can say a lot to discredit the EDF. I can tell people the colony isn't hostile. That they can come through the Gate and find sanctuary."

"That might not be the most prudent message," Carruthers said. A flood of refugees might trigger a strong response from Spacecom.

She nodded, conceding the point. "Still. The people of Earth need to know they're not alone." She scuffed a toe in the dirt. "I want to be a real journalist again," she said. "For that, I need an audience. And I need to be where the story is. And that means Earth." She folded her arms and stared into the distance for a minute. "It's not just my career, Jim. Journalists are being silenced back on Earth. Maybe a good loud voice speaking the truth can do some real good right now." She looked up at him, a pleading expression on her face. "Do you understand what I mean?"

He nodded slowly. "Maybe you're right. Maybe we need to go back."

# CHAPTER 32 – HAMMETT

As cells went, it wasn't so bad.

Hammett walked to the front of the little room, felt the tingle of the force field against his sleeve as he turned, and walked – two whole paces – to the back wall. His knee brushed the edge of the little toilet that jutted from the wall as he turned to take two more strides to the front.

If the bunk had been folded down from the wall he wouldn't have had room to walk. Still, he'd had a smaller room in his cadet days. The Captain's cabin on the *Alexander* had been reasonably roomy, but his cabin on the *Tomahawk* wasn't much bigger than this. As for the stress, well, wondering if he was going to die soon wasn't exactly a new experience either.

Pace. Pace. Turn. It was boring, but it gave him an outlet for his nervous energy.

The lack of news was the worst part.

Wondering what was happening to his officers and crew. Wondering if the EDF fleet was bombing Harlequin.

Wondering how long the people of Earth would tolerate a tyrant.

Pace. Pace. Turn.

He could handle boredom. Long journeys through deep space during peacetime were incredibly dull. Sure, the boredom here was worse than usual. The force field blocking the door was opaque. No one visited. He had no human contact. Meal replacement bars dropped from a slot in the wall at regular intervals. The lights went dim each night, then came back up the next morning. And that was it.

He would have given a lot for ten minutes with a news feed, though.

Pace. Pace. Turn.

He scratched his jaw. For the first time since his teenage years he'd gone long enough without beard suppressant that he was growing stubble, and it itched. He wondered how countless generations of men had put up with it before modern technology saved them.

Pace. Pace. Turn.

A distant boom of voices came to his ears. At first he ignored it, continuing to pace and turn. It was, however, the most interesting thing that had happened in a week, so at last he stopped, moved close enough to the force field that he could feel his hair stir, and listened.

"One of these ... Can't get ... Open."

The force field vanished, so abruptly that he

jumped back. He could see a strip of narrow corridor and a stretch of blank gray wall on the far side. This was so novel that he spent a moment just staring.

Then Sanjari stepped into view. She looked rough, her hair in a messy cloud around her head, her face lined with stress, but she smiled. "Good afternoon, Admiral. Feel like going for a walk?"

"Is it him?" A couple more people stepped into his field of view, one of them jostling Sanjari. They were civilians, strangers, young men with a breathless, excited air. The one on the left beamed at him. The one on the right shouted, "We found him!" Both men hurried away.

Hammett spent another moment just standing there, staring at Sanjari.

"It's all right," she said. "It took me a moment, too."

He took a deep breath, then stepped out of the cell.

Aside from Sanjari, the corridor was empty. He saw half a dozen cells and an automated security console, and a staircase leading upward. It was all as he remembered from when they'd brought him here, seven endless days ago.

"Nicholson was there," she said, and pointed to a cell. "He already went upstairs. Didn't even wait for me, the jerk." She smiled to show she didn't mean it. "I was there." She indicated the cell next to Hammett's.

"What-" His voice, rusty with disuse, failed him. He cleared his throat, swallowed, and tried again. "What's happening?"

She shrugged. "Social collapse? Armageddon? I'm not entirely sure." She flashed an impish grin. "I can't wait to find out, though. Come on!"

He followed her down the corridor, giving the security console a wary glance, then up the stairs. His legs trembled. He told himself it was from all the pacing. He couldn't be overwhelmed by the experience, after all. It was just seven days in a box.

His memories of the basements below the courthouse were fuzzier than he realized. He expected to find himself on the main floor, but there was another floor of cells that he'd forgotten. They had to circle around a security station to reach the next flight of stairs. Any guards were long gone, and he saw short corridors full of cells with the doors deactivated.

At the top of the next flight they walked through one last security station and reached the main hall of the courthouse. It was a grand, imposing space, with massive pillars rising toward a vaulted ceiling three stories above. A common instinct made both of them shrink back, intimidated by so much space after a week in a tiny cell.

"We're spacers," Hammett said at last. "This is nothing." He straightened up, taking on the familiar posture of a military man, and Sanjari did the same. Changing his stance had the strange effect of changing his mindset, and the last of the mindless fear that had dogged him since the cell opened finally fell away.

Together, he and Sanjari walked across the marble floor of the main hall. The air smelled of dust and furniture polish, but a faint whiff of smoke reminded him that this was no ordinary day.

The building seemed to be empty. The lights were out, but enough sunlight streamed in through high, narrow windows to make artificial lights superfluous. The two of them walked toward the main entrance, a pair of massive oak doors at the far end of the hall. One door stood ajar, letting in a brilliant bar of sunlight. Hammett couldn't see anything outside.

They were a dozen paces from the doors when a figure stepped into view. It was a petite woman, made tiny by the size of the doorway. She was lit from behind so that he could see nothing but a silhouette, but he thought he recognized her just the same.

"Admiral," said Janice Ling. "Lieutenant. I'm quite relieved to see you both." She held up a hand as they approached. "Things outside are ... unsettled. I don't think it's quite the time for you to show your face."

She stepped inside, then moved away from the doorway, beckoning for them to follow. Hammett went to the door and took a quick peek outside.

He saw chaos. The barricades were gone. Instead, crowds of people roamed the streets, some with placards, some with clubs. Someone was shouting, far off, the voice made incoherent by echoes and distance. Groups edged past each other, wary and belligerent. Fear and rage were like a tang in the air.

A small hand caught his elbow. "It's a powder keg out there," Janice said softly. "You're a spark. Think very carefully before you set something off."

He let her pull him back from the door.

"Come over here," she said, and positioned him in a shaft of sunlight. "It'll put the statue of Justice in the background." She backed away, and he glanced over his shoulder. A massive statue filled the far end of the hall, a blindfolded woman with scales.

Janice drew several silver balls from a shoulder bag. When she let them go, the balls hovered around her. She closed her eyes, and the balls moved toward Hammett. Cameras, he realized, able to catch him from three angles.

"I'll mostly use Cam Two," she said. "That's the one with the yellow light. But just look at me while you talk."

"Whoa," he said. "Slow down. What are you doing?"

"I'm putting you live on half a dozen dark feeds," she said. "The most popular ones. Ten million people will see you live. Most of the rest will see the recorded version within a few hours."

He felt his knees go weak. "Now, just a minute!"

"I'm sorry to ambush you like this," she said. "You have to do it, though." She stepped in close. "There's chaos all over the world, Richard." She gestured at the doorway behind her. "This isn't the only powder keg. The whole planet is like this. It's a turning point in history, and you have a role to play, whether you like it or not."

He stared at her, shaking his head, wondering if he could make a run for it.

"You know what's been going on," she said, then hesitated. "Wait. *Do* you know what's been happening? Just in the last four days, I mean."

"No." He wanted to keep repeating the word until she put those damned cameras away. "No, I've been in a cell. I haven't heard anything."

She stared at him for a moment, her forehead furrowed. "Okay. Here's the condensed version. There's demonstrations in pretty much every city in the world. The cops have stopped cracking down. There isn't enough military to be everywhere, and a lot of military units have been refusing to go against the demonstrators. The last straw was when Spacecom retreated to L2."

Hammett said, "Spacecom retreated?"

She nodded. "There isn't a military spacecraft on or near the Earth bigger than a shuttle, except for the *Tomahawk*."

"The *Tomahawk's* here?"

"Yes," she said, her voice betraying a hint of impatience. "It's how I got here. Anyway, Acton is barricaded in some secure war room in the outskirts of Nova Roma. He's got a bunch of loyal troops protecting him, and steel doors to keep the mobs out. A couple of dozen Members of Parliament have formed a provisional government and they're trying to get things under control." She smiled nastily. "So far, they're failing."

"What about the EDF?" Sanjari interrupted.

"Most of them have deserted," Janice said, not without a hint of vindictive satisfaction. "The rest are holed up in some of their offices and facilities." She jerked a thumb. "We've got a batch just a block from here, in Liberty Hall. They've locked the doors, and they're howling for rescue."

An ember of disgusted anger that had lain dormant in Hammett's belly for a week suddenly flickered to life. The presence of EDF goons in Liberty Hall was a travesty, and the thought of driving them out filled him with a fierce joy. He clenched and unclenched his fists, thinking of the justice that was about to be meted out.

"Things are at a tipping point," Janice said. "It just needs a tiny shove to get things moving in the right direction. People are scared. They're pushing. Some of them are pushing hard. But they're also holding back. They remember Montreal. They remember how the army fired into the crowd in Moscow and Des Moines. So they aren't pressing their advantage."

She reached out and squeezed his arm. "This is our opportunity, Richard! People recognize you. They trust you. You're the man who saved us from the Hive, and everyone knows you don't work for Acton and the EDF. They know you'll speak the truth.

"If you tell them the fleet is away from Earth, they'll believe you. You can tell them that most of the army isn't willing to fire on them. You can tell them that this is the time! They can finally hit back at the EDF. They can dig those vermin out from under every rock they're hiding under. They can finish off the EDF once and for all!" Her eyes glittered. "Then, Acton won't stand a chance. We'll go after him, and finish him off too."

It was a glorious vision, and Hammett found himself nodding. The poison could be expelled. The threat eliminated, like they'd done with the Hive. Things could be made pure and decent again, with the worst element of Earth society finally purged.

"The lights on the cameras will get brighter when they're transmitting," she said. "Just be yourself. Be yourself, and speak the truth. Okay?"

He nodded again, and she stepped back, choosing a spot with pillars behind her, dramatically lit by a shaft of dusty sunlight. The cameras clustered in front of her and she began to speak.

"Hello, fellow citizens of the United Worlds. This is Janice Ling. I've been away for a while, in exile on Ariadne, but I'm back. I'm here with a man who needs no introduction. Admiral Richard Hammett, the hero of the Battle of Earth, is with me. He's just been released from captivity." Her face hardened. "Not released by the courts, I must emphasize. No, he was released by the only people actually standing up for the laws and rights our republic was founded on. Common citizens with the courage to do what's right!"

It was an impressive bit of rhetoric, buoyed by her obvious sincerity. Hammett could feel her words swaying him. At the same time, though, he found himself growing uneasy. She'd called the world a powder keg, and she seemed determined to light a match.

As if she was reading his mind, she said, "The time of change is upon us! We tried following the rules. We tried the courts, and we tried appealing to our elected representatives. I think you all know where that got us." She scowled into the camera. "Journalists fleeing into exile. A missile fired at demonstrators in Montreal. The erosion or outright suspension of every basic right we hold dear!"

Her hands came up, slashing the air in urgent gestures. "If there is one lesson we've learned since the start of the war, one bitter lesson we've learned through blood and terror, it's that change isn't going to happen until we *make* it happen. We won't be free of the EDF until the EDF is destroyed!"

*But you are free of the EDF.* The thought felt traitorous in Hammett's mind, but it wouldn't go away. *Acton's powerless. The EDF is cooped up and surrounded by angry mobs. Their power is gone, and it isn't coming back.*

"I know that most of the people listening to me want to act," Janice said. "But you're afraid. Not without reason. We all know what happened to so many brave citizens who've tried to stand up to Acton and his goons. But things have changed. There will be no more missiles coming down from the sky." She leaned toward the nearest camera. "You may not want to take my word for it. That's okay. You don't have to. Here's someone who knows more about Spacecom and its ships than I do. Someone I think you all know you can trust. The hero of the Hive War, Admiral Richard Hammett."

The cameras flew away from her and hovered in front of Hammett. One camera, straight ahead, had an indicator light on top that glowed a bright yellow. Hammett glanced past that intimidating cluster of electronics at Janice, who gave him an encouraging nod.

He took a deep breath and looked into the camera's glowing eye.

"I've just spent a week in a cell," he said. "Before that, I was in the home system of the Hive, fighting alongside colonists and Spacecom personnel, and even a few members of the EDF. Together, we managed to destroy the Hive." He paused, fighting the urge to pant for breath. This was far more terrifying than mere combat. The worst part was, he had no idea what he was going to say.

"It was quite an ordeal," he said. "A lot of good people died. I was pretty sure I wasn't going to make it myself." He closed his eyes for a moment, remembering. "That wasn't the worst part, though." His voice firmed as he realized what he needed to say. "No, the worst part was when I thought I was going to have to battle my fellow human beings." He shook his head. "The EDF brought us to the brink of real disaster. They had some help, in the form of stubborn combativeness from the Naxos colony, and from officers like me. Among us we almost managed to start a civil war."

He jabbed an accusing finger at the camera. "You have to do better! We're all human beings. We all get stupid sometimes. We get scared, we get angry, we make mistakes. The EDF made some appalling blunders, and it was necessary to push back." He paused, breathing heavily, weighing his words. "You won," he said. "We won. There's an interim government. Acton's hiding out. The EDF has lost all credibility. It's lost the ability to harm you."

In the corner of his eye he could see Janice, looking shocked and disappointed. Sanjari was nodding, though. Janice looked at Sanjari and her eyebrows drew together as if she was starting to consider his words.

"There's been enough death," Hammett said. "Destruction feels good while you're doing it, but eventually you have to stop. Reconstruction is where the real work is. It's not exciting, but it's the only part that's actually worthwhile."

He took a step closer to the camera. "You won," he said. "Put down the weapons. It's over."

# FROM THE AUTHOR

Thanks for reading. I'd love to hear your comments.

Go to http://jakeelwoodwriter.com/ to leave me a note or to learn about other stories, or sign up for my newsletter to hear about new releases. I can be reached by email at author@jakeelwoodwriter.com.

48248794R00177

Made in the USA
Middletown, DE
13 June 2019